By S.A. STOVALL

Vice City

Published by DSP PUBLICATIONS
www.dsppublications.com

S.A. Stovall

VICE CITY

DSP PUBLICATIONS

Published by

DSP PUBLICATIONS

5032 Capital Circle SW, Suite 2, PMB# 279, Tallahassee, FL 32305-7886 USA
www.dsppublications.com

This is a work of fiction. Names, characters, places, and incidents either are the product of author imagination or are used fictitiously, and any resemblance to actual persons, living or dead, business establishments, events, or locales is entirely coincidental.

Vice City
© 2017 S.A. Stovall.

Cover Art
© 2017 Aaron Anderson.
aaronbydesign55@gmail.com
Cover content is for illustrative purposes only and any person depicted on the cover is a model.

ISBN: 978-1-63533-663-4
Digital ISBN: 978-1-63533-664-1
Library of Congress Control Number: 2017901542
Published June 2017
v. 1.0

Printed in the United States of America

This paper meets the requirements of
ANSI/NISO Z39.48-1992 (Permanence of Paper).

To Ann, for whom the book was written.
To Geoff, for always being the first reader.
To Beka, for making it possible.
To Gail, for her unwavering support.
To John, for being the first to see.
And finally, to everyone unnamed, thank you for everything.

S.A. Stovall

VICE CITY

CHAPTER ONE

GETTING HIT with a wrench hurts.

I know for a fact—I've had my jaw broken twice by thugs swinging them around—which is why I cringe every time Pete and Brisko land a blow. The crunch of bone and the wet splat of blood on the warehouse floor fill the otherwise silent atmosphere.

I light a cigarette and inhale, already disgusted with the spectacle. Perhaps I should've been paying more attention when they questioned the kid, but I don't know what Pete and Brisko are looking for. I'm just here in case trouble finds us.

"So how long have you been workin' for the cops?" Pete asks.

The kid shudders and keeps his head hung. Rivulets of blood stream from his mouth and lip, dripping onto his lap and staining his jeans. His shoulders bunch around his neck, but his hands are tied tight against the back of the chair. He doesn't have much range of movement—even his feet are secured to the chair legs, keeping him vulnerable.

Brisko grabs a fistful of the kid's black hair and jerks his head up. "Well? You want us to keep going or are you ready to talk?"

"I—" the kid says. "I… don't.…"

The blood in his mouth gets in the way of his speech. It doesn't help that he's trembling something fierce either. Those two idiots don't know the first thing about interrogating a rat. You have to give them time to recover between beatings or else they stutter, or worse, seize up from shock. Then you won't get any information out of them.

The kid fumbles with his words, and Pete backhands him, the wrench still curled in his fist. The extra weight slams the kid's head back, busting the skin of his eye socket good. His disheveled hair covers most of his face—the blood causing it to cling to everything—but I can tell he's black and blue.

Pete rubs his knuckles and snorts. "We got all night, kiddo. And there's only two ways out. Either you tell us what we want to know and we put a bullet in your head, simple and quick…. Or you keep holding out on us, like the dirty rat you are, and we go to bustin' up your organs rather than your bones. The way people scream…. You'll regret holdin' out on us. They all do."

The kid doesn't answer. I figured as much. He looks ready to die.

"Pete, Brisko," I call out from the shadows. "Go out and watch the door. I'll talk to him."

Those two thugs take a moment to process my words, like English is their third language instead of their first. It's clear they didn't think I would get involved, but Pete gives me a one-sided smile.

"You gonna make him sing?" he asks. "The boss always says you're the best."

"I'll get the information."

"You got it. C'mon, Brisko."

Brisko lumbers after Pete. I wait until they both exit the warehouse, giving the kid a moment to "recover" before I get to work. I take a long drag on my cigarette and exhale. I hate workin' late—it's almost dawn. Street work isn't supposed to be my thing anymore, but I can't sit by and watch Pete and Brisko's *Three Stooges* routine without intervening. They would have killed the kid and gotten nothing from it.

I allow the silence to thicken before emerging from my shadowy corner. The kid cringes away, keeping his gaze down and body tense. One eye is sealed shut from the swelling, but the other stares a hole in his leg. He won't meet my gaze.

"What's your name, kid?" I ask.

He flinches at the sound of my gruff voice but doesn't answer.

"Let me guess. You don't know that either? If you're a liar, there's nothing to talk about. We should just cut to the chase."

"Miles," he says. "My name is Miles."

I take another long drag on my cigarette. At least his jaw isn't broken. "Have you been workin' for the Vice family long?"

"N-no… only a couple of months."

So he's untested and thus untrustworthy. No wonder they got men questioning him at the end of a beating. They think he's some sort of mole.

"What have they been asking you to handle?" I ask, sauntering around to the back of his chair. The kid doesn't like that. He shivers when I get out of view.

"I do whatever they ask…. I-I've done everything t-they've wanted. I swear."

"What *specifically* have they asked you to handle?"

"I… I've carried a gun for them. Watched some places overnight…. Delivered messages… and things."

So he knows the location of a few places of interest. Now they'll be clearing those out…. That's a big hassle, and they need to blame someone. But the cops haven't busted anything recently.

"Why do they think you're with the cops?"

"I… went to the station. A few times."

Ah. The heart of the issue. I exhale a long line of smoke and stand directly behind the kid's chair. He sits unmoving, unable to glance back at me. Up close I can see he's a little older than I originally thought— perhaps in his early twenties. Still a kid, but not like the other teens I've seen on the streets lately.

"Why?" I ask.

He clams up and doesn't answer. I lean down on the back of his chair. He's as still as the dead.

"Why did you go to the police station?" I drawl. Maybe he needs the words slower. His brain has been scrambled pretty good, after all.

The kid refuses to talk.

I get in close and chuckle. I drag my teeth along the shell of his ear as I say, "Those two fucks outside haven't flayed as many men as I have. You think having your insides shattered will be rough? I have a goddamn nightmare worth of things to show you if this keeps up. C'mon, kid. Make life easy on yourself. You don't have much of it left. Yes or no—did you tell the cops about us?"

He shudders. I stay close, allowing my breath to wash over his neck. I enjoy the sound of his ragged, panicked breathing.

"No," he chokes out. "No. I didn't."

His conviction strikes me as genuine. "Then why did you go there?"

"My brother. He was there. I went to see him."

"Now why didn't you tell Pete and Brisko that?"

"I…." He gulps down air. I love the way he trembles beneath me, but I keep my thoughts straight. "I told the Vice family that I… I didn't have anyone. That I don't have a family."

"Hm," I say, tossing down the butt of my cigarette. "So you *are* a liar. But that doesn't explain everything. What else aren't you telling me?"

"My brother… he's part of the Cobras."

Ah. The Cobras. The street gang that's always hustling drugs and prostitutes. Pure lowlifes—no class whatsoever. They're trying to infest the Vice family's turf. I can see now why the kid would want to keep his mouth shut. If anyone connected him to the Cobras, they wouldn't hesitate to put a bullet in his head. Or perhaps use him to lure out his brother. Either way, it would've been bad news.

I stand up and run a hand down my face. Stupid kid is just in over his head. His home life must be pretty bad if *everyone* in his family is turning to the protection of gangs. I didn't have anyone when I met the bruisers of the Vice family for the first time. It made sense to go with them rather than live on the streets. What excuse does this kid have?

"Are you… going to kill me now?" he whispers.

I've been in this business too long to feel anything when he asks. I walk back around to the front of him, not bothering to answer the question. The kid doesn't look up. He just waits, his shirt and jeans bloodied enough for a crime scene. I light up another cigarette.

"Just give it to me straight," he says, his voice on the verge of cracking. The kid hadn't been cryin' before, despite the beating. I admire his grit. I'd want to have it straight if I were in his situation.

"Yeah," I reply with an exhale of smoke. "Pete and Brisko are gonna come back in and give it to you quick."

The information causes the kid to grimace, but still, he doesn't look up. The hot stream of tears running from his one functioning eye mixes with his blood. He steadies his breathing and asks, "Can you… not mention my family? I… I don't want them to… to try anything. I don't want them to hurt my brother."

"That's not how things work, kid. They're gonna want an explanation."

For the first time he lifts his gaze, staring at me through his unkempt hair. "Please. You could tell them anything. You could even tell them I was a mole…. What will it matter once I'm dead? The damage is done…. *Please.*"

"If he's part of the Cobras, we're gonna run across him eventually. You're not saving your brother with this gesture, kid."

"He said he would quit. He said he would move on. He needs that chance…. Please."

Does anyone leave the Cobras without having their legs broken? I don't think so. But whatever. The conversation with the kid is getting under my skin. I turn to the door and whistle through my fingers.

The piercing sound cuts to the outside. Pete and Brisko shuffle their way back in, arguing about God only knows what. They both look like thugs, despite their suits—oily hair, muscular, tattoos peeking out from their collars and sleeves. Brisko stands a foot taller and his shoulders are bowling balls wrapped in skin, but otherwise they're cut from the same cloth.

"You get him to talk?" Pete asks, a wide smile on his face.

I reply with a curt nod.

He snorts back a laugh. "Fuck. You didn't even get your hands dirty. He ain't lyin' to you? What was he up to?"

The kid goes back to staring at his lap. I take my time with my cigarette, mulling over the few quick interactions I've had with him. I hate when I get pensive. I shouldn't think so much, not when I'm on the job. It always gets me in trouble. Especially when I start feeling guilty….

"He was a mole," I say. "He told the police about some locations, but not much else."

"I knew it," Brisko states.

"Finish this up. It's late."

The kid exhales and I can see him resign himself to his fate. He doesn't look at me, but he sends a short nod my direction in an act of appreciation. It makes me regret the fact he's about to die. God, I'm gettin' soft.

Pete saunters over and spits on the kid. "You know what we do to moles like you?" He pulls his gun and smashes the butt of it against the kid's ear. A whole new torrent of blood spills down to the cement flooring. The kid barks out in pain but silences himself within half a second. He bites down on his lip, holding back any more noises. Crying out will only encourage them.

Brisko punches the kid in the gut, knocking the chair back a couple inches. The kid tries to double over, but to no avail.

"What're you two doing?" I ask.

"He's a mole," Pete says. "We always bust up the moles. That's what we do."

The kid doesn't protest. Still… it makes me sick. Brisko drills into him again. Kid won't be able to take much more….

"Stop."

Pete and Brisko cease their assault. They turn to me with confused wide-eyed stares.

"Stop," I repeat. "Lay off him."

The kid stirs but can't manage much movement. Pete combs back his greasy blond hair with his fingers. "What's wrong? We not doin' it right? You want us to just shoot him?"

"No."

"Then what?"

"You two have more work to do tonight, right? Leave the kid with me. Just get out of here."

Brisko screws up his face into an expression of contemplation. He obviously doesn't do it often. "But…. Big Man Vice is gonna want us to report in. What're we gonna tell him?"

The door to the warehouse slides open and we all place a hand on our guns. I can't see through the darkness, but Pete and Brisko ease up, letting me know whoever arrived is a friend. I should have been watching the door. This isn't even my operation.

"Oh, Jeremy," Pete says. "I d-didn't think you would be here tonight! What, uh, can we do for you?"

Jeremy Vice. The youngest Vice boy and by far the ugliest. He walks in, inches shorter than everyone else in the room, his ears too big for his head and his eyes wide-set. If it weren't for the suit, I would think him an inbred escapee from the swamps of the rural South. He's flanked by two bruisers, but they don't introduce themselves. They stand back as Jeremy walks by with his arms wide.

"Ah, Pierce," he says, looking directly at me. "My father *did* say you would be at the docks tonight. What a pleasant surprise." Despite his appearance he's quite articulate. I've known him his entire life—he can be clever at times, but slow on the uptake. Jeremy's gaze falls onto the kid. "What's he still doing alive? Haven't you gotten him to talk?"

"He's a mole," Brisko chimes in. "Pierce got him to talk. Just like Big Man Vice said."

"If that's the case, why is he still alive? Shoot him."

Both Pete and Brisko turn to me. Their gesture isn't lost on Jeremy. The Vice boy cocks his head to the side and lifts an eyebrow.

"Is something wrong, Pierce?"

I take a drag on my cigarette to give myself time. What the fuck was I thinking? How'd I even get into this situation? I just couldn't stand the thought of watching the kid get killed in front of me. He's got a lot of moxie… or maybe I've just gotten soft.

"We can use this kid to our advantage," I say, exhaling a line of smoke.

Jeremy narrows his eyes. "How so?"

"He's in good with the cops, right? We get him to feed them false information. Or, better yet, we give them the *Cobras'* information. If the cops are raiding them nonstop, we'll have the advantage."

Like dingbats, Pete and Brisko nod along with everything I say. I bet they didn't even listen to my words, but their immediate agreement seems to influence Jeremy. He's young—just like the kid in the chair— only twenty and still new to the biz. My plan is pretty risky. I doubt Jeremy's father would take a liking to it, but the Vice boy might not think things through.

"Interesting proposal," he says. "But how will we make sure he won't turn on us? He's already proven untrustworthy. The risk might not be worth the reward."

He's not as stupid as I pegged him. I throw down my cigarette and crush it under the heel of my shoe. "Leave the kid to me. I'll get him to agree, or I'll silence him myself."

That quells his doubt. I'm glad my reputation still gives me pull, but I already regret my statement.

Jeremy snaps his fingers. "Brisko, get this piece of trash to Pierce's car. We don't have all night."

"On it, boss."

Brisko, rough and uncaring, pulls the kid from his restraints and effortlessly slings him over his shoulders. He exits the warehouse with quick steps, no doubt trying to please Jeremy. *Someone* is going to inherit the Vice family holdings, and Jeremy's other two siblings have expressed little interest. Jeremy might one day be the man in charge, and everyone keeps that in the back of their mind, whether they like to admit it or not.

I amble after. Jeremy holds out a hand and takes my arm. I stop.

"Pierce," he says, his tone serious. "I have things I need to discuss with you."

"What is it?"

"Not here. I need you to come to my office. Maybe sometime next week? Monday afternoon, perhaps? My father always trusts you with his *difficult business*. I think I might have some difficult business all my own, and I need someone I can trust."

"I'll be there." I attempt to leave, but he doesn't release his grip on my arm. I narrow my eyes down at him.

"I *can* trust you, right? I'm not asking as my father, but as *me*."

"I serve the Vice family," is all I reply. Is Jeremy trying to say I should be more loyal to him than his father? I don't know, and I don't want to find out. Jeremy might be getting in over his head if he thinks he can usurp Big Man Vice.

He releases me and I continue to my car. It's nothing fancy—a 1980s Ford Thunderbird Town Landau painted a dark red—and she's scuffed and dinged in more ways than one. I catch Brisko yanking open the trunk and unceremoniously tossing the kid's limp body inside.

"What're you doing?" I ask.

"Puttin' him in," Brisko replies.

"You're gonna get blood everywhere. Next time use a tarp, for fuck's sake."

The lummox gives me a quick nod. I shove past him and get into my vehicle. He slams the trunk shut, and I ignite the engine. I can't get out of here fast enough—I almost peel out as I smash down on the gas pedal. The quiet of the docks is only broken by the hum of my car turning toward the exit.

I zip out once the gates automatically open, taking to the streets of Noimore at full speed. The glassy surface of Lake Michigan reflects the moon and city lights, but I've seen them a million times before. Chicago's brilliance shines in the distance, but I keep my eyes locked onto the road.

I zoom by a few cars, careful to avoid the known beats of certain cops. The driving calms my nerves. I can feel myself relaxing the longer I go. Damn kid got me riled. Living on the streets… it's a "kill or be killed" kind of place. What am I going to gain from helping some urchin? Nothing. Nothing at all.

Once the bridge comes into sight, I steer my vehicle down the maintenance road that runs near the water's edge. The gate is busted—it's been busted for years—and I park by the cement support beam, just out of sight from the road. The graffiti and trash mark the place as a hoodlum den. A perfect place to dump bodies.

With a heavy sigh I get out of my car. My best course of action is to throw the kid into the river and tell Jeremy I couldn't make it work. Simple. Easy. No hassle. Anything else will only lead to trouble.

I place my hand on the trunk handle and hesitate. If I'm lucky the kid will already be dead. He probably *is* dead, after the beating he got. Against my better sense, I open the trunk. The kid is curled up near the back, his blood staining everything from the tire iron to the car jack. I squint through the darkness, cursing my poor eyesight, but it doesn't take me long to see the kid is still breathing.

Damn. The kid's resilient. I should've known… the way he held out against Pete and Brisko… I've seen others break under less.

But I have a gun. I could shoot him and be done with it. Then again, I lied to *Jeremy Vice* simply to save him. Why waste my efforts? Exhaling, I shut the trunk and get back into the driver's seat.

I'll take him to my flat, let him rest up, give him some money, and tell him to blow town. Everyone wins and I don't have to deal with any more trouble.

Of course… nothing ever works out like I plan. Not much I can do about it now, though.

CHAPTER TWO

THE CITY outside my window hums with the music of sirens and rainfall.

I hate my flat. It's right on the edge of prosperity, a few blocks from the high-end downtown and a few blocks from the start of the ghetto. Every type of person calls my apartment complex home—businessmen, thugs—everyone. The unpredictable nature of my neighbors only adds to my stress. Are they clean-cut? Or more Cobras? I've gotta be on my toes.

The sizzling of my eggs cuts through the white noise of the outdoors. I love cooking by the window, even if my view is limited by the buildings across the street. The lights and motion of a bustling city get my blood going. I just woke up—I have the schedule of a vampire—and anything that gets me active is a good thing.

The creak of the hallway sets me on edge, however. With my gun in hand, I turn. Most lights are off, and my vision takes a hit in the darkness, but I see the silhouette of the kid and allow my anxiety to recede. He finally got up. Only took him twenty-eight hours.

I return my attention to the eggs as the kid hovers at the edge of the light. He doesn't enter the kitchen and instead just stands still, waiting.

"How ya feelin'?" I ask, trying to imitate the words of someone with a bit of empathy.

The kid clears his dry throat. "Good."

"Hungry?"

"Yes."

"You like eggs?"

"Yes."

"Sit down," I command, motioning to the island in the middle of the kitchen. It's in the light, where I can see him better.

The kid complies with my demand and creeps over to the stool. Once he's under the fluorescent lighting, I get a good look at him. He's still bruised and battered, but he healed up remarkably fast in a few areas.

Youth, I guess. God knows I wouldn't be walking a day after the beating of my life.

He straightens the white button-down shirt I left for him to change into. The kid looks good in it. He has mixed blood—honeyed skin and black hair, but wide eyes and a tall stature. He's thin too, more lithe than gaunt. I like his look.

"How old are you?" I ask, needing to sate my curiosity.

"I'm twenty."

I flip the eggs and sprinkle pepper over the top. The kid leans his weight onto the island, still weak, but he grits his teeth and doesn't mention anything. I admire that. Nothing we can do about it. I left him painkillers on the nightstand in the second bedroom—that's all I've got outside of taking him to a hospital, but I know the Vice family would be none too pleased with *that* option.

Once the eggs finish, I slap them onto a buttered piece of toast and walk over to the island. The kid looks up to meet my gaze straight on and flinches back.

I keep forgetting about my eye. It always startles those not expecting it. I guess the kid didn't get a good look at me in the warehouse. In reality it's just a cataract—I got "lucky" and developed it at the ripe old age of twenty-five—and it leaves my left pupil milky white, surrounded by a dark brown iris. I'm basically blind in that eye and most assume I got it in a fight. It leaves them feeling unsettled, which only works to my advantage.

"Here," I say, tossing down the plate of food. "Eggs."

He pulls the toast close and averts his gaze. I walk away and crack two more shells open in order to fry up my own. When I turn back, I notice the kid already inhaled his food. Figures.

I finish cooking my eggs and take my time consuming them. The kid sits in silence, and I don't even bother engaging him. I stare out the window. The pulse of nightlife intensifies. Friday is a good night to be out on the town.

The kid clears his throat. "You're Big Man Vice's personal enforcer? They call you Pierce?"

"That's right," I reply. I'm not surprised he knows of me. My reputation is well-known on the streets.

"You're the enforcer that… er, is with men?"

Tsk. I guess *everything* about me is well-known. "You gotta problem with that?"

"*No*. No. Of course not."

"Then why bring it up?"

"I was just curious...." He avoids my gaze.

It's an odd thing to ask right out the gate. It makes me wonder why it's at the forefront of his mind. People are like a grab bag of emotions—you never know who's gonna flip out over trivial details, like where I stick my dick—but I've long gotten over it. If the kid has a problem, I can throw him in the gutter and be done with this mess.

He doesn't say anything further. It's probably for the best.

"I'm leaving," I say. "I have things to do tonight. I'll be back before dawn."

After throwing my dishes into the sink, I grab my jacket and light up a cigarette. I really should cut back, but I never get around to it, even though I'm running through a pack a day.

"You're just gonna leave me here?" the kid asks, furrowing his brow.

"Yeah," I reply. "You're a grown-ass man. You can take care of yourself now that you're awake."

He straightens his posture. "But.... You trust me? In... your house?"

"You're smart, aren't ya?"

"Smart?" he repeats.

I nod and exhale a line of smoke. "Yeah. A smart kid like you would know not to cross me, right? He would know that if he fucked with my stuff, right after I stuck my neck out for him, that I would hunt him down and make him regret it? You know that, right? Of course you do. You're smart."

"Yeah. Yeah, I think I'm smart enough to know that."

"Good. Then sit tight. I'll be back later tonight."

"I can... use your shower and... eat more?"

"You better."

He tries to restrain a laugh but fails. With an unsteady hand, he combs back his hair and stares at the kitchen floor. "Why are you...?" he whispers.

I pretend not to hear and leave before he questions me further. I don't need those kinds of questions.

THE CITY of Noimore bustles with the same rhythm it had ten years ago. The same streetwalker stalks the corner of my street, and I give her a sideways glance as I drive by. She probably recognizes me on sight. Same goes for the dealers across the street and the homeless lady who inhabits the bus stop. They've lived in the neighborhood longer than I have, and I wouldn't be surprised if the post office delivers their mail to their permanent haunts.

Same shit. Different night. I feel like the literal definition of stagnation.

I pull my car up into the parking lot of my apartment complex and park. Working eight hours straight gets me on edge, but I go wherever the Vice family sends me. Lucky for me tonight was a simple "watch the location" gig. Apparently the Cobras have been in the Vice family's business more than I realized, and Big Man Vice needed me to make sure his deliveries made it to their destinations safe and sound.

Snuffing out my cigarette, I step out of my vehicle. It's an hour or two before dawn and the city has settled down, but the cry of the weekend keeps most denizens awake long after their bedtime. I cast glowers at the drunkards blocking the sidewalk and push them out of my way should they miss the hint. No one offers me any back talk. Probably better for them in the long run.

Once at my apartment door, I stop and finger my gun. A small piece of me wonders if the kid inside is going to try something stupid. He could be lying in wait, ready to "deal with me" before making his escape. All my guns are in a safe, so I doubt he has those, but that doesn't mean he didn't fashion himself a makeshift club from a chair or something. Better safe than sorry.

I open my door and swing it in. The kid isn't in the entrance hall. With careful steps, I make my way deeper inside, stopping only once I reach the kitchen.

The lights are off, but I hear someone fumbling in the spare back room. Stress leaves my body. I put away the gun and switch on the corner light. It's nothing too bright, but just enough for me to make my way into the attached living room.

I kick off my shoes, remove my suit jacket, land in my recliner, and flip on the news.

Sometimes it really does feel as though nothing ever changes. Even the newscaster reports the evening's events as though he's a time-traveler stuck repeating the same goddamn day for all eternity. *Crime rates* this and *police force* that. Occasionally they talk about the upcoming elections. It's hard to give a shit when it seems as though you've seen everything once before. All I care about is news relating to the Vice family or the Cobras. I don't want to be left out of the loop.

I scratch along the straps of my shoulder holster. I should've taken it off, but my nerves get the better of me. I still don't trust the kid—the handgun gives me reassurance. I keep the shoulder holster on despite the discomfort.

Like a ghost the kid emerges from the darkness of the house. He's walking around without limping or creeping, something I'm still impressed with, but the bruises will be there for days. He might have some cracked bones too. Those have gotta hurt.

I mute the TV.

"Hey," I say, though I don't get up.

"Hey," he replies. He's more… confident. He steps out into the living room without being prodded and holds himself straight. His old bloodied jeans make him look like a serial killer, but that's okay. Serial killers don't frighten me.

"*Miles*, was it? We gotta talk."

He stares down at the floor, losing a bit of his confidence as he crosses the room to my chair. "I need to thank you," he states. "You didn't have to help me in the warehouse, but you did anyway. They were… gonna kill me back there. And, uh, I'm sorry I lied to the Vice family in the first place. I was just trying to—"

"Forget it," I interject. "It was nothing."

"It wasn't *nothing*. It was *my life*. I know it might not mean much to you… but it means everything to me, okay?" He swallows hard enough for me to hear. "I… need to thank you."

"No, you don't."

"Yes, I do," he says, a hint of defiance in his tone. He clenches his hands into fists and hides most of his face with his hair. "I couldn't live with myself if I didn't."

I restrain a smile. Is this kid worried about his honor? Does he have some sort of code he lives by? That'll get him killed on the streets of Noimore, no doubt. Still—it's yet another detail I admire. How did he ever get mixed up with the Vice family in the first place? He should've stuck to the straight and narrow. He could've done well there.

For a moment the kid's silent and still, but eventually he regains his lost confidence. He holds his head up and stares down at me.

"Listen. *Thank you*. What can I do to make it up to you?"

"You got money?"

He looks taken aback by my sudden response. He shakes his head.

"You got any cars?"

"No. No cars."

"What about guns? Have any of those stashed away?"

"No...."

I light up a cigarette and offer him one. The kid rejects with a motion of his hand. I tuck the pack back into my pocket and take a long drag. "Whelp," I drawl. "You're just as broke as I thought you'd be. How about you send me a nice Christmas card next year? That's assuming you don't get yourself into more trouble by then. And that you have the money for a card."

"Tsk." He turns away, tense. I hit a nerve. The kid's practically red in the face, though it's hard to see, what with the black eye and busted ear. I chuckle to myself, amused by his pride. I didn't help him because I wanted thanks; the kid just needs to get over it. There's nothing he has that I want.

The kid walks around to the front of my chair. I lift an eyebrow. He's blocking the television. He drops to his knees between my legs and avoids my gaze. Heat pulses through my body the instant I realize what's going on. I go still, cigarette between my fingers, unable to bring myself to act.

With rigid movements he leans down and drags his tongue along the zipper of my pants, tracing the ever-increasing bulge of my cock. It's so brazen and sexual that my mind locks up with lust, most of my blood pumping south. I want him. It's all I can think about now.

He hesitates, losing some of his bold bravado, and I realize he's waiting for my acceptance. I widen my legs, not uttering a word, and he reaches up to fumble with my belt buckle.

This is actually happening. I'm on the verge of surreal disbelief, if only because it's never happened quite like *this* before. Everyone knows my proclivities and preferences, but I haven't known a man to "reward" me with a blowjob. The surprise and anticipation of it all gets me close, even without much contact. Fuck, it's been a while. I guess the kid *does* have something I want.

I can see his hands are shaking. Regaining a slight amount of control, I take a long drag on my cigarette to calm my own excitement. He releases my erection from the constraints of my clothing and runs his mouth along the length. His trembling… it drives me mad. It takes all my willpower to just stay seated and watch. He licks along the underside before taking me in his mouth. The slick warmth of it all causes me to shudder. I've been alone for too long. A hand just doesn't compare.

He goes halfway, sucking and licking the entire time, inching his way down. I grit my teeth when he reaches the base. He half gags and tightens his throat around my cock. Groans of pleasure escape me. I want him to go faster, but I say nothing.

The kid—no, that's wrong now—*Miles* pulls up and thrusts back down, forcing himself deeper. With each repeat I restrain a moan. He goes again until his canines catch along the side of my sensitive flesh. Pain flares through me. I grab a fistful of his hair and yank him up.

"*Watch your fucking teeth.*"

"I'm sorry," he says, gulping down air. "I've never done this before…."

Lust overtakes me. After a moment I don't feel the pain, and the submissive way he avoids staring up at me gets the blood rushing once more. I release his hair and pull him closer. He swallows and waits while I run my thumb over his lips. Like he knows what I want, he opens his mouth and I slide my digit back along the length of his tongue. He sucks on it, gentle and slow.

"Use more of your tongue," I command, rubbing my thumb along the muscle.

He pulls away, nods, and returns his mouth to my cock. I lean back and enjoy the heated pleasure as he takes it all the way the first time, despite gagging. He's good at following instructions, at least. He uses his tongue to pad his sucking—even going so far as to caress the tip.

I'm rapt by his movements. I place my free hand on the back of his head and comb my fingers through his silky black hair. It's not going to take me long, not if he keeps going with such enthusiasm. I grip his hair when he picks up his pace. He's skilled for someone who hasn't done this before.

"You look good like this," I say between husky breaths.

He turns a shade of crimson, and I swear I can feel his mouth increase in temperature. I chuckle as I tilt my head back and focus on the sensations. God, I'm close. I buck my hips, and he offers a guttural moan. Is he enjoying this? Even the mere idea that he wants cock in his mouth sends me over the edge. I tense, my hand trapping his head in place as I pump my seed down the back of his throat. He swallows—

if only because that's all he can do—and I fall back against the chair, loosening my grip on his hair.

Miles pulls away, coughing. He inhales a couple of times, but after a moment he regains his composure. I zip up my pants and allow the afterglow of the situation to settle on me. It went fast, but intense. I haven't fucked someone's mouth in a long time. It felt good. *Real good.*

My forgotten cigarette is nothing but a line of ash, and I snuff it out.

"You weren't half-bad," I tell him, somewhat out of breath.

Still on his knees and between my legs, he replies, "I'll do better next time."

My cock throbs at the statement, ready for a second round, but my mind reasserts itself. "If you're just hungry for dick, there's a good line of work for you as a prostitute."

"That's… not what I want."

"Heh. Well, there isn't going to be a *next time*. The plan is that I give you some money and you blow town. I tell Jeremy I had to put you down like a sick dog, and then no one ever finds out about *this. Capisce?*"

Miles lowers his gaze and takes a short breath. "I can't. Not without my brother. I don't want to leave town without him."

I narrow my eyes. "What the fuck are you thinkin'? This isn't a game. If they catch you around town, they won't hesitate to finish what they started. Take the money and get out while you can. It's the smart option."

"My brother gets into trouble all the time. He says he'll leave the Cobras, but if I go, I know he'll just fall back into it."

"So? Why is that your problem?"

"He's my brother…."

I don't understand. I don't have any siblings, and I'm glad that's the case. They sound like trouble.

"What if I stay?" Miles asks, glancing up to meet my gaze with his. "And we do what you said we would do? Just until I find my brother. Once I find Jayden, I can skip town."

"You aren't actually *in* with the police."

"I could be."

"Nothing's that simple, kid. I'm not workin' pro bono either. I helped you once and that's my good deed for the decade."

"Please," he says, gripping my slacks. "I won't be any trouble. I'll shadow you around and do whatever you say. Just until I find Jayden and we can leave. Maybe I can even get in good with the cops and you can impress Jeremy."

I don't need to impress Jeremy, but I can't help but feel conflicted by Miles's begging. He doesn't have anyone else to turn to? Why is this being thrown into *my* lap? I should've known this would be a bigger hassle than I originally anticipated.

I remain silent and stare. My rational side says I should get rid of him now. Then again, if he gets caught on the streets, Jeremy will blame me for letting him roam around. It'll look bad, especially after I said I would handle the situation one way or the other.

When I remain quiet, the kid tightens his grip. "Please. I don't have much, but I'll pay you back any way I can. I… haven't fully repaid you for saving my life either."

My mouth goes dry with anticipation. The look in his eye gets me excited. It's a terrible idea to actually try and manipulate the police with an amateur involved.

I know I'm thinkin' with my dick, but I offer him a one-sided smile. "You're gonna do everything I say. No questions. No back talk. Got it? I won't suffer a sad sack as company—not when life sentences and death are on the line."

Miles widens his eyes in excitement. "*Really*? Thank you. You won't regret it!"

I hope not.

CHAPTER THREE

I RUB at my good eye, struggling to stay awake.

The streets of Noimore are always congested Saturday night. I turn down a back road and continue through the grime and rain. Despite the storm, people stand on the corners—vagabonds and hookers—all asking for money. I ignore them and try to focus.

Last night was hell.

Knowing Miles slept only a room over killed my ability to sleep. A combination of paranoia and excitement kept me tossing and turning. I've worked with gangsters for so long, all I can imagine is that he's secretly out to slice my throat open the moment I give him an opening. I glance over to the passenger seat. He sits, his gaze glued to the passing sidewalks, with a relaxed posture.

He turns and catches me staring.

"What is it?" he asks.

I return my attention to the road. "You're recovering pretty quick."

"Thanks to your painkillers."

"Don't get used to 'em. Once they're gone, *they're gone.*"

"I'll be fine. I've gone through stuff like this before."

"Oh yeah? Brisko and Pete had to beat some sense into you?"

"No. My father did."

I stop asking questions.

We make it to the slummy part of town, and my nose knows it. Everything reeks of trash and marijuana, even during the rain. If anything, the rain adds its own foul soggy scent that causes my lip to curl. I hate this place. It reminds me of the first night when I struck out on my own so many years ago....

I pull the car up to a three-story "hotel" and park.

Miles fidgets with his seat belt. "What're we doing here?"

"The boss called me. Said I needed to take care of some business here."

"How is this helping me get in good with the police?"

"It's not. We just gotta wait for something to present itself. Until then you stay with me and *only me*, got it? I don't want anyone calling your loyalty into question."

"All right."

I step out of my car and squint at the flashing neon red sign that reads ROOMS BY THE HOUR. Who rents rooms by the hour? Johns and their call girls. Why get a room for the whole night when you only need six minutes and a bottle of lube? It's a cheap-ass place for cheap-ass lowlifes. I walk up to the front door—a heavy metal thing with bars and security latches—and step in.

The girl at the front desk smiles wide.

"Pierce! I knew they'd send you, puddin'. What took you so long?"

"Stella," I reply, addressing her.

Her watery blue eyes immediately hone in on Miles. She throws back one of her blonde pigtails and straightens her lacy bra, the garment clearly visible under her chiffon blouse. "Ooohhh. I see you brought a buddy. Did you two need a room?"

"You know I'm here for business."

Miles glances around the small waiting room, his attention drawn to the many pictures of half-naked women on the walls. "Uh," he says. "What kind of place is this?"

Stella lifts one of her drawn-on eyebrows. "Oh boy. He's green. *Real* green. Who is this kid, Pierce?"

"Never mind him," I snap. "Just tell me which room I need to inspect."

"I'm not *that* green," Miles says. He holds out a hand for Stella. "I'm Miles. It's nice to meet you."

The girl clearly doesn't know what to think. She holds out her hand, half in confusion, and shakes. "My, my. You're a little gentleman, aren't you? Are you Pierce's replacement?" She turns to me with a smarmy smile. "Did they say you're getting too old, Pierce, is that it? Is this Big Man Vice's new favorite?"

I grit my teeth. "Just give me the room number, Stella."

Miles looks me over from head to toe. "What're you talking about? Too old? He doesn't look that old."

Stella giggles. "Oh, you're so cute I could just eat you up. You hear that, Pierce? You're not *that* old."

I don't dignify the conversation with a response.

"How old is he?" Miles asks the girl.

"Oh, I don't know. He's just been around a long time. Longer than most in the business, ya know what I'm sayin'? It's a young man's game on the streets. Guys like Pierce are rare."

"Enough," I state. "Tell us the damn room number."

She mulls over the demand and says, "First room off the elevator on the third floor. Three A. You won't miss it. Hurry with it, won't ya? We can't rent any rooms on that floor while the mess is still there."

I walk over to the elevator and open the door. Miles shadows my steps, nodding to Stella as the door closes behind him. I hit the third floor button and sigh as I hear the ancient gears of the machine flare to life. I doubt an inspector has been out to this elevator in over a decade. If I die here, I won't be surprised.

The lift starts up like molasses.

"How old are you?" Miles asks.

"Thirty-six," I reply as curt as possible. Do we need to talk?

"When did the Vice family hire you for… this line of work?"

"Twenty years ago."

"So you were sixteen when you first started with them?"

"Oh good. You can do basic math."

He gives me a seething sideways glance. "Yeah. Of course I can do simple math. I graduated high school, ya know."

"What an accomplishment. No one has ever done that before."

Miles shoves his hands into his pockets and turns away, his posture stiff. I glance over and sigh, but my gaze trails the outline of his body. He looks better in slacks and a button-down shirt. They're mine, so they're a little too big, but he still wears them well. I glare up at the roof of the elevator, listening to the slow grind of gears.

"At least you're not an idiot like Brisko and Pete," I say as the elevator reaches the top. "I prefer workin' with someone who knows a yard can also be a unit of measurement."

He laughs once and then quiets himself, but his posture goes back to relaxed.

We step out into the hall, and I see the room we came for. The door is ajar, the inside well-lit with three lamps. I walk in and take note of the surroundings. It's a small room—a single bed and a single nightstand—but those are details I take in after the copious amount of blood splattered across the walls.

Gunshot splatters. I'd bet my life on it. I've seen 'em a hundred times.

The rank odor of coagulated bodily fluids washes over me. My gaze falls to the bodies strewn about the floor. There's a girl, half undressed and brains blown everywhere, and then there's a guy missing his pants. I get a good look at his face. He's Mikey Vice, the Big Man Vice's cousin.

I don't know the girl. Her corpse bothers me. What kind of sick fuck would kill an uninvolved party? The girl didn't have anything to do with this. She didn't deserve a bullet to the head just because Mikey wanted to get his rocks off. Her death almost disturbs me more than the Vice's—I have my standards.

Miles grimaces the instant he gets an eyeful of the room. He backs up to the elevator. "What... happened?"

I walk around, careful not to step on anything. Mikey got caught with his pants down, both literally and figuratively. Multiple gunshot wounds to the body. He bled to death. Slowly. I scan everything—it's difficult with one bad eye, but I take my time. Lucky for me, the killer *wanted* to be known. I find a calling card on the bed, tucked between the disheveled sheets. It's a business card with a snake on the back. I snatch up the scrap of paper using the sleeve of my coat.

Cobras. It's always the Cobras. I could have guessed. They wanted to send a message.

Miles ambles back to the door and leans against the frame. "How could the girl downstairs be so cheery?"

"She works in the industry of faking emotions," I quip. "Besides, I bet this isn't the first time she's seen this."

"Are the cops on their way?"

"No one here calls the cops. They deal with the problems themselves. Do you really think a bunch of hookers want cops scoping out the area? It's bad for business."

"Don't the... other women... want the killer caught?"

"Oh, the killer will be brought to justice," I say. "He's a damn scumbag who deserves everything that's coming to him."

Miles averts his gaze, unable to bring himself to look at the gore for longer than a few moments. "You care about the girl?"

"I don't kill innocent hardworking people. If some gangbanger encroaches on Vice territory, he's fair game. They knew what they had comin'. The girl, on the other hand, was just making ends meet. She isn't part of our feud. Obviously the killer didn't give a shit. He blew her brains out regardless. No moral compass whatsoever. Those types of people shouldn't be roaming the streets."

"I didn't know you felt that way."

I don't say anything, but that one rule is the only way I know I'm still human—that I still have empathy. Don't shoot the innocent people. Streetwise thugs have it coming. Gunrunners are just as bad. Dealers even worse. But the average man minding his own business? Never.

Miles furrows his brow in contemplation.

"What is it?" I ask.

"I was just wondering…. What if we could use this somehow?"

I turn to face him. Miles rubs at his neck and shrugs.

"Maybe we move the bodies and I take the card to the precinct, ya know? I tell them where the bodies are, and that the Cobras did it."

I mull over the possibility. If it were going to work, he would need to contact someone on the inside. I pull out my wallet and finger through the cards I have stored away. Detective Ambers is trusting—but is she trusting enough? Depends on how Miles handles himself. After pulling my phone, I dial up my favorite stooge and wait until he answers.

"Yeah?" Brisko says, his voice saliva-swallowing thick.

"This is Pierce. Get over to the Getaway Inn. Ya know the one."

"Whatever ya say."

"Bring some lifters, a van, and a tarp. We have bodies to move."

"I'll be there."

I hang up the phone and toss Miles the detective's card. "Later tonight you're going to call that number when you make your tip, got it?"

He flips the card over and examines the words carefully. "Detective Ambers?"

"Yeah. You know her?"

"N-no," he mutters. "It's just an odd name."

I don't like the way he answers… seems off, but I can't place it. I don't know the man like I should.

With a sigh I walk back out into the hall. "You can't ask to be her lackey or else she'll know something is up. Just say you're tired of all the death and pointlessness. Tell her you want to save people for a change, or some bullshit like that. Something she can latch on to and think you're trustworthy somehow. *She* has to be the one who suggests you're a mole if you're ever going to gain her support."

Miles follows close to me. "Aren't you tired of all the pointless death?" he asks, his voice low and his gaze fixed on mine. "I mean, that girl back there…. She got shot because she was with the wrong john, right? Pretty pointless…."

I pull a cigarette from my coat pocket and light it up. "You get used to it."

"You sounded pretty upset when you talked about her death."

"That was different."

"You saved me from Pete and Brisko. You didn't have to do that."

I shoot him a glare and exhale smoke through my nostrils. "Whadda ya want from me? To shoot you right now to make my point? Don't test my mercy. I almost shot you on my drive back to my flat. You're lucky, okay? Just lucky."

Miles turns away with the jerk of his head, grimacing in pain from his leftover injuries. He rubs at his shoulder and leans back against the wall, glaring at the tacky fake plants lining the hallway.

"Sorry," he intones. After a moment he takes a deep breath. "I knew joining the Vice family was a mistake after the first couple of weeks. I just wanted to know if you felt the same—if you ever regretted it."

I refuse to answer him. What does he expect me to say? It's a little late for that now.

"You had your chance to leave," I say. "I offered to give you money and send you on your way."

Miles continues staring off into nothing, but his eyebrows knit into worry.

I continue, "The offer is still on the table. I can make 'em think you're dead."

"No," he says. "No, that's not what I want. Look, I'm sorry. I'm grateful for everything you've done. I shouldn't have brought it up."

You should just skip town is what I want to say. The longer he stays, the more likely this will become his permanent occupation. It's not that he *can't* do the job; it's that I don't want to see him go through with it. He has a "do anything it takes" attitude, which is good for this line of work, but he still has a straight edge about him: apologizing, greeting ladies with a hint of respect and etiquette. A year or two following me around, and he'll be just like Pete and Brisko. A thug.

"Let's take the stairs," I say, shaking the thoughts from my head. "We should wait in the lobby and get some information."

Miles nods and follows me back down. The trek through the stairwell is safer than the elevator, despite the lack of fire safety and windows. When we enter the lobby, I spot Stella giving a threesome a key to a first-floor room.

"We'll give you a fifteen-minute warning knock," she says in a singsong voice.

Two men and one streetwalker disappear into the back hallway, giggling like only drunks can. I approach Stella and lift an eyebrow. She rests her elbows on the front counter and her chin in both hands.

"Pierce. You have a sour look on your face, puddin'. What's wrong?"

"Did anyone see anything?" I ask. "Before the gunshots?"

"I didn't, but Joey did."

"Joey? The janitor you ladies pay in sad hand jobs?"

"Yeah. He's the one. Said he saw a guy shadowing the hallway before everything went down. A small guy with a neck tattoo of some lady's tits."

I curse under my breath. I've seen that asshole around. Definitely part of the Cobras. Well, that makes everything a little easier—I'll track him down and make him talk. Maybe I'll put a few bullets in him for the girl's sake….

"Do you really pay a guy in hand jobs?" Miles asks, his back against the far wall and his hands in his pockets.

Stella forces a giggle. "Oh, wouldn't you like to know?"

"Anything else?" I interject before the conversation is completely derailed by bullshit.

"Hm. I can't remember anything else, puddin'. Maybe you should jog my memory."

Stella leans in closer to me, cramming her jugs together with her arms. They look like they'll explode out of her bra at any moment. I roll my eyes and pull out my wallet. "How much this time?"

She frowns. "Hey. I'll have you know that I need to make dough just like every other sad sack in this town. I got kids to feed and rent to pay!"

"I said *how much*, not *tell me about your damn kids*."

"Fifty."

"Is it worth fifty?"

"It's *definitely* worth fifty."

I wait. Stella glowers at me. I'm not paying her until I hear the information, and she knows it.

"Fine," she huffs. "Listen. I was at the front desk when it all went down. I never saw the guy, but I *did* see a car waiting outside with a big son of a bitch at the wheel. He peeled outta here fast after everything happened. I think the shooter has some serious muscle protecting him. The driver had hands like hams and a bald head. Tough. Tougher than you, I'd wager."

"Heh. We'll see. Bullets don't care how thick your hands are."

Stella licks her lips as she eyes my wallet. "Well? Pay up."

I pull a hundred and toss it on the counter. She snaps it up and shoves it down her bra, tucking it under the breast. "Oh my, so generous. What's the occasion?"

"You're just so cute," I drawl, shoving my wallet into my pants pocket.

"Oh please—don't give me any of that. Everyone knows you only get hard at the sight of cock."

"Really? The way you were shimmying out of your clothes made me think you forgot."

She giggles again, a slight hint of red peeking through her makeup. "Oh, that's just my normal way of doing things, puddin'. It works on most guys. You know the drill."

I finish my cigarette and make my way over to Miles's little corner of the room. Tossing the butt in the trash, I give him a sideways glance. Before I ask him what's on his mind, the front door opens, Brisko panting from the short jog.

"I'm here, Pierce," he says between heavy breaths. Three more guys enter behind him. Muscle. Perfect.

I motion to the elevator. "There are two bodies. Take Mikey Vice to the family estate. Big Man Vice will decide what to do with it. Take the girl and throw her under Pier Eight, all right? On the rocks, not the water. Make sure she's visible, but not visible from the street."

"Got it, got it."

"And place this card on her." I pull out the Cobras' calling card, keeping my prints off it. Brisko, with gloves, takes the card and tucks it away in his jacket. "Make sure it stays on her body."

"Got it," he drones again, stuck on automatic replies.

Stella snorts and crosses her arms over her considerable chest. "Are you really gonna do Candy like that? She was a nice girl. You're doin' her wrong with this."

"If you care so much about her, what's her real name?" I ask.

"Uh…." Stella fidgets for a moment. "I think I know this…. Uh…. Sugarlips?"

"That's what I thought," I say. "But don't worry. She's goin' to the cops after this. They'll identify her and get her back to someone who knows her."

"Oh… I guess that's okay, then. Just don't get the cops back involved in our neighborhood, or else there'll be hell to pay."

I motion for Miles to follow me outside. We still have places to go before the night is up. He complies but avoids Brisko at all costs. The moment we exit, we're both soaked. The rain didn't let up, and it doesn't look like it's going away anytime soon.

We jog over to my car and jump in, getting the seats wet in the process. Miles fastens his seat belt and gives me a half smile. "You gave her a lot of money."

"You make nice with the little guys," I reply, taking the car out of the lot. "Remember that. If she has information in the future, you know she'll call us."

CHAPTER FOUR

"I didn't know Noimore still had pay phones," Miles says as he slides his quarters into the machine. I lean on the glass wall, watching the rain from the safety of the booth. Traffic rushes by, some of them ignoring the red lights. I suspect the intersection has its fair share of accidents since the cops are nowhere to be seen.

Miles clears his throat. "Hello?" he says into the receiver.

I step out of the booth and walk under the overhang for the subway. Noimore City Bus Transit doesn't make it out to this part of the town. Trash has accumulated in every corner of the public area, most of it soaked in urine. Passengers shuffle out of the underground with their heads down. When a lady walks over to the phone booth, I step in her way and shake my head. She flinches back and hustles away. I hate busy thoroughfares.

My cell phone buzzes in my pocket. I pull it out and scan the screen.

Nicholas Vice—Big Man Vice, as most know him—calling me directly. I answer.

"Nick," I say.

"Pierce," he replies, his voice a deep rich tone that reflects his mood like a mirror. "Where are you?"

"On the corner of Twenty-Third and H."

"I want you to meet me. I'm sending you a ride."

"I'll be there."

He hangs up and the conversation ends. I tuck my phone away, dwelling on the possibilities. He's not a talkative man, and I appreciate that, but I'd still like more information than *no* information. I know he's not upset with me; I'd have heard it in his voice. Plus, he's superstitious at some level…. He's always liked me a little more than his other enforcers, simply because we share the same first name. The moment I introduced myself as *Nicholas Pierce*, he took me into his personal circle of guards. Guess I got lucky.

I glance over at my car. It's parked in a public spot, nothing too shady. A piece of me knows it'll get broken into if I leave it too long, but I'm not going to refuse Big Man Vice's ride. I'll take my chances.

Miles exits the phone booth and takes his place by my side. "Hey. I talked to the detective and told her where to find the body."

"And?"

"And she said she appreciated my tip. She didn't say anything about me being a mole."

"Of course not," I say. "It's about establishing a pattern. We do it once or twice more, maybe even something you can help prevent, and she'll ask you. Trust me. Just play the part."

I wish I had stayed in the booth to hear the conversation. I'm not sure how good a liar Miles is. Perhaps Detective Ambers pegged him immediately. Oh well. I'll deal with it later, if or when it becomes a problem.

"So, what're we doing now?" Miles asks, huddling closer to me. He didn't bring a jacket, and he shivers from time to time.

"We're waiting."

"Waiting? For what? Is this a reconnaissance thing?"

"It's a waiting thing."

Miles exhales but doesn't question me further. Another thing I like—he's copacetic and easygoing. If he had been difficult, this wouldn't work. I don't have the patience I used to.

While I stare I catch myself admiring his form. The rain gets his clothes wet and everything clings. His smooth face, slicked black hair, and discerning eyes are a pleasant sight. He drops one hand to the crotch of his pants, squeezing and adjusting, no doubt an unconscious motion, but still….

I stop my leering and force myself to stare at the traffic lights. I haven't been this horny in God only knows how long. We're in the middle of the seediest part of town; no one would blink an eye if I took Miles into the shadows of a nearby alley and forced him to his knees. Hell, they might not even intervene if I had Miles get on his knees right here, in front of the subway. There'd be a bunch of sick fucks getting off on me using his mouth…. I wonder if Miles would even do it.

I rub at my eyes. I need to stop. All night I've been stealing glances and fantasizing… now it's finally hitting a point that I need to do something about it or else it'll just get in the way.

"I'll be right back," I say.

I saunter out to my car, allowing the icy rain to pelt my body. It chills the ever-building desire, and I breathe easy. I don't know why, but I get uneasy thinking about Miles in compromising positions. I wait a few moments. All I need is to make it through the night. I'll take my "payment" from him when we get back to my flat, if he's still offering.

As I return he gives me an odd look and tilts his head. "What was that?"

"What was what?"

"You went to your car, stood around, and then walked back."

I run my hand along the back of my neck. I got nothin'. "Life's a fuckin' mystery, kid. Get used to it."

He chuckles, a bemused look on his face. "Ever think about writing fortune cookies?"

Even I get a chuckle from that. Ah, how I miss wit. I need to stop spending time near Pete and Brisko.

After a few minutes, a limo pulls up to the corner. Big Man Vice doesn't do things cheap. I open the back door and slide in. Miles hovers around, glancing over his shoulder and then back at the luxury vehicle. Before I yell at him, he gets in, taking a seat next to me in the back, despite having the option to sit anywhere along the side of the interior. Once the door shuts, the driver lurches us forward. Must be in hurry. He *did* get here quick. He may have even been in the area....

I relax back against the soft leather of the seat. The divider window is shut tight, giving the back area a bit of privacy. Multicolored lights, dim and pleasant enough, line the floor and roof, giving the back a "party room" feel. Bottles of vodka and champagne fill the side compartments, and I help myself to one. Hard liquor is my drug of choice, next to cigarettes. I don't even bother with a glass—I throw off the top of a vodka bottle and take a swig. The burning sensation doesn't last long, but the heat in my belly does. Good ol' vodka.

With a lifted eyebrow, I offer the bottle to Miles. He takes a shot glass from the side door and holds it out. I pour him a drink and he throws it back. To my surprise he doesn't cough it up or make a mess. He's had his share of hard liquor. I pour him another.

Besides the tinkling of glass against glass, the ride is quiet. Miles throws back his second shot and then exhales.

"You have any scars?" he asks out of the blue.

I give him an *of course I fucking have scars* look.

He replies with a sardonic stare. "Which one's your worst?" he clarifies.

"Some asshole stabbed me in the leg a couple of years back. I walk around a lot—it made recovery an arduous process, to say the least."

"Can I see it?"

I snort back a laugh and shrug. I pull up my pant leg and show off the gnarly piece of work left by the blade wound. It runs from the side of my knee down to my ankle, leaving a hairless line of protruding knotted flesh. I got lucky and didn't need surgery on my kneecap, though the doctor said I might if I kept running around on it.

The lighting is terrible, and Miles takes his time examining my old injury. Once he's done I release the fabric and we both lean back.

"What happened to your eye?" he asks, his tone hesitant. That's probably what he wanted to ask in the first place.

"Oh, that's one hell of a story."

"R-really? What happened?"

I smile. "I was at this bar when a fight broke out with some bruisers from the Red Spades. My buddies were surprised and got a slug to the back, but I managed to gun a few down before hiding behind the counter. It was just me and this one guy—a seven-foot-tall guy—and we ended using broken bottles as weapons. He clipped my eye, and I caught him in the throat. Blood everywhere."

Miles, wide-eyed, nods along with my words. "Wow. That's crazy. I'm impressed."

Heh. People will believe anything. I restrain a chuckle and take another swig of vodka. I cringe. Too much. After I get my breath back, I throw my arms up on the back of the seat. "What about you? Got any scars?"

"Uh, not really."

"It's a yes or no question. Don't make this needlessly complicated."

"Well, *yes*," he says with a sigh. "But it's not a *fighting* scar. It's a… well, I had my appendix removed. I broke open the stitches when I was younger, and I had to go back to the hospital a few times. It left a noticeable scar, even though I was ten at the time."

"Let's see it."

He laughs. I say nothing. He stops laughing. "Seriously? It's nothing to look at."

When the silence persists, he gets nervous and forces a smile. I wait and he eventually gets the picture. Leaning back, and with unsteady hands, he unbuckles his belt, unzips himself, and pulls down his slacks, revealing the top of his black boxers. He pulls those down without exposing himself and shows me the *V* cut of his hip just above the good stuff. There's a scar—a straight medical scar—starting from his side and angling downward, ending at his treasure trail.

The dividing window slides down, and the driver glances back at us through the rearview mirror. Miles grabs at his clothes and attempts to pull them up in a hasty fumbling ball of panic.

"Whoa, whoa," the driver says, lifting his fingers off the wheel. "I fully support your right to, uh, do *whatever it is* you guys are doin' back there. I just wanna ask Pierce somethin' before it gets thick."

"Leave 'em down," I command Miles. He stops before he gets his clothing up and hesitates. I turn my attention to the driver. "Diego? Is that you?"

"That's right," the driver replies. "I've been first driver for a while now and—"

"Ask your question and be done with it."

Diego chortles. "Have you seen Cordoba around? He hasn't been answerin' his phone. It's been a whole week since I've seen him 'round Big Man Vice's house."

"No. I haven't seen him."

Which is the punchline to most questions nowadays. So many people are turning up dead or going missing. If we don't get on top of this, everything is going to go south real fucking fast.

"That's what I was afraid of," Diego says, rolling up the divider window.

I return my attention to Miles. He's got his head down and his pants half back in position. I tuck a finger in the belt loop and pull them back down to get a better look at the scar. He gets stiff when I run my thumb over the injury and trail my hand down farther.

"What's this?" I ask, catching sight of a black line inked into his flesh and running to the outside of his hip.

"A tattoo," he says, his voice shaky. After inhaling he repeats, in a steadier voice, "A tattoo."

"Of what?"

"A phoenix."

As much as I want to inquire about his tattoo—and pull his pants off to get a good look at it—I stop to admire how hard he is. He tries to hide it by pulling on his pants and shifting in his seat, but with his zipper down there isn't any escape. I set my vodka down.

"Unbutton your shirt," I say, enjoying the way he avoids looking at me straight on.

He's obedient and does what I tell him to, getting me hot all over again despite my shower in the rain. Miles opens his shirt, and I take in his youthful, toned body. His bruises have healed somewhat—they mar an otherwise delicious piece of meat. He shudders under my gaze, but that's all right. The precome soaking his boxers is enough to know he's enjoying himself.

"You ever let another guy take you in the ass?"

Miles grows red and his dick involuntarily twitches at my question. He shakes his head. I lean in close, enjoying the raw musk of sex. Sweat beads across his half-naked body, and the close confines of the backseat make everything erotic.

I slam his back against the door and corner of the seat, trapping him in place as I loom over. He doesn't resist and, instead, leans back to give me better access. I didn't know he wanted it this badly. It drives me mad, but I maintain control. Barely.

"You're gonna be my bitch. Ya know that, right?" I whisper, my breathing heavy. I get in close to his neck and bite down on the nape, enjoying the gasp he offers in return. I lick the injury in a sensual apology, though I want the mark to show. The salty taste of his skin is just what I've been craving. He whimpers and my clothing feels too constraining.

This is gonna happen.

I rip off a few buttons on my shirt just as the limo comes to a halt.

Shit. I should've fucked him at the inn when I had the chance. I sit back in my seat, distancing myself from Miles and taking a few deep breaths. He pulls his clothes together as the divider window rolls down a second time.

"We're here," Diego says.

"I see that," I reply in a husky voice.

After the overpowering urges of lust leave my thoughts, I chuckle. I'm glad I didn't fuck him at the inn. I have higher standards than a pay-by-the-hour brothel with dead bodies in it. What the hell was I thinking? The mind goes to some strange places when consumed by carnal desire. I'm completely fucked-up sometimes.

I open the limo door and step out. Miles attempts to straighten himself, but I hold up a hand.

"Stay here."

"Why?" he asks, his heart rate still obviously high.

"I'm gonna meet Nick, and then we're gonna drive back. Simple stuff. Plus, he doesn't appreciate uninvited guests. Just wait here."

"All right. Fine. I'll wait."

The rain washes over me once more, chilling all desires and returning me to my normal state of not giving a fuck. The limo is parked in front of Big Man Vice's favorite evening hideout, the Crystal Floor Nightclub. It's high-class and exclusive—the kind of place you only get invited to. There's no line of people waiting to get in, but bouncers block the door regardless. Despite the rain they stand with muscled arms folded over their chests.

I know the two guys manning the door, Richard and Tank, and they both give me a curt nod and step aside.

The Crystal Floor Nightclub isn't cheap. The furniture and counters are made of Brazilian rosewood—technically illegal to trade—accented with ebony leather and silver. The lights are every hue and intensity, shimmering with the low-key music. The violins give my ears a good massage as I walk back to the VIP area. Nicholas Vice doesn't deal with anything but the best.

I spot him sitting at the corner table with his wife. They're a pair straight out of a movie. Both are in their sixties, I know intellectually, but they aged well, no doubt thanks to copious amounts of money and privilege. Nick eyes me and motions me over.

The dance floor bustles with the wealthiest of socialites and corporate criminals. There aren't any gangbangers here, outside of the muscle guarding the doors, and I know I must stick out like a sore thumb. The bar, lined with all sorts of alcohol, chasers, and "additives," stands on the far end of the room. The bartender, a woman by the name of Trista, holds back the muscle before they attempt to throw me out.

I weave through the crowd and stop only once I make it to Nick's table. He's stationed behind the speakers, giving the table a bit of privacy and seclusion. His wife, Anita, throws back her perfect inky locks and smiles. "Pierce. I'm so glad you could make it this evening." Her beady, overly critical eyes scan my clothing. "What happened to your shirt?"

"I got into a tussle. Nothing I couldn't handle."

"I see. Well, I have other matters for you to handle."

Of course she does. I force a smile. "Whatever you say, Mrs. Vice."

"You remember our old mortician? Juliet? She needs help with her basement. Everyone I've sent there has done nothing but anger her. I know you won't fail me."

"I'd be honored to handle it."

A mortician needs help with her basement? Yeah, this is going to be a terrible job; she's just not giving me all the details. My to-do list is getting out of control.

Nick swirls his wineglass and takes a sip. He grimaces while setting the glass down, his eyes held shut for a few seconds. His drink is laced with something potent. That's the way he likes it.

"Pierce," he says once the initial shock of the drink wears off. "Take a seat."

I comply, sliding into a chair next to him. His on-hand guards wait off in the corners, barely visible thanks to the shadows, eyeing me as I get close.

"What is it?" I ask.

"We have a problem. Those Cobras thugs seem to know every little thing about our operations, right down to where our guys stick their dicks for fun."

"I found Mikey dead at the Getaway Inn," I say, confirming his suspicions. "And last week Marty and Jay were gunned down at their house just outside of town."

"Cobras?"

"Everything points to them."

"I trust you can hunt down Mikey's killer?"

"It's already on my list."

Nick faces me, his hard black eyes as cold as the rain outside. "Do whatever it takes. I want these killings to stop. I've been cracking down on moles. Any turncoat is to be shot. No questions asked. I've lost too many family members to take this lightly. I fear they may be coming for my kids."

His wife squeezes his arm. "What did I say about talking like that? I don't want to hear it."

"*Then leave*," Nick says, half a command and half-restrained anger. "I'm talking business. You can mingle while I finish things up."

Anita slithers from her chair and stands, her magenta dress snug up against her taut skin, flat stomach, and hideously oversized breasts. "I trust you'll remember to handle my problem?" she asks me over her shoulder, her eyes narrowed.

"Of course," I reply.

"Good."

With her last remark, she leaves. Nick gives a deep exhale as he takes another drink from his glass. He slams his hand on the table as the drugs rip through his system for a brief shocking second. "Refreshing," he says. "Try some."

He isn't offering—he's commanding. I grab an empty glass, and he pours me a drink from his own personal bottle. It's just wine until he throws in a couple of dissolving tablets. I hate taking this shit, I always have, but I won't tell Nick no. Not when he's in a foul mood.

I throw back a gulp and instantly regret it. I have no idea what's in those tablets, but they break my eyesight, ability to taste, and hearing all in one intense world-shattering moment. Fucking drugs! I cough back the foul substance and thank God that my eyesight and hearing return. I'm not ready to be blind, despite what my body wants.

"Invigorating, right?" Nick asks with a chuckle. "Makes you feel alive."

Funny. It made me feel more dead than alive, but whatever. I nod to his statement. "So, what do you want from me, exactly? To catch moles spying on us for the Cobras?"

"I want you to keep an eye on my kids."

"Should be easy enough. I'll be meeting Jeremy on Monday regardless. He wants to speak to me."

"He does? He never told me about that, the little fink." Nick strokes his peppered goatee. The man has the posture of regal confidence not a lot of people possess in Noimore. His suit, unwrinkled, hugs his muscles, and his hair is clean and brushed back, white at the temples, dark up top. I get weak in the knees around the guy—the only man I think I wouldn't mind playin' bitch for—but I'm sure he gets that all the time. If he wanted a man, he could have a better man than me, that's for sure.

"Fink?" I repeat once I stop salivating. I'm not myself tonight. Drinking isn't helping anything either.

"Yes. A fink. The little rat keeps doing things against my express orders." Nick shakes his head and lights up one of his long European cigarettes. He offers me one, but I decline. I'm addicted to my knockoff brand of cancer. Paying five times as much for the same goddamn thing would only make me angry.

"You don't want me to see Jeremy?" I ask.

"I told him not to talk to you. I told him you were *my* go-to enforcer and that he should keep his ass planted in the backseat while I'm still in charge. The kid thinks he deserves more action when he barely knows what that means."

Great. Now the Vice family is having in-house conflict? No wonder the Cobras are doing so well. "I'll tell Jeremy to lay off. For his sake."

"I told you I thought he was some milkman's baby, right?" Nick asks me, a smirk on his face and smoke lingering on his breath. "I had DNA tests run in secret. Much to my disappointment, my wife *didn't* have an affair. The ugly bastard is mine."

I chuckle. As I open my mouth to continue, I spot something odd in the crowd in my peripheral vision. A pair of twentysomethings dive to the floor, covering their heads. They saw it before I did—a guy tosses out a concussion grenade.

Fuck me.

CHAPTER FIVE

I KICK up the table and push Nick down as the blast shatters lights and eardrums. I see bullets flying, but I sure as fuck don't hear them. My ears ring down to my spine, deafening me to everything. Nick opens his mouth and yells something, but it's all lost. He pulls his gun and I pull mine—it's a universal language.

Bullets rip through the expensive wood of the table. I roll out and behind the largest speaker, hoping for better cover. Nick's "guard" shoots—not at the men attacking the nightclub—*but at me*. The guard clips my jacket three times as I wheel to face him and fire twice: one to the body, one to the head. This isn't my first fight, and my body remembers all the motions it needs to survive. Adrenaline pumps through my veins, chilling my nerves and tensing my muscles.

Another turncoat bodyguard rounds the speaker to face me. I lift my gun, and he smashes it out of my hand with his own. I surprise him with a strike to the kidney—so hard he'll be pissin' blood in the morning—dropping the man to his knees. I fetch my gun and coldcock the guy in the back of the head with the metal butt. In the heat of the moment, I remember that we'll need *someone* to question after this.

The ringing in my ears dies down only to get drummed back in when I hear the explosion of gunfire all around me. I take a deep breath and concentrate.

I spot Nick leaning behind the ruined table. He's bleeding from the shoulder, one hand gripped tightly over the injury and one hand holding his .45 handgun with little conviction. I jump back behind the poor excuse for cover and lift him off the ground, offering my strength to support him. Nick holds on as I rush him back behind the speakers.

Sparks fly from the electronics as bullets chase us. I release Nick and lean out around cover, firing wildly to deter them from following. The terrible lighting and my bad eye make for inaccurate shooting at a distance. I contemplate rushing out to deal with the gunmen, but I stay sheltered instead. Nick isn't in any shape to fight off attackers.

A gunman gets the drop on me, jumping around the other side of the speaker with an automatic rifle in his hands. Nick blasts the guy through the neck, sending him back against the wall gasping down his own blood.

The shooting stops. I listen. The place sounds devoid of life. Only the creak of the damaged structure echoes throughout the dust and smoke. Nick turns to me, regal and dignified despite the bloodied wound, and offers an expression of mild exasperation. He says something. I furrow my brow, my ears ringing with a trumpeting cacophony. I strain my senses and manage to make out words.

"Go find my wife," Nick says.

I motion to his injury. "You sure about that?"

"I can handle it." No hint of reservation in his voice.

"Careful around your ex-bodyguard," I say, pointing to the guy on the floor. "He's technically still alive. For questioning."

Nick nods and holds up his gun. I return the gesture before creeping out of cover. The Crystal Floor Nightclub sits in the nicer district in town. I know the cops will be here soon, but I'll leave that to Nick. He has contacts within the authorities. No charges will stick to him, but I'm not as lucky.

The place is empty save for the bodies strewn about the floor. Most are dead, but some are writhing about in agony. Our turf war is getting out of hand—more so than I thought before. I see Trista, the bartender, slumped behind the counter. The bouncers, Richard and Tank, spread-eagle near the front door, twitch with the involuntary movements of a violent death. Even Pete, who I didn't know had been in attendance, sits rotting by the bathrooms, riddled with holes.

Damn. I've known most of them for over a decade. The realization chills me. I don't like getting pensive, and this is why. I curse under my breath as I search the corners of the room. My thoughts turn to Miles. He asked me about pointless death…. Of course I'm tired of it. Who isn't?

I finger the holes in my jacket. It could've been me.

Glancing up, I focus my attention on the mezzanine floor. There are offices up the metal wire steps reserved for the club workers. Anita Vice is a smart woman. If I had to guess, I'd say she sought shelter. I jump up the steps two at a time and knock on the metal of the door.

"Mrs. Vice?" I ask.

The door opens. She stands before me, ten or so others behind her. From the looks of it, they're nightclub patrons.

"Where's my husband?" she asks. "Where is he?"

The others push their way past each other and crowd the door in an attempt to exit all at once. I allow them through, unconcerned by their presence. The moment they leave I say, "Nick is downstairs. He got shot, but I've seen worse. He'll make it."

She half covers her mouth in as silent gasp. "They were here for him."

I nod.

"And you let him get shot?"

"His own men turned on him."

Anita glares, her eyes wet with tears. "These bastards don't know whose family they're dealing with. Pierce, you'll get my children out of town. *I know* my husband wanted them to stay here under your protection, but this is different. I won't have them harmed!"

A small piece of me remembers that Jeremy, their youngest, is twenty. I'll take them from the city if Anita wants, but her kids *are* grown-ass adults.

"Do you understand me?" Anita asks, grabbing the collar of my jacket and yanking down with enough force to rip a hole with her manicured fingernails. "If anything happens to them, I'll hold you responsible!"

Her hysterics grate, but I remain silent. She releases me and rushes by, her heels clicking against the mezzanine flooring.

Sirens ring in the distance. I need to leave. My eyes catch a bottle of fine vodka, and I snatch it up on instinct. I gulp down a mouthful on my way to the front door. I need to wash away the grit and grime of the night—it hangs on my thoughts heavier than ever before.

MY HEAD hurts.

I wake in a pool of misery and regret. I remember getting out of the limo, getting back to my car, and then… everything else is a blank. Well, I see flashes in my mind's eye of other places and people… and feeling as though I need to do something urgent… but otherwise last night remains a mystery to me. I haven't gotten blackout drunk in quite some time, specifically because I hate not remembering what happened.

It's a good way to get yourself killed or wind up naked in a back alley, missing more than just a wallet.

With an unsteady hand, I rub my face. I don't even open my eyes, but I know it's the middle of the day, too early for me to be up. Panic hits when I remember I have a shit ton of assignments on my plate. What the hell am I doing in bed?

Rolling to my side, I freeze up. The blankets are tightly woven around me and *someone else*. A combination of anxiety and confusion fuel my desperate leap off the bed. With deep breaths I stare down at Miles, the expression on his face mirroring my own.

"What's going on?" he shouts, jumping sideways and glancing around the room with a wild look in his eyes.

"What're you doing in my bed?" I yell back.

"*What?*"

"*Why the hell are you in my bed?*"

"You—*you told me to sleep here!*"

I grab my forehead in an attempt to contain the throbbing with the palm of my hand. "Stop yelling!"

"*Me?* You're the one who woke up like this!"

"*Quiet, goddammit!*"

Miles flinches back and goes silent. I rake a hand through my hair and take a series of deep breaths. What time is it? What happened last night? What's going on? There are too many questions and not enough painkillers in the world to get through them all.

I open my good eye and squint across the bed, getting a solid look at Miles. He, like me, stands in nothing but his boxers. The light streaming in from the window reveals the colors of the room I rarely get to see, but I can't rip my attention away from Miles long enough to enjoy them.

"Are you okay now?" he asks, his tone softer.

"What happened?"

"There was a shootout at the Crystal Floor Nightclub and—"

"I remember that part," I interject. "What happened after that?"

"You told me to report the shooting as an act by Cobras, and then we drove out to Big Man Vice's house to talk to his kids, but they weren't there…. Then we went looking for a guy with a tattoo of some lady's tits on his neck… and then you were a little too wasted, so I drove us back here. I think there might have been something else in your drink. You kept *rambling*, and it was hard to get you to say anything coherently."

I shake my head and groan. *Jesus Christ.* Why was I drinking in the first place? To drown out my thoughts? To escape the turf war in the easiest way possible? "This is all your fault," I say. "I haven't gotten this drunk in years."

"Hey, don't look at me! I didn't even drink that much! *You* were the one getting wasted!"

"*Shh!*" I hiss. "No more yelling!"

Miles exhales and rolls his eyes. He takes a seat on the opposite side of my bed.

"Get off," I command. "I don't let anyone else sleep on my bed."

He stands. "You told me to come in here."

"Impossible. I know *drunk me*. Drunk me wouldn't have asked anyone in here. *Ever.* Hell, I don't even bring my flings in here—I fuck' em in the guest room."

"Wait, the room you let me stay in is your *sex room*?"

I growl in irritation.

Miles crosses his arms over his chest and shakes his head. "Look. I don't know what to tell you. We got back to your apartment, and you asked me to come in here and sleep with you. At one point you even said *I don't normally do this*, and then you demanded I strip down and get on your bed. I thought… something *else* was going to happen… but then you just got in the bed next to me and fell asleep. We were practically spooning."

Flushed for the first time in years, I turn away.

"You were surprisingly nice," Miles murmurs, his eyes on the bed.

"What're you talkin' about?"

"I thought you would be an angry drunk. Turns out you're more of a talkative drunk. You were tellin' me all about when you were younger, and how you wanted to be a detective. You kept going on about how I was too good for all this and that maybe I should just go be a cop."

"*Enough,*" I snap. "Clearly I was out of my mind."

I storm into my bathroom and slam the door behind me. I flip on the shower, glaring at myself in the mirror. I look like shit. Bags under my eyes, bruises from God only knows what.… I need more sunlight. At least I still have muscle—though I'm sure that won't last if I keep smokin' and drinkin' like I do.

I exhale. I had forgotten about wanting to be a detective. That was decades ago, when I still thought the cops were tantamount to superheroes. I was naïve then. Just stupid and naïve and alone. Nick got me out of the gutter and workin'. Not the cops. Nick.

After stripping off my boxers, I slide into the shower and allow the water to wash away my woes. I use a razor on my chin, regretting the fact I have no shaving cream, and cut myself twice. My head hurts, and I got no more than a couple of hours of terrible sleep. It's better this way, considering that I need to pick up the slack and help the Vice family.

Once clean I exit the shower stall, rub myself down with a towel, and wrap it around my waist. I open the door and flinch back, startled by Miles standing a few feet away. He's dressed in the slacks and shirt I lent him, holding a plate full of crackers with a side of painkillers.

"Breakfast?" he quips, an eyebrow raised.

"You really slaved over this, I see."

"It was either this or a jar of olives. I recommend going grocery shopping more than never."

I scoop up the pills and throw them back with a cough. Miles hands me a glass of water. He thought of everything. I wash down the clunky medicine and shove a few crackers in my mouth for good measure.

Miles watches me walk to the closet, his gaze on everything but mine. He catches me staring and runs a hand through his black hair.

"You weren't kidding about the scars," he says.

I glance down at my body and shrug. "Most of them are from knife fights. A few are bullet scars. This one here on my forearm is from a fucking tin can. Goddamn can burst open when I used a can opener—the lid sliced right through my skin."

"You sound like you hate that scar the most."

"It's one thing to get a scar from a fight. It's another thing to get a scar because *baked beans*."

Miles lets out a laugh and smirks. "All right. I can see that."

I drop the towel, grab myself a new pair of boxers and slacks, and pull on a black button-down. Miles watches the entire time—it gets my blood going—but I know I'm not going to be able to perform in my barely awake state. I chortle to myself as I finish up the buttons and fasten on my shoulder holster.

"What?" I ask. "You've never seen a man get dressed before?"

"I have." He tears his attention away and stares at the ceiling. "Ya know. The Internet. And occasionally in the bathrooms at this one club downtown. I never touched any of them. I always got to thinkin' about my dad and older brother. They would… get angry… if they ever found out."

I pull on a pair of socks and then my shoes. Miles fidgets for a moment before returning his attention to me.

"So… did you ever have difficulty telling people about your preferences?"

"Listen," I intone. "I almost got shot last night. And a few nights before that. And a few weeks before that. When you live a life on the streets, death is behind every door. I don't have the time, or fucks, to give about what other people might think of me."

"That's… a good way to live. I'll keep it in mind."

"Good. Because I'm not doling out this advice for my health."

We exit my room, and Miles gets introspective. I still can't believe I asked him into my bedroom. With a shake of my head, I dispel the thoughts. I pull my cell phone and call each of Nick's children. He has three: Rodger, Guinevere, and Jeremy. Rodger and Jeremy don't answer—no surprise—but I leave them voice mails about the situation. Jeremy is a done deal—he'll meet with me tomorrow at his normal spot—but Rodger is a different story. The kid, despite being the oldest, handles himself like an eight-year-old with a no-spending-limit credit card. He could be anywhere.

I dial Guinevere and, to my surprise, she answers.

"Hello?" she says, her voice so singsong it deserves to be in its own Disney movie.

"Where are you?" I demand.

"Pierce? Is this about my father? I saw the news."

"Did he die?" I can't stop myself from asking. A part of me seizes up with genuine concern. Did he die after I left? Did his own doctor do him in?

"What're you talking about?" she asks. "All I saw was that his nightclub came under attack. Why would he be dead?"

"He got shot."

"Really?"

"Where are you?"

Her end is silent for a moment. "If it were anyone else," she drawls, "I would think they were out to get me. I'm at the country club, Pierce. I assume my father wants you to protect me?"

"I'm going to escort you out of town. Someplace safe."

"I'll be waiting."

"GIRLS, THIS is Pierce. Pierce, meet the girls."

A parade of giggles and hellos greet me as I approach the table. The Noimore Country Club, nestled in the richest district of the city, sits next to a full-sized golf course and Olympic regulation swimming pool. The outdoor seating, beautiful in the glory of the late morning sun, is occupied by Guinevere and her girlfriends. I've known her almost her entire life—the women around her are nothing more than this week's fling. Guinevere doesn't make long-term friends.

"Hello," I say. My ears pulse with pain, and my headache has yet to fully recede. I spot their mimosas and contemplate grabbing one, but I decide against it.

Unlike Jeremy, who hit every stick as he fell out of the ugly tree, Guinevere inherited her mother's poise and her father's commanding aura. She sits at the head of the white table, a large-brimmed hat covering half her face and a tight sundress sculpted to fit her body.

"You got here quick," she says, not bothering to stand. "And you brought company. Who is he?"

The women at the table turn their collective heads to face Miles. It makes the man uneasy. He goes to open his mouth, but I want this over with as fast as possible. Knowing him, he'll shake each of their hands, address them all by their last name, and take a seat for a spot of tea.

"His name is Miles," I say. "Are you ready to leave?"

"Miles? I don't remember a Miles being on my father's payroll. Tell me—is he your newest squeeze?"

The question, though audacious, is exactly what I would expect from Guinevere. She's always been fascinated by my sexual proclivities and has no filter for her thoughts. The other women, dressed in similar fashion to Guinevere and in every pastel color that Easter has to offer, whisper among themselves and coyly point between myself and Miles.

"I'm showing the kid the ropes."

She smiles. "I miss your last fling. He was so… bulky. Muscles to be proud of. Miles needs more meat on his bones. He's just *wiry*. Perhaps you'll take him to the gym as a part of showing the ropes."

"I'll keep it in mind. Now can we go?"

"Aren't these your father's enforcers?" one shrill woman asks Guinevere. "Don't they have to do whatever you say? Why is he ordering you around?"

Another woman gives a *hmpf* and nods. "He's so rude. Brunch isn't even over yet."

"He's so tough," the smallest of the group says with a giggle.

I roll my eyes. They think they're safe in the country club, but I've known men who have gone missing from the golf course on more than one occasion. If some Cobras thug wanted to kill Guinevere, he wouldn't have much trouble scaling the fence and shooting her. Doesn't she understand she's in trouble? This is all a waste of time.

The woman closest to Guinevere holds up her mimosa. "Order them to make out," she suggests, her voice slippery with alcohol. The surrounding gaggle clap, nod, and giggle in delight.

I need to nip this bullshit in the bud. "I don't *make out* with my flings."

"Tell that to drunk you," Miles quips.

I wheel on him, and he flinches back. "*Not another word*," I mouth through clenched teeth. He offers a half smile and a nervous laugh, but I just glare. I'm not here to discuss anything about my life—Miles needs to learn to keep personal things private.

Guinevere laughs into her hand. She stands, silencing the group. "Excuse me, ladies. Pierce isn't a patient man. I'd hate to see what he'll do if you continue to pester him."

Despite her jovial tone, the women at the table grow pale and ever quieter. So Guinevere told them about my preferences *and* my history of violence. I'm surprised they had the testicles to try my patience at all. Eh. I don't care. I'm in no mood for anything—entertainment or violence. I just want the job done.

"Good-bye, Guinevere," one lady murmurs.

The others nod to the sentiment, but their attention remains on me. Guinevere flips back her black hair and waves, not even bothering to address any of them by name. Miles holds out his hand, and Guinevere takes it. "I'm Miles Devonport," he says, gently squeezing her knuckles. "It's a pleasure to meet you, Ms. Vice."

She lifts an eyebrow and gives him an amused smile. "I like this one, Pierce. He's more articulate than the last."

"Doesn't have a six-pack, though," I drawl, taking Miles by the shoulder and pushing him toward the door. He glances back at me with a confused, somewhat indignant expression.

"Don't fool yourself, Pierce," Guinevere says, taking my arm and walking toward the entrance. "If you wanted abs, you would still be with the meat machine you were with years ago. I think you like a little repartee."

Girl knows me too well. I blame Nick. He doesn't trust any of his other enforcers to protect Guinevere—and it has everything to do with me fucking men instead of women. I've watched Guinevere since she was a kid, and now she thinks she knows everything about me. It gets insufferable at times.

"Do you have a vehicle here?" I ask her.

"I have one of my father's tactical cars. He insisted. It's parked in the club's garage."

"Perfect."

Miles opens the door for Guinevere and me, which gets her smiling wider. "Why are we changing cars again?" he asks.

"You gotta avoid recognizable patterns if you're gonna work the streets," I say. "You don't want the cops to catch on, you don't want the Cobras to know your routine, and, most of all, some missions require vehicles with protection."

"Oh good, another chance to get shot at. I was disappointed I missed out on the last time."

"Smartass," I mutter, unable to think of a retort in my current state of headache.

I'm sure Guinevere is amused, but I trudge on, unconcerned. The country club workers hover close by. They don't get too close, not while I'm around, but Guinevere is a high roller—they don't want to disappoint her. They have orders to see to her every whim. When we near the garage, the lanky security guard stands at attention.

"José," I say to him.

José relaxes and nods. We walk through the door and into the multicar parking facility.

"Do you know *everyone*?" Miles asks. "I swear you seem to know everyone's name...."

"You should remember people's names. It's a simple sign of respect. They'll be a lot more copacetic and reasonable, then."

Guinevere tilts her large hat to the side and glances up at me. "Wow. You're not just showing him the ropes; you're training him to be a little gentleman."

"Everything I've taught him is just basic information he needs if he's going to be working for the Vice family."

"You never answered that meat locker of a man you were dragging around before."

"That's because he was more a trained dog than a man. He couldn't string four words together without losing his train of thought. Remembering people's names? I'm surprised he knew his own half the time."

The "tactical vehicle" Nick provided his daughter isn't as nice as a limo, but it's damn close. The windows are tinted, the siding is reinforced, and the insides are skinned in all the most expensive and comfortable animal hide one can obtain. I hold my hand out for the keys. Guinevere hands them over and heads for the back door. Miles opens it for her.

"Ma'am," he says.

"I hope you stay with the family," Guinevere replies as she gets situated in the back. "I appreciate a man with class."

Miles shuts the door, and I grab his collar before he walks around to the passenger side. He stops and stares at me, confusion in his stance.

"You fuck women?" I ask.

"N-no."

"Then don't make it look like you're sniffin' around Big Man Vice's daughter." I pull him close. "You're *mine* for now. Got it?"

His honeyed skin grows red. He forces a laugh. "Right. Of course. I said I'd do whatever you say." He leans in close, hesitates for a fraction of a second, then nibbles my neck, getting my blood hot the very next moment. I'm ready to stop everything and take him, but the feeling is fleeting. I quickly regain my senses.

Miles pulls away, still flushed, and I let go of his shirt. I guess I shouldn't be too surprised with his brazen moves—he *is* the one who rewarded me with a blowjob without asking. Neither of us has had a chance for relief, apparently. I'm gonna get a case of blue balls unless I fuck him soon.

Burying my lustful thoughts for later, I open the driver's door and get in. If I take Guinevere to Chicago, she can take one of the family planes to Canada. She can stay in a hotel—plenty to choose from—and change every few nights, at least until everything here blows over.

I pull out of the garage and speed out of the country club, despite the protests of the staff. The heavy-duty car—some sort of Ford— handles surprisingly well. I swerve through traffic without the tiniest hint of trouble. The downtown area is packed, as always, and I steer us down some back roads to avoid the traffic. Guinevere lights herself a cigarette, and the smell gets me jonesing for the same thing. I light myself a smoke.

Within seconds the car is filled with the sweet, sweet cloud of cancer. Miles wrinkles his nose but doesn't complain. His discomfort grates on me, however. I snuff out my cigarette and roll down the window. He gives me an odd sideways glance but, again, says nothing.

Right as I pull the car onto the corner of the red-light district, I catch sight of a man and slam the brakes. Miles and Guinevere lurch forward, their seat belts trapping them in place.

"*Pierce*?" Guinevere shrieks. "What was that?"

"Shh," I hiss, pointing. Miles follows my gesture, and he sees it too.

Across the street, heading toward the hotels, is a scrawny guy in a heavy coat and boots. He's unremarkable in every regard but his neck. The ugly tattoo, which I can see despite a bad eye, is of a gnarly set of tits, the head of the woman up by the man's ear. He walks with a gang of four others, laughing and talking.

Guinevere cranes her head to get a better view. "Who is that?"

"The guy who shot Mikey at the Getaway Inn."

"Uncle Mikey?"

"Yeah. Uncle Mikey."

She sits back and takes a drag of her cigarette. "Well? What are you waiting for? Sideswipe the fucker. No one kills a member of the Vice family and walks free. Kill him, Pierce."

I chuckle. The car *could* easily plow the man over and keep going. I bet it's even designed to do so. We could always shoot from the windows, for good measure. This part of town doesn't have many cops, and all the cameras are blacked out or ripped down thanks to the prostitutes, not to mention our tinted windows block a good view. We could probably get away with killing the guy in broad daylight. Him *and* the rest of his crew, if I angle the car just right.

The man and his gang turn down a narrow road, putting themselves even farther away from prying eyes or crowds.

Cars honk behind me. I pull forward and stop at the nearest red light, keeping an eye on my target. Miles stares for a long moment, tense and silent. Once the light is green, I flip around in order to get a good long running start….

Miles grabs the wheel and jerks it to the side, throwing the car into a small side street. I pry his hand away and, again, slam on the brakes. He meets my gaze as though he's seen a ghost.

"What the fuck was that?" I ask. "Start talking."

Guinevere glares at me through the rearview mirror. "Pierce. What's going on? Is your protégé having second thoughts about serving the Vice family, or is he just suicidal?"

Miles exhales. "It's my brother," he murmurs under his breath, low enough that I suspect Guinevere can't hear. "He's here."

CHAPTER SIX

I BITE back a slew of choice words. Bitching isn't going to help us.

Guinevere narrows her eyes, waiting for my explanation. Miles offers nothing more—he doesn't even look at me—he just stares down at the floorboard. It's on *me* to solve this whole situation.

I face Guinevere. "Miles has a point. He said we shouldn't risk getting run down by Cobras gangbangers. They infest this area, obviously. If we're reckless, they might swarm us. Even chase us down in their cars."

In reality I suspect if we did a hit-and-run, there wouldn't be anyone to follow us, but there's *technically* a chance that it could happen. All I need is to convince Guinevere of a different plan that doesn't involve killing Miles's idiot brother.

"And?" Guinevere snaps. "What're you trying to say? What're you going to do about it?"

"We'll follow them from a distance," I say, cutting off Miles before he gets a word in edgewise. "Do some recon and then get the guy when he drops his guard."

"Sounds like a waste of time."

"Your father was never prone to making rash decisions. I submit to you that it worked for him."

She mulls over the comment and nurses her cigarette. "I suppose I'm not really involved in the family business. You would know best. Very well. We'll do recon."

"*We?*" I repeat.

"Yes. I'm invested now. Before I go running out of town, I want to see this man brought to justice."

The mention of justice gets me thinking. "Miles. Call the detective. We'll follow the gangbangers and report their location to her. We can make some bullshit up about them having drugs and guns—they probably do anyway—and get a whole nest of Cobras at once without getting our hands dirty. If Detective Ambers doesn't ask for your assistance after that, I don't know what will convince her."

Miles gives me a pleading look as he says, "But then they'll *all* go to prison. I mean, some of them could have *just been released* and, if they go back, they'll be there for years."

"Maybe they would *be safer in prison* rather than the streets."

"Maybe some of them will be off the streets in just a few days, and we should *think of something else.*"

Guinevere isn't stupid. Our doublespeak raises her ire. She snuffs out her cigarette on the back of my chair and glowers. "Pierce. Explain."

"One of the Cobras guys is"—Miles tenses—"a mole for us," I say, digging myself deeper into a never-ending rabbit hole of lies. Miles releases his breath, his posture slumped.

"And we don't want to send him to jail?" Guinevere asks, her gaze flitting back and forth between me and Miles. "Why not say that? What am I missing?"

"I forgot about our mole. Miles was just trying to subtly remind me."

"Liar."

I glare back at her. "Maybe I should call and ask your father about whether I should take you straight to the airport or not."

"Touché," she says, straightening her hat. "I'll accept that you don't want to tell me, so long as I get to participate in a little fun. Nothing too bloody, though. I don't want to sully anything."

Guinevere leans all the way back in her seat as I turn the vehicle around. It's painted black, and I think it'll blend in, despite being bulkier than most, so I drive along the far sidewalk where I first spotted the man with the tattoo.

I almost jump when I feel Miles's hand slide its way up my thigh. I turn to him with a cocked eyebrow, but he doesn't meet my gaze, instead allowing his fingers to feather along my crotch. The hell? Is doing recon his fetish? Fuckin' bizarre.

With gritted teeth I chortle to myself. It's so obvious I should've seen it right away. He's "rewarding" me for helping him out. That and I think he's still horny. Good enough for me. I *am* sticking my neck out for him, after all. I could get used to this kind of arrangement.

I spot the men as they turn into a back alley behind buildings. I drive by, taking my time, and see the door they open and enter. The hotels in these parts have back entrances for long-term visitors, which consist of gangsters in between permanent residences. They pay the hotel a portion of their earnings, and the hotel lets them occupy a room for an extended visit.

"He's going there to sleep," I say aloud. Miles keeps with his petting, and I'm starting to lose my train of thought. A piece of me wonders if Guinevere is watching, but I don't really give a fuck. His strokes grow ever more purposeful.

"Why don't we get him while he's sleeping?" Guinevere asks. "Sounds easy."

"If we go in on foot and get into a firefight in the middle of their base of operations, I guarantee you'll *sully* something." And there's a good chance we'll all get gunned down.

"So we'll wait. He'll come out at night, like all the street scum do, and then we'll be waiting for him."

"Street scum? Ya know *I* wake up at the crack of dusk, right?"

"Oh, I wasn't talking about *you*, Pierce. You're different. You're classy."

Waiting the entire day in order to catch this one asshole isn't the best use of my limited time. On the other hand, I didn't get much sleep and I'm running on fumes. I *need* to get this guy, but I also *need* to rest. The priorities are fuckin' with my mind, but sleep and revenge beat out protecting grown-ass adults. I have Guinevere. Rodger might not even be in town. Jeremy will show up tomorrow. I've got time.

I drive by the hotel, eyeing the foot traffic outside. Miles points to a building on the other side of the street. Another hotel, just as run-down and sad-sack as the others.

"We could stay there," he says. "And keep an eye on them instead of driving around the entire time."

He just wants to get into a hotel room. Then again, it's not a bad idea. I nod. "Fine. We'll watch 'em through the windows." I pull the vehicle around the block and to the backside parking lot. Guinevere doesn't protest the plan, but I can practically hear her seething. The hotel is far, *far* below her standards. I would suggest she go somewhere else, but I'm not letting her out of my control until I get her to the airport. Not in this territory.

I park in one of the covered spots to avoid anyone getting a good eyeful of the vehicle. Miles lets go of me when we separate to exit, but I can tell he's not done. Guinevere is out of place for anything but a Hollywood movie premiere or a debutante party. I roll my eyes and take her hat. I would offer her my jacket, but then it would expose my shoulder holster, which I can't have happen.

She frowns but doesn't say a word as I toss the clunky hat into the trunk. At least she has common sense enough to know my judgment is best.

I'm not familiar with the hotel, but as I enter I know we won't have any trouble. The man behind the counter—skin like a potato, accent thick—is neutral in all this turf-war bullshit. Everyone leaves the foreigners out of the fray. They're good hardworking people minding their own business. There aren't many of them, and they accommodate both sides. Win-win.

Miles fidgets as I pay for two rooms. It takes a bit to get the rooms I want—street-view rooms on the fourth floor—but eventually it happens. The smell of the lobby… it reminds me of a gas station. I light a cigarette and allow the smell of smoke to replace everything I inhaled. We walk to the stairwell and begin our climb to the fourth story.

"If I'm to stay here, I want some basic amenities," Guinevere says halfway up. "Strawberries and champagne will do."

"For fuck's sake," I groan. "Strawberries? That might give us away faster than me screaming our identities out in the middle of the street."

"Champagne, then."

"Box wine or bust."

She snaps her heels down on the steps as she walks, but I know that's her way of accepting the terms. I stop and turn around, intent on getting her wine from the mini-mart next door. Miles trails after me.

"Do we have to do this right now?" he asks, his tone low. "We could go up to our room now and get her stuff afterward."

"Eager?"

He shoves his hands in his pockets and turns away. "Are you saying you aren't?"

I chuckle. Lack of sleep and a headache make it easy to contain my lust, though I feel it coursing through me nonetheless.

Miles grits his teeth at my blasé attitude.

"I guess I could turn around if you want it that bad," I drawl as I return to the bottom step of the stairs. "But that means I won't be buying any of the stuff that makes it easy on you."

Miles furrows his brow and glances over. "Like… condoms?"

I let out a single laugh and stifle the rest. No, I wasn't planning on getting condoms. I'm pretty sure my fate is to die via bullet to the face, so why limit what pleasure I get before the inevitable? Still, Miles isn't a Boy Scout, but his request shouldn't take me by surprise. I guess he still has a chance to live life in a suburb. Perhaps he's only playin' this smart.

"Sure," I say. "Like condoms. But, more importantly, lube."

He says nothing. I stop at the door to the lobby and hold the handle.

"If you want it bareback, you should let me know now," I mutter. "Otherwise I'll be right back."

Miles remains silent. I throw him the room key, and he catches it.

I head back into the lobby and out onto the street. I hate the daylight. It glares off the chrome and glass of every passing car, hurting my bad eye and causing me to squint. I hustle to the mini-mart—owned by another foreigner—and admire the bars, cameras, and security. The place could be a mini-Alcatraz.

I grab the most "expensive" box wine they have and amble over to the glass safety room surrounding the front counter. Exhaling smoke, I nod to a box of condoms on display, along with lubricant. The man behind the register waggles his eyebrows. I smirk. He rings everything up with a snicker on his breath.

Without a word I slide my money under the safety glass and the transaction is complete. I like this mini-mart.

I return to the hotel without delay, keeping my brown paper bag of goods close. With a flick of my wrist, I toss out my cigarette on the stairwell and stomp it out on my way up. Winded, I make the fourth floor regretting the fact I smoke in the first place. I really need to quit.

To my surprise, Guinevere is out in the hall waiting for me.

"I found them," she says once she spots me. "Come look."

I pass my room and walk into hers. The brown-on-brown color scheme floods my vision. The blankets are brown, the dresser chestnut, the blinds a shade of feces—the room has all the glitz and glamor of a mud puddle. *I'm* disappointed, so I know Guinevere is unhappy, but I don't say anything lest she gets into a habit of complaining.

She points me to the window, and I walk over. Across the street, standing in the third-story window, is our target. A piece of me can't believe they didn't shut their blinds, but perhaps they're too stupid to take even the most basic measures to hide themselves on their home turf. Or maybe it's hubris. Either way, this is to our advantage.

As I stare I see four others—including a man so large it's noteworthy. Stella hadn't been lying. The little tattooed freak has some backup. I'll need to think of some way to kill that bastard without getting caught in a compromising situation.

"Don't leave your room looking like you do, understand?" I say. "We shouldn't draw attention to ourselves here."

"Of course."

"I mean it."

"What's this?"

I turn and see Guinevere rummaging through my bag. She gives me a coy smile as she holds up the box of condoms.

"Are they ribbed for *her* pleasure?" she asks.

I half smile and move away from the window. "You know that means something else out on the streets, right?"

"Oh? What does it mean?"

"Forget it." I snatch away the box and toss it back into the bag.

"These walls are thin, Pierce. I might hear things if you two shirk your duties to fornicate."

"You're gonna hear things, then."

Her smile widens into something devious. "Oh. This is already getting interesting. You should've taken me on more of your assignments when I was younger. This is what I've always imagined your little outings were like."

"Can I trust you to keep an eye on our targets?" I ask, ignoring her frivolous musings. "I'm certain they aren't going to move until the evening, and I need to get some rest, but the more information we have, the better."

"Don't worry. I'll watch them."

Her eagerness to comply raises my suspicion, but I don't have time to deal with it. Whatever. She gets to watch them. Hopefully she won't fuck it up. I leave her the wine and exit the room. My thoughts turn to Miles, and I lick my lips.

I walk into my room to find the blinds shut and the lights off. Only a hint of sunlight dapples through, leaving everything silhouetted. Miles sits on the bed, shirtless, resting his weight on his posted arms. He straightens himself as I step in and lock the door behind me.

Good. He knows I don't want to bullshit around. I need this.

I place the paper bag on the dresser and remove my jacket, holster, and shirt in one swift motion. I'm ready to go, but I'm not overclocked like last night in the limo. I can take my time—I'll enjoy it more this way.

Unbuckling my pants, I hear Miles follow suit. He fumbles and fidgets while I dump out the bag, remove a single condom from the box, and snatch up the lube. When I turn back, I see he's stripped down to the buff, his unkempt hair hanging over most of his face. He backs up as I climb onto the bed. His trembling does wonders for my excitement.

Miles audibly swallows.

What's wrong with this guy? He was all over me five minutes ago, but now it seems like he has cold feet. I rip open the condom wrapper. "You ready?"

"Y-yeah," he murmurs. "I want this. I've, uh, wanted this for a long time."

Longer than he's known me, no doubt. He just wants the experience, then. That makes sense—and makes this easy—but I'm a little disappointed it wasn't *my* cock specifically that got him all hot and bothered.

I unroll the condom over my semihard erection. Miles clears his throat. "So, uh," he says, his voice still just above a whisper. "What… position… should I be in?"

I wanna say *any way I can get my dick inside you is fine*, but I hold back my sarcasm. Without the precursor of foreplay or overbearing lust, he's overthinking everything. I chuckle to myself and grab his leg, manhandling him as I like, despite his nervous grunts. I roll him onto all fours and shove his face down onto the bed. He shudders as I smear lube into the cleft of his smooth ass.

Miles waits beneath me as stiff as a rail, his hands gripped so tightly on the blankets it's like he's choking them to death. I run my hand over his back, enjoying the feel of tense muscles beneath my fingertips. Damn. I want to fuck him so bad, but….

He flinches as I run my hand down across his balls and grip his rock-solid cock. He's leaking enough to slick up his shaft as I stroke him, and with my other hand, I circle the entrance of his ass with my thumb. Now that he knows what's happening, I slide my digit into him, testing the waters, so to speak. Miles sharply inhales but doesn't pull away. Even in the dim lighting, I can tell he's coated in sweat. He smells like sex.

Little by little I increase the speed, depth, and pressure of my thumb, enjoying the hot insides of his body that practically pull me deeper with each passing moment. He wants it, and he starts to relax the longer I go. I feel his dick twitch, and I cease my stroking, causing him to whimper and buck. I smile to myself. That's enough prep—the agony of my own cock is driving me insane—and I pull Miles back by the hips.

I align the tip and force myself halfway inside. Miles lets out a sharp cry but stifles most of it as he bites down on the blankets. He's tight. Even with a condom I feel like he's trying to cut off my circulation. I gulp down air as I rock back and forth, inching ever deeper, digging my nails into his hips to make sure he stays in place. Miles grunts into the mattress, his noises desperate, needy, and pain-laced.

It only adds to my lust.

I straighten my back and revel in the sensation of being balls-deep in another man for only a moment before withdrawing to the tip and slamming it back in. Miles, again, cries out, clawing at the bed and quavering. I almost want him to try and run—to *try* and get away from me now that I have him—but he doesn't. Instead he offers nothing but shallow breaths.

As I continue my full thrusts into his untested ass, I lean over and bite the back of his neck and shoulders, relishing the salty taste of his skin. He gives me an appreciative whimper as I reach around and return to stroking his cock—which is considerably limper than before, but still somewhat hard.

"Relax," I whisper in his ear.

"I'm trying," he breathes, his tone apologetic.

I grit my teeth, stop my thrusting, and jerk him around onto his back, not bothering to pull out before doing so. I spread his legs and push them back, angling to go deep, and I return my hand to his cock. With forceful pumps I continue, jerking off Miles like I would myself. He moans aloud, unable to hide it in the sheets, and reaches up to grip the headboard. My efforts rock the bed, adding a symphony of creaks to his panting. His dick hardens in full force, precome slicking my hand.

Dripping sweat everywhere, I drop forward, desperate to catch my breath and bracing myself over Miles with my spare arm. I'm breathing heavy but enjoying every second of pleasure. I latch my mouth on Miles's neck and run my teeth along his flesh, lapping up his sweat with my tongue and coating him in my hot saliva.

He wraps his arms around my neck and licks at my ear. "Faster," he begs, his voice so laced with need it causes my mouth to go dry.

I bite down on his shoulder and comply with his wishes—I thrust fast and hard, slamming my flesh against his like I aim to bruise, heat building in my gut as he whines and groans right into my ear. Even my hand on his cock goes faster and harder until I feel him clench every muscle in his body. His spine arches, and a guttural moan fills the hotel room as he covers us both in his sticky seed, his cock twitching with release. His nails leave bloody furrows in my back.

I can't stand it. The sharp pain, his scent, the heat, the tight grip of his body—I rut into him with everything I have, stretching his ass to take every inch of my cock. He keeps his arms tight around my neck even as his grunts turn to whimpers and muffled cries. My teeth break his skin, and the coppery taste excites me.

"I'm gonna fuck you every night like the whore you are," I growl into his neck.

"Whatever you want," he forces out, his voice unsteady.

His act of submission sends me over the edge. I bite down on him again out of instinct, blowing my load into the rubber that surrounds my dick. Miles shudders but keeps his embrace with me as I slowly come down from my high. After a few seconds, I realize I haven't even been breathing—I pull away from Miles and gulp down air.

Sex does wonders for headaches. I feel like a whole new person, albeit an exhausted person. I withdraw from Miles—going slow but still feeling him tense and grit his teeth as I exit—and then peel off the condom. It's thick with juices and easily thrown into the nearby trash can. With a contented exhale, I fall onto the bed next to him, forgetting that I'm covered in sweat and semen.

Eh. Whatever. There are two beds. I roll onto my back and regret that decision as well. Miles really did a number on my back with his nails.

He snuggles up next to me, unconcerned with his own state of cleanliness, and runs his mouth along my neck and jawline. He goes to kiss me, but I turn away with a hiss.

"I don't do that," I say.

"We did it last night."

"Yeah? Well, I was drunk then. Don't expect it to happen again."

He gets unresponsive. I stare at the ceiling, feeling his steady heart rate through his rib cage.

"How bad is it?" I ask.

For a moment Miles doesn't answer.

"It hurts, but not too bad," he finally replies. "I expected as much."

"You didn't ask me to stop. That's pretty good for someone who's never had a guy ride his ass before."

"I've used… toys… in the past…."

I chuckle and close my eyes.

"Thank you," he murmurs.

Thank you? I laugh to myself even more. I've never been *thanked* for riding a guy. Miles continues to amuse me. "There's no need to thank me."

He doesn't reply. Or maybe I just don't hear him. The sounds of the city outside the window are a lullaby I can't ignore. Sleep takes hold of me before I even know it.

CHAPTER SEVEN

I JERK awake, haunted by nightmares that linger in my thoughts.

Death.

All I can remember is death. People getting shot, living in fear, running from danger, fighting for my life, dying without a purpose.... God, it's so bleak I feel like I need a stiff drink. I glance around looking for Miles, yearning for his presence, though I can't articulate why.

The room sits quiet and dark. The window is aglow with twilight. It's dusk.

I fumble to the nightstand and switch on the lamp. Light assaults my eyes, and it takes me a few moments to adjust. I'm alone—Miles is nowhere to be seen. To my surprise there's a granola bar and bottle of water waiting for me next to the bed. I'm famished and I rip open the food without delay.

In a blur I pull myself from the bed and shamble into the bathroom. I'm in the shower and washing with barely any memory of doing anything in between. I stumble out, dry off, and dress myself all while reviewing my nightmares. My mind can't get over the shootout in the Crystal Floor Nightclub. My time is coming. I can feel it in my bones. I won't be lucky forever.

The brown-themed room is still empty when I exit the bathroom. I walk out into the hall and turn to Guinevere's door. I knock, but no one answers. I knock louder. Nothing. I slam my fist on the door. The neighboring room opens, and a scraggly man in boxers gives me a confused look.

"Mind your own business," I say.

He continues to watch.

I rear back and kick the door with enough force to shatter the wooden doorframe around the lock. The man down the hall ducks back into his room. Smart move.

Furious, I storm inside and see Guinevere's room is *also* empty. Panic overtakes my anger. Where are they? I silently curse myself for not checking my phone before breaking into the room. What if they left me a message?

I pull out my cell phone and see twenty-two missed calls, all of which are from Anita Vice. She left several voice mails. I listen to those first.

"*Pierce*," it begins, her voice so sharp it could cut skin. "Where're my children? Have you taken them out of the city? My husband is asking for you, but don't show your face at our home until you've secured Rodger, Guinevere, and Jeremy, understand?"

I don't even bother listening to the others. Anita has always been high-strung, especially when it comes to mollycoddling her adult children. I'm working on her assignments—all I need is more time.

No other calls or messages. Not from Guinevere. Not from Miles. Panic turns to dread as I wonder where they could have gone to. What if the Cobras came into the hotel while I was sleeping? What if Guinevere and Miles are gettin' their knees broken right now while I'm just standing around staring at the walls?

I rush out of the room, down the stairs, and out the front door of the hotel. The streets of Noimore sing with activity, though it's low and subdued compared to Friday and Saturday. Sunday night isn't the liveliest.

My bad eye doesn't help me search the crowds of people on the streets. I push my way through them, glancing back and forth in an ever-desperate attempt to catch sight of anything I recognize. I stop at the corner and catch sight of Miles down the street. I jog over, a mix of relief and rage coursing through my body.

I take him by the arm, and he turns to me. "What do you think you're doing?" I growl.

"Pierce," he says with a sigh. "I know why you're upset, but I can explain."

I wait, my grip tightening on his bicep.

He continues, "I know you said I shouldn't be around Guinevere because of what people might think but…. Look, she wanted to go out, and I didn't think it was a good idea. She said she was in charge and went, so I followed to keep her out of trouble. I figured it was what you wanted, but you were sleeping and—"

"You didn't think to call me? Or leave a message?"

"I don't have a phone."

I find it hard to argue with his logic, but still. He could've left a *physical* note. I loosen my grip. "Tsk. Fine. I'll correct that."

As the paranoia leaves my system, I examine Miles. He's still got hints of damage from his beating a while back, but now the base of his neck is raw with bite marks and bruises. He's "hidden" them by propping up his collar and angling his head down, but anyone who knows what they're looking for would spot them in a heartbeat. A twinge of guilt strikes me. I'm a fucked-up guy sometimes.

He notices me staring and covers the injuries with one of his hands. "Hey, aren't you here for Guinevere?"

Guinevere? Oh, right.

"Where is she?" I ask.

Miles points. I follow the gesture to the door of a card club. If Miles hadn't been pointing, I wouldn't have known the woman by the door is Guinevere Vice. She leans against the outside of the building in slack jeans, a T-shirt, and a baseball cap, her long hair tucked away and out of sight. Slung over her shoulder is a sports duffel bag. She spots us and saunters over, her high-heels the only indication she might not be what she's presenting.

"Ah, Pierce," Guinevere says. "I'm so glad you could make it. I've been watching our marks like a hawk."

"You weren't to leave the hotel room," I snap. "What're you doing out here?"

"Well, sometime before sunset those thugs left the hotel. I couldn't let them get away! I followed them out here, after getting a disguise, of course, and saw them enter that establishment over there. They're in there right now."

"All right. Let's get back and—"

"They're the only ones in there," Guinevere interjects. "The tattooed guy, four bruisers, one of which I assume is our mole, and some old guy I think that runs the place. That's it! Six guys! Now's our chance! Before they open!"

I grab her and shove her into the nearest alley, whipping my head from side to side to see if anyone noticed. "Keep it down," I say, my voice on the verge of full-blown anger. "We're in the middle of Cobras territory. What if they heard you? *Common sense. Use it.*"

Guinevere exhales and narrows her eyes into a glare. "Very well. What should we do?"

The front sign on the card club indicates they're closed. If it really is run by the Cobras, it'll be opening any moment for the "night rush" of criminals who scour the streets once the sun sets. I turn to Miles. "Watch her while I investigate."

He nods but stops me when I go to leave. "Wait. Don't you want some backup? I can watch your six."

Can I really trust him to in a fight? I don't know. And I'm not about to risk it. "I said *wait here*."

"All right." He lowers his voice. "The… mole… looks just like me, okay? You'll know him when you see him."

"Good to know."

I pull my jacket tight and zip it up, leaving the alley as inconspicuously as possible. I realize the weight of my gun is less than normal. Of course—I shot it at the Crystal Floor Nightclub and haven't replaced or reloaded the magazine. I check the clip, keeping the weapon inside my jacket, and count three bullets. Perfect. Not even one per hostile. Just my luck.

The card club sits between buildings much larger than it. The club must've been built some time ago, and it sits awkwardly on its lot, giving plenty of space on all four sides. I slink into the darkness of the alley and crane my head around the corner, scoping out the back of the building before turning. The back door is open and an older man, hair white as snow, leans against the wall with a slumped posture. No one else is around.

I turn the corner and walk toward the guy, hunching over and avoiding eye contact. The guy gets nervous and straightens himself, but he doesn't go inside. When I get close I give him a reverse nod, jutting my chin up and offering a one-sided smile.

"Got a smoke?" I ask.

The man is displeased. He sneers and waves his hands. "Get outta here, ya freeloader."

"C'mon. Ya gotta have a spare. Help a guy out."

After a moment of glowering the man shakes his head and, with arthritis-ridden hands, searches the pockets of his sweatshirt. I see the bulge of a gun at his waistline. Just as he's found his smokes, I lunge forward, pulling my own handgun and slamming the man against the wall in one swift motion. I jam the barrel of my weapon under his chin.

"You one of the Cobras?" I ask.

He reaches for his weapon, but I grab his arm and twist it against his body, pinning him to the wall. He grunts in pain, and I loosen my hold, but only by a small amount.

"*Answer me.*"

"I just let them use the club," he spits. "I'm not part of them."

Just as I thought. These thugs in the Cobras do this shit all the time. Unlike Nick, who builds his businesses and shady hideaways, the Cobras impose themselves on the denizens of Noimore. We're all bad guys, but at least Big Man Vice has a little dignity about it.

I pull my wallet and slip a hundred dollar bill into the man's pants pocket. "You were out gettin' supplies," I say. "That's what you tell the thugs when they come asking about what happened here. Got it?"

The man nods.

I reach into the waistline of his pants and draw his gun. "This is mine now."

Again, he nods.

"Now get outta here."

I release him and he stumbles away, shaken. He glances back several times as he jogs out of the back alley, bewildered by my mercy, no doubt. The Cobras wouldn't have been so generous, but I stand by my advice to Miles. I don't kill hardworking innocents. Gangbangers, on the other hand....

I check the old man's handgun—a .22, weaker than my .45—but at least it has a full clip. I tuck it into my own waistband and creep into the card club through the back door.

The place is dim and uninviting. Perfect for sneaking around. I stay to the shadows and keep my back to the wall as I make my way deeper into the building. Card tables, playing chips, and classic fifty-two card decks are stacked around the place, making it easy to shift from one position of cover to the next. The light under the bathroom door catches my eye. I slink over, straining my ears to pick up even the slightest of noises.

The sound of water hitting water echoes in the bathroom. I crack open the door and steal a glance. There's a man—dressed in leathers, a cobra tattooed on his upper arm—standing in front of a urinal, his piss coming out in short spurts. He groans and fidgets, his attention consumed by his arduous ordeal.

I walk in, but he doesn't look up.

"*Caesar*," he grunts. "It's happenin' again. It hurts every time I go, man. *Every time*."

I restrain a laugh as I cross the room and, without answering, wrap my arm around his neck and yank back, trapping him against me and preventing him from yelling. He gurgles something, half flailing to pull up his pants and half clawing at my arm to remove it. I grab my wrist and wrench my arm harder, cutting off his air and blood flow. The man kicks forward, slamming his boots on the wall—calling for help—but I pull him away after only a few strikes.

Through the twisting and the thrashing, I struggle to maintain my hold until, finally, the bastard loses consciousness and goes limp in my arms. I hold him a few seconds longer, determined to make sure he's really out, before hauling his body to a nearby stall and throwing him in. I probably should just kill these guys, but they're not why I'm here. I came for Miles's brother and some asshole with a tits tattoo on his neck. That's it.

I hear someone walking up to the bathroom, and I hide in an empty stall, crouching on the toilet seat. My shoulder and arm hurt from fighting with the last guy. I pull my belt out of its loops and hold it taut in my hands.

"Rio?" a man asks, his smoker's voice echoing off the tiles of the bathroom. "Was that you I heard bangin' round in here? Jeez, man. You need to stop fuckin' chicks with bumps. That's your problem, right there."

He takes a few steps in and stops. "Rio?"

Silence.

"*Rio?*"

I hear him strain to bend over and, I assume, spot his buddy's feet in the stall over.

"What're you doin', Rio?"

Poor bastard makes the wrong decision and walks farther into the bathroom, straight to the body-occupied stall. He slams on the door, and I leap from my hiding place, catching the thug off guard and wrapping my belt tight around his throat. I loop the strap in the buckle before he has a chance to slip his fingers underneath, and I yank back.

"Arg—!"

The guy, quick as a whip, pulls a knife from his pocket. I grab his arm and wrestle with him, struggling to take the knife without getting cut. The man chokes out barks and grunts, the belt preventing him from swallowing any of the saliva building in his mouth.

In the chaos the guy slices through my jacket, down to my forearm, but I knee him in the side, right in the soft spot. He doubles over, clutching his side and unable to breathe. Blue in the face, he collapses to the floor, drool running from his mouth in rivulets. After a few moments, I remove my belt.

I glance down at my arm. The cut is superficial, but it bleeds everywhere nonetheless. I wrap my belt around my forearm, tightening it place to prevent any more blood loss. I'll deal with it later.

The fight with the two men leaves my blood pumping fast. I rotate my head and stretch out my sore arm, trying to calm my excitement. Probably best Miles didn't join me—the last fling I took on assignments only slowed me down at times like these. Then again, nothing beats post-fighting-for-your-life sex. Those are some good times.

While I fantasize about conquests long past, I pull the belts from the two guys lying around on the bathroom floor. Just in case they wake early, I tie them to the bathroom sink, their arms behind their backs. Good enough. I need to get this over with.

I slip from the bathroom, pull the gun from my waistband, and head for the main room. I see light underneath the door, just like with the bathroom, and I sneak up to it. Right as I place my hand on the handle, I hear someone else in the hall behind me.

"Who are—"

I turn on my heel and spot the monster I've been dreading—the muscled bruiser Stella warned me about—fists like hams and a slick bald head. The hulk of a man widens his eyes in surprise. Moving on instinct, I fire… and miss. Fuckin' lack of depth perception—he's only ten feet from me! I fire again, grazing the beast in the shoulder as he barrels down the hall. He slams into me, sending us both through the door and tumbling into the main card room. I hit the floor hard, my back flaring in pain, and I feel my grip on my gun fail. The weapon slides off, just out of reach.

"What the fuck?"

"Santiago, what's goin' on?"

The two new voices inform me that I'm now in a fight with *three* men instead of one. Fuck me. Santiago, the man with muscles in places most men don't even have places, straddles me and punches down. His knuckles are jagged—a single punch opens a gash across my face—and for a second I see nothing but black.

I pull my personal gun from its hostler and fire, slamming a bullet through the man's right bicep, crippling his dominant arm. The harsh bang of a powerful handgun fills the room, drowning out Santiago's shout of pain. I slide out from under him and jump to my feet, the room spinning with my dizziness.

Someone else fires a gun and sharp agony floods my upper arm. I throw myself behind a table, desperate to get my bearings straight.

Santiago, despite the gaping bullet wound, gets to his feet and charges, flipping card tables out of his way like they are made of paper. I fire again, miss, and fire *again* only to hear the click of an empty clip. That's it. No more bullets.

I throw the gun at his face, and he lifts his functioning arm to shield his eyes. I go for the punch, striking him hard in the gut. He stumbles back and kicks, slamming me in the stomach and sending me back, reeling. Jesus Christ. I'm *definitely* going to lose at this rate.

I hear another round of shots and glance over. The two other guys— the man with the tits tattoo and Miles's brother—are by the back wall, Miles's brother the one with the blasted gun. The tattooed guy grabs the gun and yanks it away. "You'll hit Santiago!" he shouts.

Santiago lunges forward, telegraphing a swing from his left arm. I duck, just barely, and stumble back, watching as Santiago crashes into a nearby table. I pick up a chair and swing, battering Santiago across the spine and splintering the wooden furniture. Taking deep breaths, I step away and, to my horror, the other man shrugs off the attack. He's not even breaking a sweat—only the bullet hole seems to be causing him any trouble.

Rage in his eyes, Santiago rushes me with a football tackle. I fall back right as he hits me—allowing his momentum to carry him over top—and I plant a foot in his chest, kicking up and sending him headfirst into the wall. Unfortunately for me, he shrugs that off as well, jumping to his feet long before I do and then kicking me midstand.

I fall forward and feel an organ-crushing stomp crunch down on my back. I'd yell if I had any breath. Instead I writhe, helpless and unable to recover from the shock in time to stand. I've gritted my teeth, preparing for the worst, when I hear the door slam open.

Santiago glances up and gets a solid punch to the face from Miles. The larger man winds up to return the favor when Miles, using his off hand, jabs forward with a knife, burying the blade deep into Santiago's right side before he can finish his swing. Miles twists and slams Santiago with his shoulder, sending him back into the wall. Santiago shudders and falls to one knee, his shaky hands holding the injury.

"Miles!" his brother shouts.

More gunfire. I tense. Miles crouches down and helps me into cover behind a tipped-over table. I thank whatever god is watching that Miles decides to follow. The tattooed guy fires as fast as his finger can pull the trigger, ripping up furniture all over the room.

"Stop! *Stop*! That's my brother!"

Miles's brother lurches forward, fighting for his gun. The tattooed man, just as spindly and gaunt as his attacker, punches the kid in the jaw, ripping the gun away at full force. "I don't care who he is! They all die!"

Miles's brother doesn't give in—he jumps for the gun again, fighting the man with gusto. The door opens a second time and, to my dismay, Guinevere walks in. I try to call out, but I'm still in a mild state of shock. I watch, unable to act, as she crosses the room straight to the two fighting men. She opens her duffel bag and withdraws a Taser, then shoots it, nonchalant, right into *Mr. Tattoo's* chest.

Electricity pumps through his system—he spasms and twitches— before falling, face-first, onto the floor. Guinevere faces Miles's brother. He holds up his hands, surrendering, and she smiles, the Taser still smoking from the discharge. She turns to me and returns her gun to the duffel bag.

"Pierce, why is it you never use these? They're wonderful."

I wipe blood from my face and roll my eyes. If I had hit the guy with my car, there wouldn't have been a need for melee combat in the first place. Besides, guns are better in every situation. Why would I carry nonlethal weapons when the Cobras aren't going to show me the same courtesy?

"Where did you even get that?" I ask, glaring at her duffel bag.

"I went shopping while the two of you were preoccupied. I figured we would need a few items for our mission. Seems I was right."

Guinevere withdraws a roll of duct tape and throws it to Miles. He takes it and ties up the tattooed man.

"Miles, what're you doing here?"

I turn to Miles's brother and take in the kid. He's Miles's doppelgänger—they're almost identical—the same honey shade of skin, the same black hair and mixed race features. Miles's brother is shorter, though, and he wears facial hair like he glued black sprinkles to his face, but their blood relation is undeniable.

"What're *you* doing here, Jayden?" Miles demands. "I thought you said you had a way out! You said it would only be a few days!"

"I *was*! I swear!"

Jayden runs both his sweaty palms over his black jeans. His sleeveless shirt exposes his shoulders, along with the fresh tattoo inked into his shoulder in the shape of a cobra. I shake my head in disgust. Kid doesn't understand what *joining a gang* entails. I let the brothers argue for a moment, turning my attention to Guinevere.

"I told you to wait for me," I say under my breath. "Your father would kill me if he knew you were here."

"Well, I *would* have stayed, but Miles was anxious to help you. I don't think I could have stopped him even if I wanted to."

Taken aback, I say nothing. I would've bet money that Guinevere instigated their assault. It didn't even cross my mind that Miles would be that concerned with my safety. Then again, perhaps he was just concerned for his brother….

"You're *always* doing this!" Miles shouts. "Why can't you just listen to me for once?"

Jayden tucks his hands into his armpits and glares. "Listen? *Listen*? Listen to what? You were gone, Miles! What else am I gonna do?"

"Gentlemen," Guinevere says, her voice commanding enough to silence the argument. "Enough. If you're going to listen to anyone, listen to me. Miles, you help Pierce. I'm going to go get the car. We're going to load up our tattooed friend and then leave this place as quickly as possible. Who knows who heard all these gunshots? We shouldn't take any risks."

I glance over at Santiago. He's not dead. He glares at me, conserving his strength through shallow breaths and not moving much. I leave him be, if only out of respect for his skill. The man sure does have some endurance. I hope he lives, though there's a piece of me that wonders if he'll ever come calling for revenge.

Miles offers his shoulder and I lean onto it. He smells good, but the pain sets in the moment my adrenaline drops. Jayden goes to open his mouth, but I silence him with a glower.

"You keep your trap shut, got it? Not another word until we're out of here."

Miles nods. Jayden shuts his mouth.

CHAPTER EIGHT

BACK TO good ol' warehouse thirty-six. The location on the docks has it all: isolation; easily cleaned concrete floors; security that won't report the screaming. It's where I like to do most of my interrogations, though outside of this weekend, I hadn't been doing that many. I'm sure the place is familiar to Miles, since he was just here, and he glances around with a nervous look in his eye. Guinevere has seen me work here a few times—she left the car as a kid and spied on me manhandling a few guys, despite my express orders—but she never got involved.

I finish duct taping Tattoo Guy to a chair.

"What's your name?" I ask him.

"Malloy," he replies, squinting up at me.

Up close the man is hideous. His tattoos, which he has more than one of, seem to cover pox marks and scars—even the naked woman along his neck and the side of his head covers acne marks. His oily hair, elongated neck, and mismatched denim and leather clothing do nothing to help the matter either. I step away, attempting to gather my thoughts.

I need to know why he went after Mikey and, more importantly, how he knew where Mikey was staying. Mikey was a secretive guy who didn't frequent many brothels. He also never went to the same one twice.

"You guys aren't going to do anything to me," Malloy says. "I'm important, ya know. I'm Harlan's cousin!"

"Who's Harlan?" Miles asks.

"The King Cobra," I say. "The guy in charge of their whole damn Cobras gang."

"Ah. I didn't know."

I force myself to walk to Miles's side without limping or making a show of it. My body hurts from the fight—especially my back—but I can't quit until the evening is over. And it's gonna be a long evening.

Miles looks me over, his discerning eyes lingering on my stance. If he knows I'm in pain, he doesn't mention it, which I'm grateful for.

Unless he has any of those painkillers left, there's nothing he can do for me.

Guinevere tilts her head to the side. "You don't look like Harlan's cousin," she says. "You're a little on the pale side."

Malloy spits on her high heel. "Shut up, bitch. I wasn't talkin' to you."

She frowns at her shoe and narrows her eyes. "My, my. You don't have much in the way of manners, do you?"

"You're gonna be sorry you were involved in this, *whore*. When the other guys hear what you did—*when Santiago gets back to them*—they're gonna track your asses down and make you all pay! I wouldn't be surprised if every cock in the Cobras gets into your prissy little pussy before they finish you! *That's* what's gonna happen if you don't let me go!"

He's a talkative son of a bitch.

Malloy turns his head to Jayden, and he spits again, this time missing. "And *you*! You sorry traitor! I knew taking you in was a mistake! They're gonna carve up your legs and feed you to their dogs, ya know that? It's your fault this all happened, ya chink weasel!"

Jayden slinks back into the shadows of the warehouse, shaken. "I-I never said I was with them," he mutters. "It's just my brother. It's my brother who's—"

"Try tellin' that to the others, ya little piece of shit! They ain't gonna listen! You're as a good as dead!"

Malloy takes a few deep breaths and quiets himself. All his raging got him winded—he's a small man, despite wearing three layers of everything in order to appear bulky.

Guinevere turns to me and smiles. "Can I interrogate him, Pierce? I would love to give it a try."

I'm not in the mood to do this bullshit. I nod. "Knock yourself out."

She smiles and Malloy offers up a breathless laugh.

"Her?" he balks. "She doesn't have the stomach for it."

Guinevere drops her duffel bag on a nearby chair and unzips the main pocket. "So, Malloy. You look like a clever boy. Answer me this: What's brown and bad for your teeth?"

He sits for a second, bemused. "Uh, sugar?"

"A baseball bat."

She pulls a bat from the contents of her bag and twirls it around in her hand. The color drains from Malloy's face, and Miles lifts both eyebrows in surprise. I chortle to myself—she loves to be dramatic.

"Would you mind securing his head, Pierce?" Guinevere asks me, her tone sickeningly sweet. "I don't want him moving around too much."

I walk over and wrap duct tape over his forehead, pulling his head down and securing it to the back of his chair. He quivers and jerks about, but I'm stronger. After repeating that process a few times, I tug on his restraints. The jackass isn't going anywhere, that's for sure.

He watches me with bulging eyes as I take a step back. "I hope you have dental insurance," I quip.

Guinevere saunters to the chair, her heels the only sound for miles around, and takes a few practice swings, the thick of the bat aimed for his mouth. "I've never done this before," she drawls. "So I might have to swing a few times…. That's not going to be a problem, right, Pierce? This is just like hitting a piñata? I just keep going until candy hits the floor?"

"W-wait," Malloy chokes out, sweat soaking through his denim. "Don't let her d-do that! Let's make a d-deal!"

"Don't *let* me do that?" Guinevere repeats. "You know I'm in charge, right? That technically Pierce and the others work for me?"

"O-okay. Fine. Let's you and me make a deal…. I'm ready to talk."

The guy can't move his head, so he scrunches his eyes closed and waits with his lips tight over his teeth.

"Very well," she says. "Why kill my Uncle Mikey?"

"You're gonna let me go after this, right? You're gonna let me go?"

"Of course we'll let you go. Now, why kill my Uncle Mikey?"

"H-he was on our turf!"

"How did you know he was going to be there?" I interject.

Malloy swallows hard. "*I was told*! I had an informant! Some g-guy on the inside of the Vice workings! He called up! Paid us to do it!"

"Who?"

"I d-don't know! That's the honest truth! I don't know!"

I sigh and recall that Nick's bodyguards at the Crystal Floor Nightclub turned on him the moment the shooting started up—insiders ready to pounce. Maybe there's some legitimacy to what Malloy is saying…. Maybe we really are being undone by someone on the inside.

"Who does this mystery man contact when he gives you all this information?" Guinevere asks.

"He, uh, talks to Diver! He works directly under Harlan! He gets all the calls!"

Malloy's yelling grates on my nerves. He's loud and likes to talk. A terrible combination. I rub at my temples and light up a cigarette. Hopefully the nicotine can ease the pain.

"Did you get all that, Pierce?" Guinevere asks me. I give her a curt nod. "Do you have anything else you need to ask?"

I shake my head. "I got everything I need now."

"Good. Then I trust you can let him go without me?"

"I'll handle it."

Rotating my shoulders, I grab a moving dolly from the side of the warehouse and wheel it over to Malloy's chair. Miles jogs over to me, glancing between the chair and the dolly.

"Do you… need help?" he asks, confused.

I shake my head. "Take your brother back to the car. We're heading to the airport after this."

Miles stares at me for a long moment. I exhale a line of smoke and lift an eyebrow.

"You don't wanna be around for this," I say, my voice low. "Watch the others till I get back."

"All right."

He turns and walks off, glancing over his shoulder once before grabbing his brother and leading him away. I use the dolly to scoop up Malloy and move him with ease. The gangbanger grunts and shakes.

"What're you doin'?" he shouts. "*Let me go!*"

I wheel him out the back of the warehouse. The night greets us with a chill wind. I pull my jacket tight and keep my sights forward, ignoring Malloy's incessant complaints as I take him to the end of the nearest pier. His disapproval turns to outright panic as I set him on the edge, his back facing the water. I ignore his screams and outcries as I grab a cinderblock from a convenient pile and duct tape it to the solid wood of his chair.

"W-what is this?" Malloy barks, struggling against his restraints. "What're you doing?"

"I thought it obvious."

"You said you'd let me go!"

"That's what I'm going to do."

I stand in front of him and tip his chair back. As he's about to careen into the frigid water below, I grab the collar of his shirt, keeping him suspended midfall. Only the back two pegs of his chair are on the pier—the instant I let go he'll tumble off.

I wait for a second, and the wide-eyed panic of Malloy drains enough for him to speak. "W-what is this, man? *What is this*? Killing Mikey was just business, man! Business! He was on our turf! That's the rules!"

"None of Noimore is your turf."

"It is! We took it! That's what happened! We outplayed the Vice family! They had a stranglehold on business, but now *we* have business! This isn't fair, man! I was just following orders! *Don't let go*! Don't do me like this! I answered your questions!"

The fear in his ragged gasps causes my skin to crawl. He's about ready to piss his pants. Empathy gets the better of me. Maybe I don't have to do this—but does a guy like Malloy deserve a second chance?

"You let Mikey suffer when you killed him," I say, my voice calm, betraying none of my discomfort. "It wasn't a quick death."

"Mikey was a scumbag!" Malloy barks. "Who cares if he suffered? He probably had it comin'! He's probably burnin' in hell right now! What're you gonna do? Go after the devil too? If you kill me like this—*after I had reasons to kill Mikey*—you're gonna start a full-on gang war! *Not just a turf war*! We'll be hunting you down! You'll have drive-by shootings! I'm Harlan's cousin! There'll be consequences!"

At this point I think he's just throwing out words and hoping they stick. I loosen my grip on his collar. He gasps and stiffens, blubbering things through tearful sobs.

"W-wait!" he grunts. "Please don't! Not like this! *Please*!"

"What about the girl?" I ask.

"G-girl? What girl? What the fuck are you talking about?"

"The girl you shot. The one in the room with Mikey."

"*Girl*? That wasn't a girl! It was some cunt hooker! Who gives a shit about her! I can't even remember her! It's not like she was that good-lookin'!"

"She wasn't a part of this. She didn't deserve a bullet through the head."

"*Are you serious*?" Malloy chokes out with a forced hoarse laugh. If he could, he'd shake his head, but he just continues to sweat profusely. "You're upset over some *whore*? She wasn't even important! She's a nobody! Gutter trash! I can get you prettier ones if that's what you want!

You can't seriously be thinkin' about lettin' me fall over *scum* like that brothel skank!"

Not even a hint of remorse. He doesn't care. All he wants is to save his own disgusting hide. He'll never change.

I let go.

He splashes into the water, his cries gurgled and muffled by the waves. He'll drown like the snake he is.

I step away from the edge, a lump in my throat. His cries are going to haunt me—they always do—and with an unsteady hand I pull the cigarette from my mouth and flick it into the water. I let out a powerful exhale to clear my thoughts. It's going to be a long, *long* night.

Hard liquor sounds amazing right now.

I walk back through the warehouse and out to Guinevere's vehicle. She's in the passenger seat, with Miles and Jayden in the back. I make my way over to the driver's side door and let myself in, not saying a word.

"Where's Malloy?" Jayden asks.

"We let him go," Guinevere replies.

"But if he tells the other guys about what I did… they'll all come for me and—"

She smiles and motions for him to lower his voice. "Don't worry, sweetie. He's not going to tell anyone."

Jayden shakes his head. "B-but you don't know Malloy like I do! He'll break his promise. He'll tell everyone in the Cobras, even if he said he wouldn't."

"Trust me. He *isn't able* to tell anyone."

Her definitive tone silences the car. If the kid doesn't understand *now*, he won't until it's spelled out for him. I start the engine, and we circle out of the docks parking lot. Next stop—O'Hare International Airport.

THE TWO-HOUR drive to the airport is done in silence. The two brothers in the back stare at each other, no doubt communicating nonverbally, but I don't have the understanding or patience to try and keep up with it. I'm driving. My attention is on the road.

I park the vehicle on the far end of the last parking lot. Guinevere grabs her duffel bag and steps out of the vehicle. I turn to Miles. "Wait here."

He nods.

I exit, shut my door, and join Guinevere twenty feet from the reinforced car. She removes her baseball cap, allowing her long black hair to fly loose, then faces me with a smile.

"Pierce, this was an exciting evening."

"I suppose."

"Thank you."

Those words rub me wrong. I instantly think of Miles.

Then again, there's a reason Guinevere never keeps any friends. Her father and mother would never allow it—never allow her to do anything or get close to anyone—for fear that she would be spirited away or deflowered. Anyone she got too close to would go missing. And risk or adventure? She had very little. No camping. No sports. If it weren't for me breaking the rules and taking her on a few assignments, I doubt she'd have seen much outside her parents' estate. Maybe she's thanking me for the excitement.

"I was impressed with your baseball bat trick," I say with a genuine laugh.

"I learned from the best."

"Hm."

Guinevere takes a deep breath, her mood shifting from jovial to solemn in the blink of an eye. "I've always wanted to know what my father does for a living. After tonight… I know for sure I don't want anything to do with it. I'm sorry you go through it day in and day out."

"Malloy deserved what he got."

"I agree, but…."

I say nothing.

She continues, "I know I didn't show it but… I was nervous, and when Miles and I came looking for you in the card club, I was certain we'd find you dead. A life like that isn't for me. That kind of fear takes a toll on a person."

"Listen—"

"No, *you* listen," she interjects, glaring at me. "I'm trying to tell you something." Guinevere steps closer and wraps her arms around me in a tight embrace. "Pierce. I've known you for as long as I can remember. You're like the nanny who raised the kids in all those shows where the parents are horrible people."

"How specific," I say, my voice dry and sarcastic.

"I wanted to tell you… I'm leaving and I'm not coming back."

I return to my silence.

Guinevere releases me and steps back. "I'm getting on the plane, but I'm not going to any of our safe houses or known locations. I'm getting on the plane, and I'm leaving for good. I don't want to get involved with any of *this*. My father can handle it and, when he's done, Jeremy can take over since that's what he wants anyway. I'm escaping while I still can."

"You're not telling your father or mother where you're going?"

"No. And you shouldn't tell them either."

"You know I don't deny your father anything."

She rolls her eyes. "I know you have a man-crush on him, but you have to promise me. I'm even ditching my phone—I planned everything out ahead of time to disappear off the grid. Well, not entirely off the grid… just far enough away that my parents won't find me."

"Why tell me?"

"Because… I was hoping you would join me."

I catch my breath, a little confused by her statement. "What?" I ask, like I'm some moron incapable of mulling over the conversation in my head.

"Come with me, Pierce. Maybe not *right now*. But someday. When my father finally keels over. When you retire. *Sometime*. You don't deserve all this. You could do better."

"You don't know me that well. I'm just as terrible as any other mobster. You'd be better off by yourself than with some old coldhearted killer." I regret saying anything. I don't like talking about myself, and the hurt look in her eye irritates me. If she wants to leave, she should just leave. I know where I'm going to die. If she wants to escape a similar fate, I applaud her.

"That kid we pulled from the card club isn't a mole," Guinevere states matter-of-factly. "They're brothers. We went to save your boy toy's brother. That's what we did. Maybe we also got my uncle's killer, and that's a bonus, but we also saved some kid simply by virtue of your mercy. Now look me in the eye and tell me you're a coldhearted killer."

"That's different," I say. "You don't understand. It's my lies that got him mixed up in this in the first place. It's an obligation now."

"You could bring him with you. When you retire." Guinevere opens her duffel bag and removes a small index card. She writes out a note with a handy pen, folds up the card, and then passes it to me. "That's my new number. The one I'll use once I'm out of state. Give me a call in the future? And don't give it to my parents."

"Fine."

"Good-bye, Pierce. I'm going to miss you."

I say nothing. She really does have a flair for the dramatic. She says I was her nanny, but in reality I was just some bodyguard. They aren't the same.

Guinevere turns on her heel and gives me an energetic wave before heading off toward the airport terminals. I watch her go for quite some time before glancing at the card and realize it's a California area code. She's been planning on leaving for some time. I sigh. At least I did my job—one kid is safe, two to go.

Her offer weighs on me as I drag my feet back to the vehicle. I won't leave Nick. But… maybe when he dies…. No. I shake my head. What would I even do? I have no skills other than street smarts. Right? I guess any asshole can flip a burger. But is that what I want to *start* doing at the age of forty? What a way to go. I might as well blow my brains out.

I throw myself into the driver's seat with a heavy exhale. Miles and Jayden are in the back, bickering. They silence themselves as I shut the door. It'll take another two hours to drive back to Noimore from Chicago. There isn't much evening left.

"Pierce," Miles says, breaking the silence. "Can we take my brother home?"

Jayden sits forward. "We can't go! I told you already—Dad kicked me out. I'm not allowed back. Where am I even going to go?"

"We can get your things, and maybe Mom will—"

"Mom wants nothing to do with me! How many times do I have to tell you? You know it. You should've just let me stay with Malloy and Santiago."

Those two won't make plans, not acting like siblings.

"Where's your father?" I ask Miles.

He half smiles. "Do you know that trailer park on the east side of town? Little Trees Trailer Village?"

"I know the place."

"That's where he lives."

THE LITTLE Trees Trailer Village is the type of trailer park with mobile manufactured homes rather than trailer homes that hitch up to the back of a vehicle. It's nicer than I expected, but still a white trash stereotype straight out of the movies. The streets are narrow, the houses ramshackle, and the vegetation lacking—which is ironic, given the name of the trailer park. I see more broken-down cars than I do people, but that might have something to do with the time of day. Dawn is approaching, though the sun isn't yet visible.

The unpleasant silence of the vehicle gets to me. The radio is off, and the two brothers seem content to stare out opposite windows. I wonder what Miles is thinking. I don't have any brothers or sisters, so his dedication is foreign to me, but it's yet another trait I admire. *He* didn't choose to have a brother, but he took up the responsibility of caring for him nonetheless. Anyone willing to take on extra responsibility is a hard worker in my book. Which reminds me of something Nick said: with hard work you have a garden; without hard work you have weeds. So it is with people.

"That's it," Miles intones. "The one next to the tree."

The tree is a black, twisted oak, long since dead. It's a corpse, nothing more, nothing less.

I pull the vehicle up and around, parking so the passenger door faces the front door of the trailer. Miles and Jayden go stiff at the sight of the house—it's like they both stop breathing for fear they'll stir something within. The home is a faded blue thing with steps leading up to the rickety front door. A porch light attracts all sorts of insects, and the trash piled up the side covers a few windows. Reminds me of my own home growing up.

I glance back at Miles. He stares at me and then looks away. "You can… wait here."

"This has nothing to do with me," I say.

"Okay. Good. We'll be right back."

They exit, straighten their clothes, and walk together up to the front door. Jayden takes the steps and attempts to go in, but the door is locked. He pounds on the flimsy entrance, almost knocking it off its hinges, until it flies inward. A man steps out—tall, muscular, wearing a shirt and jeans—too young to be their father, but they both respond to him with familiar tones.

"Lawrence," Miles says. "Where's Dad?"

"What're you two doin' here?" Lawrence asks, his small eyes shifting between Miles and Jayden. He has the complexion of mayonnaise, but his nose and face are similar to the men in front of him. If I had to guess, I would say he's their older half brother.

"Where's Dad?"

"He doesn't want to see you two ever again. Beat it."

Another man emerges from the trailer—fatter than the rest and just as pale as Lawrence. He has a two-week beard, a balding head, and a gut that holds most of his weight out in front of him. The man walks with a fighter's confidence right up to Jayden.

"I told you that I didn't want you here again!" the older man shouts, waking the neighbors. "If you want to act like an ungrateful piece of shit, I'm going to treat you like an ungrateful piece of shit!"

Classy.

"I just want my stuff, Dad," Jayden says, crossing his arms over his chest. "Just give me my stuff so I can leave."

"That's *my* stuff now, boy. I took you in under my roof for all those years, and you never paid rent. All that stuff you left—I'm no storage unit! It's mine!"

"Give it back to him so we can leave," Miles says. "We don't want any trouble."

Lawrence pushes Miles and Jayden back away from the front of the house, blocking their ability to get inside. "Dad already sold it. You don't have anything here. Now leave."

"You sold it?" Jayden asks in disbelief. "My clothes? My things? You sold them?"

"Some of it," their father states. "The rest I'm keepin'. For everything *you owe me*."

Miles shakes his head and tenses.

His father glares. "Whatta you gonna say, boy? It looks like you got some spare cash. What's that you're wearing? A fancy suit? You never paid me rent either, ya know. Where's my cut?"

"I don't have any money," Miles says through gritted teeth. "And this isn't about me. Jayden wants his stuff. He doesn't owe you a damn thing."

"Why, you're a lyin' sack of shit," Lawrence says, his enunciation the exact opposite of eloquent. He grabs Miles by the arm and shakes him—he's at least twice Miles's size in muscle, someone Santiago would be proud of. When he slams Miles against the trailer, I feel my blood pressure rising.

Lawrence rummages through Miles's pockets. "You have money. Look at you!"

Jayden sits, passive, as his brother is groped for cash. The look on his face… it's like he's glad it's not *him* getting assaulted. Miles offers no resistance and, true to his word, he has no money on him regardless. His half brother ends up empty-handed.

"No wallet?" Lawrence asks. "You're keepin' stuff from us, aren'tcha, faggot?"

"You were always the most ungrateful," their father says. "You think you're better than us? Do ya? That why you brought Jayden here? To tell him *he's entitled* to his shit back? He's not."

Lawrence slams a fist into Miles's gut, taking him by surprise and causing him to double over in pure unmitigated pain. Miles bites back a yell as he hits his knees. Jayden, flinching back, says and does nothing.

I'm done with this.

I step out of the car and walk around the front. I pull my firearm and tap it across the roof of the vehicle, the metal-on-metal clacking drawing everyone's attention. They see the shiny silver of my handgun long before they take me in. I lean back against the car and shake my head.

"I've had enough of this," I say. "I've got a schedule keep, and I don't have time for an impromptu episode of *Jerry Springer*. Let the kids take their stuff."

"Who the hell're you?" their father barks, the fat of his gut jiggling with his outrage.

"I'm the guy with the gun."

Lawrence takes a step away from Miles, his hands in the air. Jayden snickers to himself and runs into the mobile home, leaving his family outside to fend for themselves. Miles staggers to his feet and follows in after, but not before giving me an odd sideways glance.

I pull my pack of cigarettes and light one while I wait. Lawrence and his father keep their eyes on me, but eventually relax back into their default hostile postures. Lawrence even gets bold enough to walk a few steps toward me, always managing to stay at arm's length. Technically I don't have any bullets, but I'm certain I would win if it came down to a fight. His skin is a little too smooth and his hair a little too neat to be someone who gets into regular brawls.

Good-lookin', though. He's the kind of guy I'd *love* to show who the alpha of this situation is. I bet he'd be a lot more docile with a dick up his ass.

"What're you starin' at?" he asks.

I blow smoke in his direction. "Trash."

He sneers and goes to say something but stops when he notices my bad eye. "Can you even see with that thing? Where'd you even get that?"

"Your mom. She's a scratcher."

Every verbal jab, no matter how obvious or stupid, gets him just a little angrier and just a little closer. I want him to try it. I want him to throw the first punch. I'm half tempted to just start the fight myself, but I rein it in. I'm thirty-six years old, and I should probably act like it.

The door to the trailer opens. Miles and Jayden walk out, Jayden holding a black trash bag filled with miscellaneous goods—some hard and some soft, judging by the protrusions. They both avoid looking at their older half brother and father as they jog over to the car. Miles takes the front passenger seat, and Jayden takes the back.

"You're stealin' my things," their father says as I walk around to the driver's door. "I'm gonna call the cops. I'm gonna see you're prosecuted. I'm get my due whether you little ingrates like it or not."

I'd like to see him try.

I start up the car and peel out onto the street, more tense and angry than I realized. I release the gas pedal from my death stomp and return to driving like a sane person. Miles and his brother, silent like they've been for the entire ride, remain that way. That's fine. I don't want to talk about their deadbeat father or abusive brother. The moment I saw Miles struggling to fight for his brother's safety, I figured their life sucked. Assholes will be assholes. What're you gonna do about it?

FOR ONCE in ten years, I'm happy to see the front door of my flat. The sunshine, however, is a different story. It's too late—early?—for all this bullshit. In a few short hours I need to meet with Jeremy, and just thinking about it gets me agitated.

"Where are we?" Jayden asks, holding his black trash bag close. "I don't want to be here."

"Don't make a scene," I say.

Miles holds his brother close. "It's an apartment. Calm down."

I unlock the door and shuffle inside, sore and ready to bury myself in bed. Miles mutters things to his difficult little brother as I flip on the lights and throw open the refrigerator door. Nothing but a jar of olives. Fuck.

"I can get something from the corner store," Miles says, tracking my movements.

I pull my wallet and toss him a stack of bills—way too much for a bag of food—but I don't care. I want something to eat. Anything will do.

Jayden glances around my apartment with greedy eyes. I see him stare at my television, take stock of my sound system, and crane his head to glance down the hall toward my bedrooms. The kid might have a drug problem—druggies are always lookin' for things to pawn in order to get quick cash.

I walk over to the hall closet and rummage through a box on the floor. I pull a pair of handcuffs as cold as the wind outside. Miles watches me finger the cuffs, and he flushes hard. I stifle a laugh.

"They're not for you," I mutter.

"What're they for, then?" he asks, his tone indignant.

"I don't trust your brother. I'm gonna lock him in the guest room."

"You didn't do that to me."

"Yeah, well, when I met you it was different. You were weak and injured. When I met your brother, he was shooting at me with a gun." I motion to my arm. The bullet grazed my bicep, leaving a long slash through the skin and muscle. "He almost got me. You understand why I don't trust him, right?"

Miles relaxes. He flashes the money and shrugs. "I'm gonna get some food. Hopefully my brother isn't too difficult." He hustles from the apartment, and I suspect he's hungry as well. I probably should have stopped to get something to eat when we drove through Chicago....

The front door slams shut, startling Jayden. I stare at the kid and then motion to the back. "I have a spare room."

"You do?"

"Yeah. You'll sleep there and we'll deal with you tomorrow."

I guide the kid back. He holds his bag close, and I let him keep it. We walk into the spare bedroom, and Jayden takes everything in. It's nothing special—just a bed, a nightstand, a dresser, and an empty closet. The dresser has a collection of sex toys and lubricant—hopefully the kid doesn't get too curious.

I shove him into the bedroom and swing the handcuffs around my index finger. The frightened animal look in the kid's eyes is unexpected. He gulps down air and backs away from me, shrinking into himself and bunching his shoulder around his neck.

Uncertain of his fright, I walk over and push him toward the bed. He throws his bag at me and jumps up onto the mattress, stuffing his back into the corner of the room. "Get away from me!"

I can't stop myself from chuckling. What's this kid's malfunction?

"Get down here," I say. "Put your hand by the headboard."

"Fuck you!"

I'm really not in the mood for games. I exhale, grab his leg, and yank back. He kicks and thrashes as he falls back onto the mattress, landing one mild blow to my chin. I grit my teeth and wrestle him to the headboard, taking the cuffs and fastening one around his wrist and the other to the metal post.

To my surprise, the kid—lightning quick—reaches into my jacket, draws my gun, and pulls the trigger three times with the barrel against my chest. The clicking of an empty magazine is his only reward. I wrench the gun from his grasp, and he flinches.

"Don't do this!" he pleads.

I stand up and holster my firearm, curling my lip in disgusted confusion. "What the fuck are you talking about?"

"I-I heard about you! You're that… *creepy enforcer*! The one Nick Vice calls on!"

I snort. "Yeah. That's me."

"You… you…." He grips his clothing tight to his body. "Everyone knows what you do to… to… *boys*."

In that single moment I'm both furious and amused. Is the kid trying to imply that I'm going to rape him? Is he trying to imply I have a reputation for fucking little boys?

"I don't do anything to boys," I state, my tone more threatening than I wanted it to be. "I never have and never will."

"Malloy s-said the Vice family gets you kids and—"

"He was *wrong*," I say. "But ya know what I *do* like to do? Shoot druggies who steal my stuff."

The color drains from his honeyed skin. His instant turn to silence confirms every suspicion I had. He's a drug addict. I wonder if Miles knows.

I force a smile. "Now stay in here and be good. You and your brother are gonna be sharing a bed. Got it?"

"Yes."

"Good."

I walk out of the room, tense and angry all over again. Of course the Cobras would make up stuff about me. I guess I'm scarier to them as a pedophile. I sigh and let the breath take some of my anger with it. Pent-up and frustrated, I make my way to the master bathroom. The bathtub, wide and luxurious, is calling to me. I run the water and strip off my clothing, including removing the belt strapped around my forearm.

Sliding into the tub, I wince in pain. My face is cut, my arm has a bullet injury *and* a knife wound, and my back is killing me. The hot water does everything good, but the few moments of adjustment are agonizing. I have salve in the cabinet by the toilet, but I don't have the strength to pull myself from the water. Instead I just sink in, my head on the back of the porcelain. Once the water fills to the brim, I switch it off.

Life passes at a snail's pace while I watch my own blood seep into the water. I'm contemplating sleeping in the tub when the handle to the bathroom turns and Miles ambles in.

CHAPTER NINE

I RELAX at the sight of him.

Miles is holding an armful of packaged food and drops most of it on the floor next to the tub. I watch, silent, as he turns around and walks back out the door, leaving it open. I can hear him enter the guest room—he must be leaving *every* door open—and when I close my eyes I can faintly make out his conversation with his brother.

"—he's not going to hurt you."

"He's a psycho! Everyone knows it! That's what Malloy said!"

"Would you please just listen to me for once? I'm trying to help you!"

"I'm just doing what *you* did! Why are you trying to stop me?"

"I was just making money, okay! *For you*! So that you didn't have to! So that you could stay in school!"

"School? I don't want to go school! You're not helping me by putting me in school! I could be making my *own* money!"

"Jayden—" Miles cuts himself off for a long moment and, when he returns to talking, he's harder to hear. "Please just trust me. Let me take you to Mom. I think she'll help."

"I don't want her help! I don't want to be here!"

"Can't you just…. Never mind. We'll talk about it tomorrow."

The conversation cuts short, and I can see their cold glares in my mind's eye. If Jayden were my brother, I probably would have dropped him like a bad habit. I'm surprised Miles gives two shits about what his brother does.

I'm also surprised when Miles walks back into the bathroom, shutting my bedroom and bathroom door behind him.

"You don't mind if I eat in here, right?" he asks, his voice just above a whisper.

I glance around the dull blue, black, and white of the bathroom. It's no French table with a candelabrum, but it's clean enough to eat off. I shrug and motion him in with a weak flick of my wrist. Movement takes a lot out of me. I return to my sedentary bathing.

Miles takes a seat on the floor, right next to the bathtub, his posture slumped. He picks up a plastic-wrapped sandwich and hands it to me. The meat, pale and dubious, is half soaked into the bread itself. I take the food—I'm too hungry not to—and peel back the wrapping. I eat without tasting. It's better this way.

Miles passes over a bottle of vodka, and I lift an eyebrow.

"Aren't you too young to purchase this?" I ask.

He shakes his head. "The cashier didn't ask for my ID."

I can see that. Miles is wearing my clothes, after all. I bet the owner thought he was one of the Vice family enforcers and didn't want to risk getting in trouble. Lucky for me, I guess. I undo the top of the bottle and take a powerful swig. The burning is everything I could've hoped for. I let it warm my insides as I sink farther into the tub.

We eat in silence. The sandwich disappears long before I want it to. I sigh and take another long drink.

Miles, once finished, leans over the side of the tub and brazenly scans me. I don't move, but at the same time I know I'm no stud on a magazine cover. I'm pretty sure I'm bruised down half my body, and the blood only gets the water a sick shade of pink. He's probably just curious.

"Are you okay?" he asks.

"I've had worse."

"Are you in a lot of pain?"

"Take a wild guess."

"Do you have anything for your injuries?"

I motion with my good eye to the cabinet. Miles slides over and finds my salve—he's quick with his wits—and grabs a few hand towels while he's at it. He places them on the side of the tub, but I have no energy to use them. They sit on the edge and the bathroom remains silent.

Miles opens the salve and gobs some out on his fingers. He sits up and gingerly rubs it across the bullet injury on my shoulder, covering the cut with a solid layer. When I offer no protest, he moves to my forearm and repeats the process on the laceration.

This is new. And bold. Then again, Miles just *does things* without asking, most of which are gutsy to begin with. He slides his thumb across the gash on my face, applying the salve to that injury as well. I stare at him directly, and he gets nervous under my scrutiny. He doesn't meet my gaze and instead focuses his attention on my body.

Once he's done with the salve, he rolls up his sleeves and rubs soap on a hand towel. He runs it over my chest, neck, and arms, careful to avoid most wounds. He scrubs my gut, and I grimace—good ol' Santiago kicked me there—but he pulls away before I have to stop him. Miles continues down to my thighs, taking his time and gently caressing everything sensitive.

I have to admit, it's erotic as hell. I've never had anyone bathe me, or whatever this is. I spread my legs and relax further, content to receive a massage.

He stops for a moment to push the bottle of vodka closer to my hand. I take it and throw back another swig. Miles returns to rubbing me down, and I chortle to myself. A guy could get used to this.

"Thank you for helping my brother," he says.

I ignore the comment.

Miles continues, "I… know he can be a handful… but I'm all he has. If I don't look out for him, who will, ya know? That's why I appreciate all your help."

I savor another mouthful of vodka.

Apparently discouraged by my silence, Miles stops his gratitude.

"Tomorrow," I drawl, staring up at the ceiling, "I'll pull some cash for you and your brother. I have to meet Jeremy at our usual spot, but I can drop you both off at the bus station just on the edge of town."

It's Miles's turn to be silent.

"I'll tell them you couldn't get in with the police, and they'll forget all about this," I say. "No one will come looking for either of you."

"Th-thank you."

There's an unsteadiness about his voice that makes me glance over. He's still focused on his work. I exhale and don't allow it to bother me. I've done everything I can for the man. The real question now is whether he can keep his slob of a brother on the right track.

Miles stops his kneading. He slides down the bathtub and leans over me, his breathing uneven. Without waiting for me to stop him, he presses his mouth against mine, sliding his tongue over my lips and slipping it past my teeth.

I'm not drunk enough for this but… he tastes good. And the way he presses harder into me—like he's desperate for this—it gets me going. I'll just pretend I'm drunk enough.

He laps his tongue against mine and sucks my upper lip. When he breaks away, it's to nibble on my jaw and trail his lips down my neck. I lean back to allow him better access. Miles latches on to my flesh, allowing me to feel his canines without inflicting any pain. He stops to catch his breath and waits a moment longer.

"When are you planning on getting out of the tub?" he asks.

I shrug. "I dunno. I was giving serious thought to sleeping here."

Miles chuckles. "My brother thinks you're gonna break into his room while he's sleeping and molest him."

"Your brother is gonna have to crawl into this tub and molest himself with my soggy body if that's what he wants to have happen."

"Are you really gonna sleep in here?"

"No. Of course not."

Miles jumps up and gathers my discarded clothing from the floor. Guinevere's index card falls from my pants pocket. I tense as Miles picks it up. He turns it over in his hand and gives me a questioning look.

"It's from Guinevere," I say. Her offer rings in my head. People are leaving Noimore all the time—either via death or vehicle—and I know her words will hang on me like a wet blanket if I keep her card. "Get rid of it," I command. "I'll never need it." Nick will be around for another couple decades, and I'm sure I'll be dead by then.

Miles crushes the card in his hand. "I'll take care of it."

I pull myself from the tub, feeling twice my age, and grab a towel. Miles lingers nearby as I make my way to the bedroom, drying as I go. I throw the towel in the hamper, and he tosses my clothes in after. With a sigh of contentment, I throw myself back onto my bed. What a long fuckin' day. I glance at the clock. I have to be up in four hours and I set the alarm. Perfect. Just… perfect.

Miles crawls onto the bed and gets over me, bracing himself on all fours and craning his head down to continue his kissing. I go to say something only to have his tongue invade my mouth. Fuck it. If he wants this so bad, I guess I'll chunk out some sleep time to give it to him. I grab his arm and roll him over onto his back, pinning him under me.

To my surprise he goes stiff. "Wait," he breathes, placing a hand on my chest. "I'm still sore."

"You gonna tell me no?" I ask, my face inches from his. "After everything you've been doin'?"

"No—no, of course not. Please… just… be gentle."

His request is laced with fear. It drives me mad—I want him more than ever, but not in a *gentle* way. I force myself to roll back onto the bed, my gaze locked on the ceiling. He doesn't know what that kind of language does to me. He doesn't know I *was* being gentle with him before. I don't normally take the time to make sure my flings are enjoying the experience....

"Never mind," I force myself to say. "I'm not into it."

Miles sits up stares at me with an unreadable expression. "You look like you're still into it."

Eh. My dick's still into it, sure, but the mind and the dick are two separate creatures. If my dick had its way, I'd be some rent boy, fucking twenty-four seven.

"Don't worry about it," I say.

"What if I did all the work?"

I mull over his suggestion. "Fine. Get to it."

Miles reaches across me and grabs a box of condoms off the nightstand. He must have purchased them at the store—of course he did—and he opens one with a steady hand. He unrolls it over me and right away I know it's one coated in lubricant and it's a tad too large. I glance over at the box. It reads MAGNUM XXL. I stifle a laugh. I'm flattered, and maybe that's what it *felt* like to him, but I'm not *that* big.

He rips off his shirt, undoes his pants, and removes his boxers. The midmorning sun reveals his tattoo better than the dim lighting of the hotel room we first fucked in. The tattoo is of a phoenix—some sort of tribal design done in solid black—starting from his right knee and ending with its wings at his hip. I've never seen a tattoo in that location before, but I like the look of it.

Miles straddles me, bracing most of his weight on my chest with his posted arms. His expression... it's as if he's wrapped up in his own thoughts, barely seeing anything around him. He takes my cock and guides it into place, easing back until it no longer needs a guiding hand. He grits his teeth as it breaches his body.

I tilt my head back, enjoying what mitigated sensation I can feel through the excess rubber. He takes it slow, holding his breath the entire time. He's tight and the feeling of stretching him is impossible to ignore. Halfway down and I have to stop myself from flipping him over and finishing this myself. The agony of anticipation is killing me. I run my hands over his hips, urging him to go faster and digging my nails into his skin.

"*Fuck*," I groan.

He picks up his pace and rocks back and forth, gradually lowering until there's nowhere else to go. Miles takes a few ragged breaths, clearly not yet used to the sensations, and stares down at me with a mix of lust and deep contemplation. He's lean and smooth—his sweat a pleasant sight in the glow of the morning—and I enjoy the hint of muscle under his tight skin. Even the bite marks…. I like seeing them too. Like they're proof he's mine.

I reach up and grab his neck, pulling him down. I bite his bottom lip and lick it afterward. With a need to taste him, I force my mouth onto him and twist my tongue around his. He increases his force until pulling away midkiss, his expression almost one of anger.

"I thought you didn't like making out," he says, his voice shaky. "Why are you…?"

I snort and narrow my eyes. "That's what you wanted, right?" I ask between husky breaths. "What're you complaining about?"

He stops his movements and turns away from me, his longer black hair obfuscating his expression. I wait, confused, for him to do something, but the moment continues. Hot wet droplets hit my neck and chest as he pulls away. I prop myself up onto my elbows and graze the wetness with my fingers. Is he crying?

"For fuck's sake," I say. "If it hurts that bad, stop!"

He punches the headboard, the crack of the wood hitting the wall enough to get me tensed for a fight. I sit up and Miles wraps an arm around my neck. I grab his hair and yank back, instinct telling me I should fight. He glares at me, his face wet with tears but his eyes so rage-filled they chill my aggression.

"*Pierce*," he says, his tone curt. "I…."

I take a deep breath and release him. He closes his eyes and slams his forehead against my collarbone.

"No one is there for me," he continues, his voice clearer than before but still raw with emotion.

"What're you—"

"*No one.*"

"You better start makin' sense. I'm losing my patience." Was *he* drinking? What the hell is he so angry about?

"My mom, she… she left. She didn't take me or my brothers—but she took my sister. *Her favorite*. And then there was Lawrence…. Well, you saw Lawrence."

He takes a ragged breath. "My father kicked me out. I slept on the streets; the kids at school were relentless in their mocking… every day it was the same. You get it, right? Afterward… when Jayden went to school, I thought I could make it different for him—because no one made it different for me—but *even he* doesn't want anything to do with me. He dropped out, shot up, and got involved with the Cobras…."

Miles holds himself close. I say and do nothing. His anger isn't directed at me.

He continues in a breathless whisper, "It's my fault. *I had to do something*. No job, no experience… no clean clothes. No one wanted me. The Vice family took me in as an extra gun but… but Jayden wouldn't listen. And then the Vice family wouldn't listen. Even they turned on me."

His grip tightens and he speaks directly into my neck. "*Pierce*. I can't… I can't repay what you've done for me because… no one has ever done it for me. My life, my brother's life… I just… *thank you*."

His ramblings are a little less coherent now, but I'm certain I understand. He was lost and alone, and I was the first sad sack to throw him a handful of crumbs. They're just *crumbs*, but to a starving man, they're more valuable than all the gold in Fort Knox—more valuable than one can put words to. I smirk. That's how I feel about Nicholas Vice.

"I get it," I say. "I really do. Calm down."

"Come with us," Miles mutters. "When Jayden and I leave… come with us. I'll spend the rest of my life paying you back."

That's two times in one night. I swear I'm not superstitious, but that's an omen if I've seen one. "I can't," I tell him straight up. "I owe Nick a debt I can't repay."

He shivers. "Then let me stay with you. Let me help Jayden and then… and then let me come back and help you."

"Fine."

He's throwing his life away to repay me for a few crusty crumbs, but I won't deny him his honor or gratitude. I wrap an arm around him. God, it's like I'm holding a younger version of myself—right at that moment I agreed to fight for the Vice family.

Miles pulls himself off me. It's easy, considering how flaccid I've become, and he exhales in relief. Before I speak he drags his lips over my own and trails tender kisses. I indulge the moment and return his affection, if only because it's rare to feel such raw intimacy. He runs his hand over the back of my neck and up into my hair, pulling me deeper. I like it—I like that he wants it—and I caress the ridge of his spine.

He breaks away but keeps his mouth against mine. "Fuck me," he says.

Heat sluices through my body. I'm ready to go, despite being cold not but ten seconds ago. I push him off, throw him down onto his stomach, and grab the box of *overcompensation condoms*, tossing the old one into the trash.

Miles shakes his head. "Don't bother."

I don't argue. I never liked them anyway. I do, however, grab some lube and apply it to myself. Miles waits patiently through the process, even as I settle in behind him, rapt by his naked body.

Needy, I thrust into him a little too fast. He cries out and seizes up, clenching hard but not pulling away. It's fucking hot and slick and, without a condom, I swear I can feel his pulse. He whimpers something apologetic and forces himself to relax by collapsing on the bed and taking long, even breaths. I silently curse myself for being such an asshole. Miles isn't like the other guys I've been with—the ones with all the experience and a taste for pain. I think he loves playing bitch, which suits me perfectly, but I'm not a full-blown sadist. I need to ease him into rougher stuff, like I did in the hotel.

I reach around and stroke him, not bothering to move despite my body's urgency. Miles gets half onto his knees in order to better accommodate me, pushing himself harder up onto my cock and moaning as he does so. I lean down and lick the flesh of his neck, moving my hand on his dick slow but steady. I don't thrust or move my hips in the slightest and, after a few solid minutes of nipping at his skin, he begins to honestly relax under me.

With each heavy breath, I can tell he's enjoying himself.

"You can go faster," he breathes. "I'm fine."

"I know."

"I want you to… give it to me like before." His voice gets weaker with each word, almost like he doesn't like saying it aloud.

I chuckle into his ear. "I thought you said you were sore."

Miles pulls his hips forward and then pushes back, fucking himself on my cock. He twists his body and head around, meeting my mouth with his. His hot breath mingles with mine as he speaks. "I wanna feel it tomorrow. I wanna feel it and think about what we did here."

Jesus Christ. It's like he knows what buttons to push to get me into it.

I shove him back down and start my thrusting. The flesh-on-flesh contact of bareback is everything animalist that I enjoy. Licking my lips I lean back to grab his hips in both hands. The slap of skin reverberates throughout the room. Anyone listening would know what the heavy breathing and rhythmic noises meant. I don't stifle my groans of ecstasy.

"Play with yourself," I command. I want to feel him shudder underneath me at his climax, especially now that there isn't anything between us.

I can tell the moment he starts. He clenches and sucks in his breath, the muscles of his body betraying how close he is. The longer I ride him, the tighter and hotter his body gets, building to the moment of sweet release.

"From now on you're only to come with my dick in your ass," I say through gritted teeth.

Miles nods into the blankets and forces out, "If that's what you want."

"Tell me you want it."

"I… I want it. Of course I want it."

"You wanna feel it tomorrow?" I ask between ragged breaths. "You're gonna feel my seed leakin' out of you all day, ya know that, right?"

I guess all my husky musings get to him because he convulses under me the instant I'm done speaking. His back arches and his muscles grip me with uncontrolled intensity, his breath forcefully exhaled from his body in one low moan. God, it's like his muscles are milking me, begging for my sweet seed. He bites his lip to keep from getting too loud and starts bleeding.

The sensations are intoxicating. Heat pools in my lower gut, and the sudden release of pressure fills me with overwhelming pleasure. I fill him deep with semen, enjoying the grip of his body on my now-satisfied cock. I'm panting louder than I should, tired and filling my lungs with air at a desperate rate.

Holy hell I'm tired.

I withdraw, twitching, and roll to my back, staring at the ceiling. I glance at the clock. Only two and half hours remaining. Where has all the time gone? Fuck me.

Eh. Unlike at the hotel, I'm gonna have to clean this up. I go to sit up, but Miles catches me.

"Wait," he says, his voice breathless. "Stay for just a minute...."

I comply and rest back on the bed. If I'm not careful, I'll fall asleep here.

"Thank you."

I don't respond.

"Can I... sleep here?"

Did he have to ask? If he'd have just fallen asleep, I wouldn't have said anything and we could've avoided this. Then again, I don't like sleeping next to guys I can't trust—are they going to kill me in the middle of the night? But Miles is different and I know it deep in my gut.

"The bed's big enough," I say. "Do whatever you want."

"And... did you mean what you said? That you should... be in me... every time?"

"No." I bit back a laugh. "I can't fuck as often as some twenty-year-old can yank it. I just say things sometimes in the heat of the moment, anything I think would get my rocks off."

"I like it."

"Yeah, I can tell." I yawn.

Miles cuddles up to me like a damn puppy. Whatever. It's hard to get angry at someone you just had a great romp with. I wish he wouldn't idolize me, however. I feel like I'm lying to him on some level. It's not like I'm going to make his life fantastic. My life isn't a glamorous one. It's pretty shitty, if I have to be honest.

I bring my hand up and brush his hair with my fingers. This is nice. Is this what life would be like living in some suburb house? Probably. I close my eyes and allow myself to imagine watering a lawn. It's boring and stupid and I can't believe I'm fantasizing about it. What am I thinking? *Miles* could water the lawn. I smile at my own internal joke.

Maybe giving up life on the streets has some merit... even if I have to flip burgers for a living to have it. At least then I could sleep in.

THE ALARM wakes me.

I don't want to be awake, but here I am. The sun shines through the window, burning the carpet. My mouth is dry; my system low on nicotine... and everything hurts.

"Hey, Pierce. You need to get up."

I roll to my side and force myself into my normal routine. Get up. Wash down in the shower. Get dressed. Everything moves in a blur, so much so that it's like living in a jump cut sequence. As I pull on my boxers, Miles shoves another plastic-wrapped sandwich into my hands. The thing could have been rancid and I wouldn't have noticed. I eat it, one-handed, as I attempt to pull up my pants.

"Pierce!"

The shout jump-starts my system into overdrive. I leap out of the bathroom, through my bedroom, and into the hall. Miles is standing in the doorframe of the second bedroom, his eyes wide with disbelief. I glance inside and roll my eyes so hard I swear I've strained something.

His. Fucking. Brother. Left.

The window, ajar, signals his escape route. I storm through the rest of the flat, checking every inch. Nothing stolen. Even the handcuffs are left half secure to the bedframe in the second bedroom. The kid must've taken my warning to heart.

His black trash bag, on the other hand, is nowhere in sight. I silently curse myself for not taking it from him. A lowlife like Jayden no doubt had burglar tools on him. He probably picked the lock to his handcuffs minutes after I left the room.

"What am I going to do?" Miles asks me, running both hands through his hair. "What if the Cobras blame him for what happened?"

Good riddance.

Miles turns to me with worry in his eyes. "What if he tells them about me or you? About this apartment?"

Goddammit. I rub my forehead. Why was he so desperate to leave?

"What if he heard us in the other room and assumed…."

"For fuck's sake," I mutter. That's what happened. Miles called it. I can see it in my mind's eye. "Listen. Your brother isn't that bright. I'm sure we'll find him before he gets himself into too much trouble. I know Noimore like the back of my hand—there are only so many people he's going to buy drugs from, and I'm sure he's jonesing for a hit."

Miles nods.

I return to my room and throw on the rest of my clothes. My safe, which I keep in my closet, has a complicated code, but I've used the same one for thirteen years. I type it in without even looking at the pad. Inside sits five .45 handguns, a whole case of ammo, ten loaded magazines, a few extra shoulder holsters, and one box of hollow-point bullets.

Miles hovers around, watching me gather my materials. I replace my empty magazine, take a few extra, and then grab a second holster. I motion Miles over, and he jumps to my side.

"You ever put one of these on before?" I ask.

He gives me an *are you serious* look before taking the holster and effortlessly slipping it on. I offer a one-sided smile as I tighten the straps and slip a gun into place. I throw him a jacket, to conceal his firearm, and he hesitates.

"You trust me with a gun?"

"You're gonna watch my six, right?" I ask, handing him a second magazine.

Miles stares at me with a newfound confidence. He stands a little straighter as he slips the clip into his pocket. "You always seemed a little reluctant to…."

"You looked like you held yourself well with Santiago, especially when you got your blade in him. You have some skill with a knife, right? That wasn't a fluke?"

"Yeah. I know how to use a knife."

I walk over to my nightstand and remove a KA-BAR knife from the drawer—nothing beats the military-grade weapon when it comes to hand-to-hand combat. I toss the thing hilt-first over to Miles. He catches it without a hint of uncertainty. I toss him the belt holder and he secures it to his person. I've never been good with knives.

"You know how to fire your gun?" I ask.

He nods.

"You know about the safety?"

"Yeah."

"How to clean it?"

He lifts an eyebrow. "You know I was a hired gun for the Vice family, right? They ran me through the drills."

"Just makin' sure."

"Are we going to look for Jayden now?"

"Not yet. First we're gonna go talk to Jeremy Vice."

CHAPTER TEN

JEREMY VICE has his own little section in the industrial district. He's had it for years, ever since he turned sixteen. His mother keeps funneling him money in order to "refurbish" the place to his liking. Jeremy turned it into a strip-club-meets-game-room combo, complete with an area in the back he calls his office. The office part resembles his father's aesthetics—expensive wood, leather, crystal, wines—while the game room and strippers have a poorly lit thug den filled to the brim with all sorts of things a teenager would jerk off to. It's low-class meets high-class in all the wrong ways. The only upside is that the two areas are separate.

To my surprise, his strip club operates in the middle of the day. I spot a couple bouncers by the door and hear the music half a block down. The men give me odd glances when I park. I've never met them before. I nod as I walk by, heading straight for the back. They don't give me any trouble, but they do eye Miles as he waits in the car.

Jeremy's office and the strip club are two neighboring buildings. Smokers and strippers alike gather around the back of the club, a handful of bouncers getting an eyeful of the workers. I guess they're not busy, considering how many of them are outside, and I wonder what else goes on in the club if the dancers can take a break from time to time.

I do a double take when I realize that *three* of the dancers are men—effeminate, small, and could easily pass as women—but still men. I almost didn't recognize their form under all the glitter. Three seems a little high for this kind of establishment. I don't know many coed strip clubs. Actually, I don't know *any* coed strip clubs. The mystery gnaws at my mind as I walk up to Jeremy's office door.

The enforcer waiting there, another guy I've never seen, motions me in without a word. I step past the threshold and into the luxury I've come to know from the Vice family. Jeremy sits on top of his solid wood desk, chatting it up with another group of enforcers I'm unfamiliar with. He abruptly ends his conversation and flashes me a toothy smile.

"Pierce!"

Jeremy hops off the desk, standing a good foot shorter than any other man in the room.

"Who're these guys?" I ask, motioning to the three enforcers and ignoring Jeremy's cheery posturing.

"This is Brett, Donnie, and Rico," he says, pointing to the men in respective order. They say nothing, but they nod to acknowledge me. I nod back, a little uneasy given their muscle and guns. I don't like guys I don't know, especially when there are more of them than me. It's not smart practice to hang with a group of sharks in unfamiliar territory.

Jeremy gestures to the door. "Get out of here, you three. I'll talk to you all later. Pierce and I have some *serious business* to attend to."

Brett, Donnie, and Rico mutter acceptances as they shuffle past me and out the door. Once I hear the click of it shutting, I relax. Jeremy walks around to the front of his desk, leans back, and kicks one foot over the other, lacing his ankles together.

"I'm glad you're here, Pierce," he drawls.

"Since when did we get so many new enforcers?"

"I've been hiring men to replace the ones we've lost. They're good with a gun. And reliable too."

"Your father let *you* do the hiring?"

Jeremy shrugs, his ugly mug scrunched in a forced look of confusion. "He *has* just been shot. I'm picking up the slack for him. It's only natural, given my talents."

"Uh-huh. Listen. Your mother wants you to leave town." I don't have time for bullshit—I'm gonna take Jeremy to the airport and send him off like I did Guinevere. "I have a car ready. Let's go."

"Didn't you hear me? My father's preoccupied with recovering. Someone needs to take over."

"Your mother is capable."

Jeremy rolls his wide-set eyes in an overly dramatic fashion. "My mother micromanages everything like a fussy hen. You know it. I know it. My father knows it. I'm capable of running things while my father recovers. Look, I even have your bonus ready."

He motions to a briefcase sitting idle on the side of the desk. I walk over to it and pop open the latches. A few thousand dollars sits inside—at first glance I'd say close to forty thousand—but I don't count it in front of him. I shut the case and throw it down next to one of the guest chairs. I take a seat. I'm still tired.

"That's for killing Malloy," Jeremy says, a wicked smirk on his face. "I'm impressed with how quickly you caught my uncle's murderer. Then again, I shouldn't be surprised. Even all the guys I hired figured you would do it in no time flat."

He already knows about Malloy? Fuck—word must travel fast. "Yeah, well, that's my job. I'm told I'm pretty good at it."

"Which is why I called you here," Jeremy continues, his voice so false-cheery I'd swear he's trying to sell me something. "I have something big. Something I can only trust a few people to know." He lowers his tone and leans forward, meeting my gaze straight on. "Because… we've got spies in our midst. You know that, right? My father got shot by his own guards. We can't trust people like we used to around here."

"Malloy said as much," I say. "When I interrogated him, he said someone from the Vice side was feeding information to the Cobras."

"Did he?" Jeremy asks, leaning away and scratching his weak, barely pronounced chin. "I should've known you would've gotten information before you killed him. You're so efficient." He pulls a case of cigarettes from his pocket and offers me one. I shake my head and take out my own pack. I light a smoke, but Jeremy just tucks his away—the pack isn't even open. Does he smoke? I've never seen him smoke.

I take a long drag and wait for Jeremy to hurry and tell me his secret. What's he got that his father doesn't?

Jeremy continues with his car-salesman smile. "Pierce. You're the only man I can trust to carry out my plan. See, in a few months' time, Harlan, the King Cobra himself, will be attending an underground boxing event. Ya know the kind—bloody, cages, the fighters die, stakes are high—Harlan loves 'em."

I laugh, exhaling smoke. "Yeah. I seen 'em. They're filled to the brim with bruisers. No one gets in or out of that place without gettin' patted down for weapons. They probably won't let anyone in unless they have a cobra tattoo either. And damn near *everyone* on the streets knows me by my bad eye. What makes you think that, just because you know where he's going to be, you can kill Harlan himself?"

"Oh, that's the fun part. In a few months the boxing matches will take place in the Nightquarter Café. It's an old historic building, used to be a speakeasy and smuggling den for bootleggers and rumrunners. There's even an old shaft that leads to the basement… no one uses it anymore, though. No one knows about it but me and the old man I shot getting the information."

Jeremy, unable to stop his smiling, waits. I take another drag on my cigarette.

"So," I say. "Let me get this straight. You want me to crawl through some old bootleg tunnel to shoot a guy in the middle of a jam-packed speakeasy basement? *That's* your plan? What's my bonus? A casket made of silver?"

"No, of course not. Listen to me. You're going to pack the bootleg tunnel with explosives. Then, when Harlan and his closest men are in attendance, we're going to *blow* the tunnel and the whole speakeasy basement with it. Get it?"

I go silent and nurse my cigarette.

Jeremy fingers the red tie of his tailored suit, his gaze drawn to the floor. "You know street gangs, Pierce. Once the head of the organization goes down, the rest of it goes with it. The Cobras don't have a contingency plan once Harlan is gone—they're not like us and our dynastic rule. They'll fight amongst themselves, ripping apart at the seams."

I must admit, I like the idea. This turf war has gotten out of hand, and after Malloy threatened that it would escalate, I've been having my doubts. Killing Harlan would be a swift decisive blow for the Vice family.

"Have you told your father?" I ask. I wonder what Nick would think of this.

"We can't let the Cobras figure this out," Jeremy says, returning his gaze to mine. His smile turns coy, and he looks me over, leering. "Besides, I've come to trust only a certain kind of man in this world. Men like us. Men that don't need women."

I exhale a line of smoke and cock an eyebrow.

Subtle. *Real* subtle. I've had guys admit to me they like dick, but never quite like that. That explains the strippers…. Jeremy wanted something for himself to enjoy.

"So you haven't told your father about the plan?" I ask.

Jeremy places a finger to his lips and half laughs. "You've known my father for a long time, Pierce. Tell me… now that it's just the two of us… has he ever ordered you on your knees?"

I chortle and shake my head. Oh, Jeremy. Clearly he doesn't know his father in the least. I would happily suck Nick off if he asked—but he's not that kind of guy.

"Your father has never asked me to do any of that," I reply with a few smoke-laced chuckles. "He's old-fashioned. He's got Anita. He never touches anyone else. You know that."

"Well, I've also seen the way you look at my father and brother, Pierce. I know you have a thing for *Vice men*." Jeremy leans back on his desk and grabs a fistful of his crotch. In a voice that I can only assume he *thinks* is seductive, he whispers, "You want a taste?"

Coughing and choking on my own cigarette, I stand.

I can't backpedal out of this situation fast enough.

"*Jeremy*," I force myself to say between strangled-back laughs. "Listen. You know your father doesn't want *anyone* touching his kids, right? And your mother—what would she think?" I gulp down smoke and take control of my vocal cords. "Your offer is *very appealing*. It is. But I can't risk it. Your plan, though—it's a good plan. I want to be part of it."

I grab the case of money and motion to the door. Jeremy crosses his arms over his chest and narrows his eyes, a dejected frown on his face. "Really? You follow my father's orders even when he's not around? Even if he wouldn't find out?"

"What can I say? I'm loyal to the Vice family. I follow the rules."

It's true. Nick would kill me if I fucked his kids, even Jeremy, who he's not fond of. When Rodger goes on his "sabbaticals," Nick even sends men to watch him and make sure he doesn't get into too much trouble. All that aside, Jeremy isn't my type. He wants me to get on my knees? I might have to sit down to be a crotch-level with the man. Plus, I like playing the top—Nick has a commanding aura that makes him the exception to the rule—but Jeremy didn't inherit any of *that*. If anything, Jeremy makes me want to scratch out my good eye in an attempt to stop looking at him.

"Pierce," Jeremy says, halting my escape. "You can't tell anyone about the bootleg tunnel or else we could lose this opportunity. Not even my father. He'll surely tell some of his enforcers, and you saw what they did to him at the Crystal Floor Nightclub."

"All right."

"Leaving so soon?"

I've made it a few feet to the door by backing up, but I'm not yet there. I smirk. "Yeah, well, I have a full schedule. I came to take you out of the city, but it looks like you have all the protection you need here. And boy toys. I saw the strippers. They must love a guy like you. Guys like that always gravitate to the one in charge."

Jeremy combs back his hair with his fingers, basking in what little praise I lavished on him. "Eh. They're not what I expected. I enjoy men like you. I've always admired your masculine qualities and quick wit, especially when Father assigned you to protect us as kids." He offers me a devious smirk. "I would think to myself, *when I'm in charge I'll have him work for his money*…. My father isn't using you properly."

Oh God. This is only getting worse. I regret every decision that brought me here.

If he were *any other man*, I would just give it to him straight… but he's not. He's Jeremy Vice. There's a good chance he'll be in charge, and he's apparently already pulling the purse strings. What am I going to do? Tell him to fuck off? Tell him he makes my dick shrivel every time he talks? He's never been quite right in the head. Maybe when Nick dies I'll be *forced* to join Guinevere—if only to escape Jeremy afterward.

"Yeah, well, I gotta go," I say, snuffing out my cigarette in a nearby ashtray.

"Wait, Pierce. Before you go, tell me about the kid you have in the police force. What's his status?"

"We're making headway. I'll have the police hitting Cobras' locations all over the city."

"I want to stay informed."

I open the door and take a step out. "I'll do that. Give me a call anytime." I stop right before I exit completely. "Actually, there's one other thing. Where's your brother? Where's Rodger?"

Jeremy shrugs and steps away from his desk, his mind clearly on other things. "Last I heard he joined some cult or religion or whatever he was doing."

A cult? Jesus Christ. No wonder Anita is worried about her children. They're like turkeys—they might drown themselves in the rain if you don't watch 'em close enough. Then again, Guinevere turned out all right. One out of three is as good as any parent can hope for, I guess.

"Where is it?" I ask.

"I don't know. I've been looking for it, but apparently the place *moves* periodically."

I leave the office, case in hand, and make my way back to the car. My back is killing me. Stiff and sore, I take the time to stretch and loosen my muscles. The strippers and enforcers give me sideways glances, some outright staring, but I ignore them. I spot Miles by the front door of the strip club, chatting with the two bouncers, laughing it up. Once he notices me heading to the car he stops, nods to the men, and hops to the passenger door.

I take the driver's seat. Miles takes his seat next to me.

"What was that?" I ask.

"Just getting to know the people," he replies. "Learning their names. That's Dorian and Gene, but they call Gene by his nickname—*Lucky*—'cause he won it big in some casino when he was younger and then lost it all in some scheme he took part in. They're funny guys."

"Heh. Good to know." I'm glad he's quick to pick up on my lessons. I throw him the case of money and start the car. "Count it."

Miles cracks open the briefcase and stares down in mild shock. He glances over at me like I might be joking. When he realizes I'm not, he picks up the stacks of cash and fingers through them, counting in his head and adding everything together.

"There's fifty thousand here," he says. "And a card? It says, 'Remember to call me.'"

I jerk my head to the side and spot the business card with Jeremy's number on it. I snatch it away from Miles and crumple the thing as I toss it to the back.

Miles chuckles. "What was that?"

"Never mention this to anyone," I drawl. "Understand? It goes to your grave."

"All right. I won't mention it."

"And take twenty-five thousand for yourself. That's bonus money for killing Malloy. You were part of it, so you get part of the cash."

In reality I could have killed Malloy with my car and been done with it, but Miles *did* jump in to save me from Santiago. Half the cut is fair.

"*Half?*" Miles balks. "You want me to have half?"

I flash him a glare. "Did I stutter?"

He fidgets with the case and closes it. With uncertain movements he hesitates between putting the case on the floorboard or keeping it in his lap, his train of thought clearly derailed and impairing all other mental functions. He's probably never had that much money in his life.

"Where're we headed now?" he asks.

"We're going to Big Man Vice's house to tell him about his son's plan." I give him the once-over and mull over some options. He's still wearing my clothes—which don't fit right—and his hair is out of control. "I've changed my mind. First I'm gonna get you looking proper."

"Why?" Miles asks with a laugh in his voice.

"Because Nick appreciates clean-cut appearances. You need to look the part if you're gonna be one of his enforcers."

OF COURSE he looks good. He's lean and young, and Sandora—the best tailor in Illinois—knows how to craft clothes like Michelangelo knows how to paint chapels. She put him in a snappy little number complete with fitted black slacks and a smooth charcoal-gray shirt.

His haircut brings it together for me. His silky black hair is cut short on the sides and round the back and his longer locks have been tamed and trimmed. He looks like a goddamn professional, and it gets me hard just starin' at him. He had the aura of a timid kid before, but now he stands a little taller and walks around exuding confidence. Clothes really do wonders for a man.

Miles straightens his shirt using my car's side mirror. The chill wind rustles the privacy hedge surrounding Nick's palatial mansion. The driveway runs half a mile from the road up to his house, ensuring that most don't get a good look at the place when they drive by. Nick's a private guy and hates unexpected guests. The cameras in the nearby fountain and trees track our every movement.

"I've never worn stuff this expensive this before," Miles says.

"You get what you pay for. You look good."

"Still…. A few thousand for a couple of shirts and slacks? Is that what you pay every time you get new clothes?"

"Yes."

"But you get pretty messed up all the time. Getting shot and stabbed…."

"Don't remind me," I groan.

I motion with my head toward the mansion. Miles jumps to my side and shadows my steps as I walk to the front door. The tranquility of the property is a welcome change from the commotion of downtown Noimore. I admire the landscaping, and my thoughts go back to watering the lawn. I chuckle aloud. Miles cocks his head and lifts an eyebrow.

"Just a stupid thought," I murmur.

"Hey, after this, will we search for my brother?"

"I called some guys I know who deal on the streets. I'll call them again after we're done. Trust me. This is more efficient than just driving around."

"We found him last time just driving around," Miles quips, though his tone has an edge of seriousness.

"Are you saying you *want* to just drive around a massive metropolis searching for your brother? Do you at least have any *ideas* about where he would be?"

"No," Miles says. "I don't. I'll trust you. But… do you think we can make one stop once we're done workin' today?"

"I'll make it work," I reply.

Nick's humble abode doesn't have any blatant enforcers milling about, but I know they're inside. I get up to the front door and knock, my announcement echoing in the entrance hall. Miles glances around with wide eyes, his attention lingering on the brass knocker, the detail work of the masonry, and the intricacy of the iron bars around the windows. The place is expensive without being gaudy, but his gawking has got to stop. I elbow him.

"Keep it together," I say. "Don't look like such a green hand."

"A-all right."

He keeps his gaze straight ahead as the door opens. Anita greets us, a tight smile on her face and a tight red dress across her body. She motions for us to enter with a curt gesture, no doubt holding back choice words.

"*Pierce*," she says. "Here you are. I've been calling you."

I pull my phone from my pocket and see I've missed another forty-seven calls. I delete the notifications and shrug. "Phones are fickle sometimes."

"Get in here," she commands. "Where are my children?"

Miles and I walk into the entrance hall. Anita doesn't allow us to sit or get comfortable; she takes us straight up the stairs.

"Guinevere already took a plane out of town," I say as we climb the steps. "Jeremy is still in the city—fucking around in his *playpen*—and Rodger… well, I haven't found Rodger yet."

Once we reach the top, Anita stomps down the hallway and slams open the door to the workout room. A large full-wall window on the opposite end of the room allows light to stream in, giving the place a holy glow thanks to the time of day. They have way too many machines for two people—it's almost a full-blown commercial gym—but Anita and Nick don't share well. They have two treadmills, two weight-lifting stands, two bikes…. They even have two personal trainers, though they're not around at the moment.

I spot Nick running on his treadmill, and I have to adjust my pants for a moment before anyone notices. He's in sweatpants—a rare sight— and a tight ribbed tank top. His shoulder is bandaged up from the gunshot wound from the Crystal Floor Nightclub, but it only adds to the sight. The bandages are spotted with blood from the injury underneath.

"*Nick*!" Anita shouts, her voice shrill. "What did I tell you? He hasn't found Rodger *and* Jeremy is still in the city!"

Nick continues running. Not jogging. Running. Sweat coats his shirt and most of his pants. Damn, he's in good shape for his age. Hell, he's in good shape for *any* age.

Anita storms up to his workout equipment and slams her heel down. "I told you he wouldn't handle this! He doesn't listen to me like he should!" When Nick *still* doesn't answer, she wheels back around to me. "And what about Juliet? Have you seen her yet?"

Juliet? Oh, right. Juliet is the old mortician. Anita wanted me to help her with something in her basement. I shake my head. "No. I haven't gotten around to it yet."

"Are you hearing this, Nick? He's done nothing! Our children's lives are on the line, and you're letting your *dogs* walk all over you! You need to take control of the situation and get your men back in line!"

Nick stops his machine and jumps off. He pats himself off with a nearby towel, wiping the sweat from his face and neck. Anita huffs and glares as he loosens his muscles with a few quick stretches.

"Pierce is my best enforcer," he says, his definitive tone stoking my ego. "If he hasn't gotten to it, he hasn't gotten to it for good reason."

"You're playing favorites! Pierce is getting slow, and you're making excuses for him." She turns on her heel, glaring at me with the intensity of death itself. "Pierce, I swear I'll have you put down if anything happens to my children. *I swear it*."

I offer no response as she flounces past me. She slams the door, punctuating her exit with an echoing smash of wood on wood. Nick, unfazed, throws down his towel and takes his pulse with his smart wristwatch. He ambles over and, half glancing up, examines Miles.

"A new enforcer?" he asks.

"My name is Miles Devonport," Miles replies, holding out his hand. "It's a pleasure to meet you."

Nick doesn't return the gesture of a handshake. He lifts a perfect eyebrow and gives Miles a thorough once-over, his eyes lingering on the bite marks just beneath the collar of Miles's shirt. Nick turns his attention to me. "Your new toy, Pierce?"

Miles awkwardly returns his hand to the side, his posture cold.

I nod. "He's a little more than that, though. He helped me kill Mikey's murderer—some Cobras scum by the name of Malloy. Miles has potential."

"I didn't think you were the kind to think with your dick."

"It's not like that. He's trustworthy. That's worth a lot these days."

"Does he have any notable skills?" Nick asks, rubbing at his wounded shoulder and walking over to a mirror mounted on the far wall. "Can he drive better than most? Shoot better than most?"

I remain silent. As far as I know Miles is new to most things on the street. Sure, he can use a knife, and he knows his way around a gun—but Nick doesn't want to hear about knife skills or how Miles can reload without instruction. He wants to hear about talents he can put to work *right now*.

Nick allows my silence to stew before continuing with, "You're making me look bad, Pierce. I endorsed your work, and then you bring me some kid because you liked the shape of his ass? Too many enforcers have died during our street brawls. I need good people to replace the ones who have died. *Reliable people*. Not fuck-boys."

"I have the ear of the police," Miles says. I can hear the anger in his tone, though he does a good job of suppressing it. "Their top detective knows and trusts me. I bring more to the table than just being Pierce's *fuck-boy*."

Nick stares at me via the mirror, our gazes locked in the reflection. "Is that true, Pierce?"

"No," I state. "It's a potential long-term plan, but—"

"It *is* true," Miles cuts in, turning to me with a glower.

"No. It's not."

Not another word, I mouth to him. *You're only making this worse.* Why would he lie to Nicholas Vice? Is his pride really that important to him? If he had just stayed quiet, Nick would have made a few more insults and then let it go. But now….

Miles shakes his head, his eyes saying a million words in a foreign language I can't understand.

"*Toy*," Nick snaps, addressing Miles. "Watch the door."

A long second of silence passes over the room. Miles—thank God—does what Nick says without protest and exits the room. This isn't how I imagined the encounter going, but it could be worse.

"Is that the same kid we suspected of being a mole for the police?" Nick asks. "The one caught visiting the police station a few times? The one that Pete and Brisko took to the docks?"

My mouth goes dry. Fuck. "Yes," I say. I won't lie to Nick. I won't.

"Shoot him."

My heart stops for a moment. "What?"

"I don't trust him. He's either lying to you or he's lying to me. Either way, he deserves what's coming to him. Take him out back and get it over with. Meet me back here when you're done."

CHAPTER ELEVEN

I LIGHT a cigarette to allow myself time to think.

"Nick, you're gettin' paranoid," I say, chuckling to mask my nerves. "He's young. He's just sayin' things to impress. You know how all the new enforcers get, especially if you cut 'em down with insults."

Young men like to posture. Nick sees it all the time when he hands out guns to the new muscle. They peacock and parade for the first few months before everything starts to get serious. It's standard procedure— I'm sure that's what happened with Miles. At least, it *better be* what happened.

"Do I need to remind you that I was shot by my own guards?" Nick drawls. He rips off his bandages, glaring at his reflection in the wall mirror. His skin is torn open and blood weeps from the injury. "The doctor said I should take it easy. How can I take it easy when every ballsy asshole in town thinks he can kill me? How do I know your new *toy* isn't one of them?"

"When have I ever brought you an enforcer who went turncoat?"

"You've *never* brought me one of your whores and pawned him off as an enforcer."

"No, I usually just fuck a preexisting enforcer," I quip. "What's it matter?"

Nick plunges his hand into a bowl of water on a nearby chair and pulls out a wet cloth. He dabs the cloth around his bloody injury, no doubt mulling over the conversation in his head. If he pushes the matter—if he *forces* me to kill Miles…. The thought puts a lump in my throat. The kid *just* told me that no one had his back…. He put his trust in *me*, and if I turn around and *shoot* him…. God, I can't imagine looking him in the eye.

"Why is Jeremy is charge of hiring new men?" I ask, hoping to put distance to this topic.

"*Jeremy,*" Nick growls, his eyes cutting daggers wherever he turns them. "I give him an inch and he takes a mile. I told him to hire a couple of men. *A couple*. Two, three tops. Now look at him…. He's hired a whole goddamn army. He's part of the problem. Everyone he hires is suspect. His priorities are skewed."

"I think he's trying to impress you."

Nick scoffs. He throws the rag back into the bowl, splashing the water onto the floor. He turns and walks over to me, anger and disgust etched into his face. "I think he wants me dead."

I exhale a line of smoke and offer him a half smile. "He wants to kill the King Cobra. He wants to kill Harlan himself."

"*And*? What of it?"

"He's got a plan to bring down some old speakeasy right on top of him. It's a pretty good plan too, so long as no one catches wind about the tunnel he hopes to bomb."

"Where?"

"The Nightquarter Café."

"Hm. You're a good man for bringing this to my attention, Pierce. I know I can always count on you." Nick crosses the gym and grabs a clean towel from the wall. For the first time since we started talking, he looks tired. He takes his time drying off the last of his body. "You're one of the few people I still trust. Don't fuck this up. Keep an eye on Jeremy and all his *plans*."

I walk over to him and nod. He gives me a curt nod back. Normally I would leave at this point, but his decision about Miles looms overhead like a circle of vultures waiting for carrion. I take a long drag on my cigarette and Nick gives me the once-over.

"I don't trust him," Nick states, no doubt talking about Miles.

I wait.

"Tsk. If you think you have him handled, fine. Keep the toy. But he *never* contacts the police. I don't want to risk giving him the chance to double-cross us. You keep him under your surveillance until we get rid of Harlan. After that we'll reopen this discussion. If I *still* don't trust him…. He's gone. Understood?"

"Completely," I say, relaxing. Close. Too close. I can't believe I almost had to shoot him—and I would have *had* to shoot him or I'd have been shot myself.

"Oh, and do all the bullshit my wife is harping about," Nick groans. He rolls his eyes and mimics a mouth flapping with his hand. "She's been riding me about Juliet and her basement for *days*. Every guy I send out there either can't handle the problem or—get this—that old crone chases them off. And *find Rodger*. My *doofus* of a son needs to be brought back before Anita gets the whole damn city involved."

"I'll handle it."

"He joined some religion. They called themselves the 'Pillars of Valor' or some other sort of pretentious load. The guys I had watching him said Rodger joined because of some whore. Drag Rodger back here if you have to."

Again, I nod. With my cigarette held in my mouth, I turn toward the door. Same shit, different day. No doubt I'll be busy until dark, and *then* I'll have to do something else. Death, guns, corpses, finding grown-ass adults and treating them like kids…. And what makes it all worse is that it could all go south if Nick wants it to. I'm at his mercy no matter the time of day—I could have been forced to kill Miles at his whim.

I stop at the door, gripping the handle.

"Nick," I intone.

The man turns to me, silent.

"What do you think… about me retiring?"

He laughs. "Has my wife gotten to you? You're too young to retire. You've got another thirty years in you, maybe forty if you stop smoking like a chimney."

"What if it's because I want to?"

Nick stifles his laugher and his posture gets stiff. "Don't joke with me, Pierce. Not now. I'd hate to have to put a bullet through your head, but if you keep talkin' like *that*…."

I get stiff and my blood ices. He thinks of me like a dog. I knew—I've always known—but right now it's difficult to hear. He'll throw me away when he's done with me. Just like he does everyone else. Without a second thought.

"Don't do this," Nick snaps. "I treat you good. Better than you deserve. You were nothing but an uneducated street urchin when I found you. Now look at you! Why're you questioning everything now?"

"I was just curious," I murmur. With my body numb, I turn and exit the home gym.

Miles straightens himself the instant I emerge. I shut the door and walk past, Miles falling into step behind me. Besides the stomping of our shoes as we travel down the stairs, the house sits silent. Miles doesn't talk and neither do I. We make our way through the entrance hall and out the front door without so much as two words. Once outside I wheel on him.

"What the fuck was that?" I bark. "Explain. Now."

"I told the police about the Cobras," Miles replies without a sigh of hesitation. "When I went to get my brother. Before I joined you. I followed Jayden around for days just so I could give the detectives something. They said they would be lenient with the charges, so that's what I did."

I grab Miles by his shirt collar and jerk him closer. "That's not everything."

He takes a deep breath and shivers. "N-no. It's not. I started calling them when you told me to. To get their trust but… I already had their trust. I spoke to Detective Ambers before, and… and she knew I was with the Vice family. She asked me to give information on Nicholas Vice and… and his closest associates but…." He turns away, his eyes shut tight. "They were just using me, Pierce. Like everyone else. They said… they said if I helped bring in Big Man Vice's hitmen, they would drop all charges on Jayden, but I know they can't do *that*. They're just telling me things so that… so that I'll do what they want."

"Men like *me*?" I ask. They're going after Nick's enforcers? Why? Why not the man himself?

"Yeah," Miles answers, returning his gaze to meet mine. "But I had no intention of turning you in. I just told the detectives I would help so that they'd let me and Jayden go. I figured we would be long gone by now."

"Why didn't you tell me?"

"You wanted me to get in good with the police, and I thought I could just… tell you after. I'm sorry, Pierce. I thought you might try to kill me if I told you sooner… if I told you that they wanted me to turn men like you in."

So Miles has some sway with the cops because they think he's a mole. He could summon them somewhere, but the moment his information is bunk is the moment they drop all association with him. That's a one-time gamble of a police summons. It doesn't matter, though. He can never use it.

I shake my head. I'm angry at Miles, but I'm still cold from Nick's comment. I might be misdirecting my anger, but I don't give a shit. Miles shouldn't have kept this from me.

"You're not going to call the cops ever again, got it?" I say, keeping him close. "If I so much as *hear* about you calling them, I'll shoot you myself."

"I understand."

I take a drag on my cigarette, exhale, and grit my teeth. I hate being lied to. I hate that the moment I trusted him *this* came up. It's not like we have a long history I can rely on. I *want* to trust the kid, but maybe Nick is right. Maybe I *am* thinking with my dick.

My blood pressure is high, and I feel like punching some asshole in the face. Miles stares at me with a hint of fear, though I don't think he's afraid, per se. He makes no effort to defend himself when I let go of his shirt and shove him back. Under his breath he mutters another apology, and it grates me the wrong way.

"Words are cheap," I drawl.

"I'll do whatever you want to make up for this," he says.

"Then get on your knees."

The words come out without me even thinking them. I know what I want. I want Miles to know his place—that *I'm* in charge and, no matter what else, he doesn't keep secrets from *me*. He wants to apologize? He'll do it with his mouth.

Miles glances over his shoulder. "Out here?" he asks, his brow furrowed.

I take a step back and lean against the front of the house, right next to the door. I let out a line of smoke and glare. "It was a simple instruction."

He grows silent and red. After a moment of internal contemplation, he walks over and gets to his knees in front of me, his gaze straight ahead and his body stiff. The hard concrete of the entrance walkway no doubt is hell on his knees—he shifts about for a moment before reaching up and unbuckling my belt.

I watch him with a keen interest, excited by the way he takes shallow breaths and trembles with each motion. He unzips my pants, opens my boxers and, right before he takes me into his mouth, I reach down and grab him by the chin, forcing him to look up at me.

"You tell me everything," I say. "No matter what."

Miles swallows hard and half nods. "I will."

I release him. "Now get to it."

He uses his tongue to guide my full-on erection into his mouth. Once he takes me all the way in, he places his hands on the wall, one on either side of my hips, and braces himself into position. He pulls back and moves forward, slowing when he gets it deep and semigagging, though he forces himself through the sensation.

I love seeing him like this—on his knees, submitting to me, right where anyone could just come by and see. I take a drag on my cigarette and eye the property as Miles caresses me with his tongue. There are cameras—some security guard is getting quite a show—but otherwise the area is secluded and empty. Anita or Nick could walk out the front door any minute, on the other hand. Anita would demand I stop, but I'm betting Nick would carry on a conversation like nothing was even happening.

Miles lets out a tiny mew of a moan, and I smile. With each back-and-forth, he seems to be getting more into it. He reaches down and rubs his crotch through his pants, but I exhale smoke as I growl, "Keep your hands on the wall."

He complies with a whimper. I pet him across his new short hair, enjoying the sweat that lingers on his scalp. Miles tilts his head back and my cock slides even deeper into his throat, the tightness around the tip an intoxicating pleasure.

"You're gonna take it deep when I come," I say.

Miles offers a curt nod and continues harder than before. I love that he follows instructions like a well-trained dog. It's fucking exciting the way he takes me deep and holds me there, urging me to come by forcefully sucking—begging for it.

I rest my head back against the façade of the house and breathe deep. With a flick of my wrist, I discard my used cigarette and allow the growing pressure in my gut to overtake the last of my senses. For a moment I forget where I am until the crescendo hits me hard. I grab Miles's head and hold him against me as the ecstasy floods my system.

He coughs and chokes, swallowing without spilling anything. Needing air, he pulls off and hangs his head, saliva running down his chin. I glance down, still enjoying the sight of him. Before he stands I pull him close a second time.

"Clean me," I command.

Miles hesitates before leaning forward and licking my semihard erection. He doesn't take it in his mouth—he laps at the sides, removing the last of the excess fluids. The odd sensations of his nimble tongue cause me to shudder and flinch. Any and all anger I had disappears with the pleasure.

I pull away. "Enough."

Buckling my pants back into place, I step away from the wall and motion for him to follow. Miles gets back to his feet, rubbing his knees the entire time, and jumps back into step behind me.

"We're going to go visit an old mortician," I say.

"All right."

THE DRIVE across town is infuriating. At night the traffic is predictable. During rush hour the traffic is enough to get me angry all over again. It doesn't help that I'm mostly blind on one side either. I know I'm paranoid, but a piece of me fears that, while I'm sitting idle in traffic, some Cobras thug will take the opportunity to shoot at me from a car over. What would I do then? Get out and run? All it would take is one jackass on a motorcycle to run me down.

Eh. My mind goes to dark places when I'm frustrated.

I glance over at Miles. He's been quick to please since we left the Vice house. Looking him over, I find myself questioning every detail of every story he's ever told me.

"So you have a tattoo," I drawl.

Miles turns and nods. "Yeah."

"A pretty large one too. Those can get expensive. Weren't you telling me that you never had much money? That you were using it all on your brother?"

He looks away and focuses his attention out the passenger window. "My other brother, Lawrence, fancies himself a *tattoo artist*. That's what he calls himself. It's what he does for a living."

I say nothing.

Miles continues with, "He used to practice on me and Jayden." He lets out a halfhearted laugh. "He tattooed the soles of our feet. He's not the best with an ink gun so… it got bad. Jayden couldn't walk for a while. I said he could practice a large piece on my side so long as he left Jayden out of it. He let me pick what I wanted, and I guess he didn't do a bad job, but it was painful. I wouldn't do it over again."

Again, I remain silent. His tone and posture are convincing. I believe him. His brother didn't seem like the caring or empathic type.

"You still think I'm hiding something?" Miles asks.

"I don't know. I'm just asking all the questions I should've asked."

Miles is quiet for a moment before asking, "Have you ever thought about getting a tattoo?"

"I've never been interested."

"You could get one to cover your scars."

"I don't mind my scars."

"What about your bean can scar?"

I open my mouth to retort but close it once I realize I have nothing. That's a good idea. I hate the scar on my arm… and I can think of a few images I wouldn't mind seeing inked into my skin. Damn kid already knows me too well.

The frivolous musings take my mind off the traffic. We turn off the main road, and I'm not as irritated. Having a "partner" takes away from the sting of solitude. I'm glad Miles is with me despite our earlier falling-out. Miles must agree, or he's trying to distract me from my anger, as he points to anything and everything interesting on the side of the road. Noimore has a lot of trash, but it also has homeless men pissing in the alleys, a ball of dead rats, and a full-sized refrigerator banged up in a gutter. I find myself distracted until we reach our destination.

The residential areas in Noimore are hit-and-miss. Some are high-class and worthy of any aristocrat while others stand half a step above a hovel. Juliet, Big Man Vice's last mortician, lives in an older neighborhood of brick and black wood. Her front yard has overgrown bushes and vines, giving the place a bit of privacy, but I imagine in a few years the place will be completely hidden.

I step out of the car and Miles follows suit.

"What're we doing here?" Miles asks.

"Checking out a basement."

We walk up to the front door, and I heave a sigh. Anita and her fucking assignments…. I shouldn't be dealing with this. I knock on the door and muffled irritations are my only answer. I knock again. More noises. I knock harder.

Finally the door opens. I step back and stare at a sixtysomething woman in a wheelchair glaring up at me with the intensity of someone out for murder.

"Who're you?" she grunts.

I give the woman a thorough once-over. Her short curly hair, frizzing out enough to be its own light brown afro, covers the top of her head. She wears makeup like she needs to draw her eyeballs into place, including green eyeshadow thick enough to be ooze. I almost miss the fact she has naturally dark tan skin.

"Anita sent me," I say.

The old woman sneers. "You're a little old to be one of Anita's enforcers. Get in here, then. Get in here. Call me Juliet. *And don't touch my things!*"

I walk in without further comment, and Miles nods to the woman.

"I'm Miles Devonport. Nice to meet you."

He holds out a hand, but the woman turns away and offers an *hmpf*! Miles ignores her disregard, and we enter the living room with wrinkled noses. The place smells of death. And ass. I glance over at Juliet and eye her a second time. She doesn't look so old that she would smell of corpses…. Then again, she was once a mortician. Did the smell of dead bodies ingrain itself in her skin?

Miles gives me a baffled expression. I shrug. This situation is new.

Juliet wheels her chair past us. "This way! This way!"

The walls have more pictures of birds than an aviary. Among them I catch sight of a few family photographs, but otherwise the woman has an obsession. The wallpaper itself is a horrid floral design, and the furniture she stole straight from the 1940s. Everything is jam-packed in narrow spaces thanks to the overabundance of stuffed cats frozen in "cute" poses through the magic of taxidermy. I'm surprised Juliet can get around without knocking everything over.

I hate this house.

"In here," she says, gesturing to a door at the back of her kitchen. "Clean this out."

"*Clean it out?*" I repeat. "I'm not your servant."

Juliet picks up a cane and whaps me hard on the side of my thigh. I stumble back and rub at the bruised area, gritting my teeth to stop a whole slew of curse words. What the fuck is wrong with this woman? She's crazier than a soup sandwich!

"We'll handle it," Miles says. "Anita knew we could get the job done."

"Hmpf," Juliet huffs. "The last three boys she sent only made the problem worse. You better clean this up. It smells in here."

I straighten myself and face the door. "We'll look over the situation and see what we can do. But I'm not guaranteeing anything."

She thwaps me again, and I turn to glower at her with a slow, cold precision. If she does it again, I swear I'll kill her myself.

Miles steps between us. "There's not much Pierce can't handle."

I open the basement door and grimace when the wave of stench hits me. I hold back a gag and push forward. Miles flips on the lights—floodlight-type things—and the entirety of the basement is illuminated in one go. The place is huge, no doubt some sort of bomb shelter in its original design, but that only adds to the horror of the situation.

Rats cover the floor. The entire floor. They writhe and squirm and scamper over each other, a carpet of live bodies.

Why are rats in the room? Probably because of the corpses chained to the far wall. Two of them. Big men too, by the looks of it. Or, they *were* big men. They're half-eaten and liquefying from the rat saliva and heat of the unventilated basement. Well… the mystery of the rotting aroma is solved.

"They made me hold two Cobras thugs in my basement," Juliet yells from the top of the stairs. "And then they forgot about them! And then rats got in. It's not my fault I have this problem. I was barely a part of this."

I notice hunks of cheese and rat poison boxes littered around the edges of the room. The rats ignore these treats and scurry about without fear. The mousetraps I spot are either triggered, killing a single rat, or they hold a gnawed-off foot. There are over a hundred rats—perhaps more—and such small-scale solutions wouldn't even account for the breeding.

Juliet slams the basement door.

Miles walks down to my step and stands next to me while he surveys the situation. Half coughing and half gagging, he glances over and shrugs. "So what do we do?" he forces out.

I pull my gun and look it over. I don't have enough bullets for this… "I don't know."

"Really? You don't have a plan?"

"I'm standing in a basement full of corpses and rats. Clearly I don't have all the answers to life."

He lets out a single laugh and smiles.

I contemplate calling an exterminator, but they'll go straight to the cops. Anita gave me this assignment because she hates me, I know it. This is the worst problem I've ever had to solve, and I'm not even ten minutes in.

The basement door flies open. "Have you started yet?" Juliet asks.

I'm going to kill her. It's just a matter of time.

Miles must sense my deep irritation because he turns to the woman and forces a smile despite the smell. "We're going over our options."

I glare. "We'll tell *you* when we're done. Keep to yourself until then."

"I worked for the Vice family for thirty years," she says, waggling her cane like *Crotchety* is her middle name. "If I wanted, I could call in favors and have you two dealt with." She shuts the door, leaving Miles and me to our work.

"Hey," Miles says. "What if we pour a whole shit ton of bleach and ammonia down here?"

"I'm not physically cleaning this place no matter what the old woman threatens. They can put a bullet in my head before I pick up a scrub brush."

"No, not for cleaning the place...."

"Then what're you talking about?"

"When you mix ammonia and bleach, you make chloramine gas. It's fatal. It burns your lungs and stuff. If we poured it all over the basement floor, I'm sure it'd kill the rats... but then we have hundreds of rat corpses here."

I turn to him and narrow my eyes. "Where'd you learn that?"

"Chemistry class," he replies. "The one I took getting that high school diploma that *everyone* can get and is in no way impressive."

I scoff. "You're becoming a regular smartass."

"I learned from the best."

I crack a smile and huff out a laugh. "How dangerous is this gas?"

"Fairly dangerous. People die by accident from time to time when cleaning their house. I think Juliet would need to live elsewhere for a week or so, and then her basement would need to be thoroughly cleaned, but the pests will be dead."

"Fine. I'll get the chemicals. You deal with the woman."

"That's fine. I think she wants company anyway."

What an optimistic kid. That'll change before long.

Miles walks back up the stairs and opens the door. Juliet is waiting right there, her wheelchair practically touching the door itself. He smiles, and she frowns but doesn't say anything.

"We have a plan," he says, his cheer cutting through the stench. "And we'll be taking you to a hotel for a week or so. It'll be a nice vacation, and when you get back, everything will be fixed."

"No one better steal my stuff," she replies. "I'm friends with the Vice family, ya know. I rearranged corpses for them. Did dentist work and everything. They owe me some favors for makin' it look like specific men turned up dead. You better not be stealing my stuff."

Miles motions her back into her cramped household. "No need to worry. Anita Vice made it clear that you were a dear friend."

"She did?"

"Oh, yes. We know what'll happen if your stuff goes missing. We just want to clear your basement."

"Good.… Good. That's what I want to hear."

With his carefree smile, Miles helps Juliet by steering her wheelchair. I must admit, he seems to have some charm with the ladies. I never would have had the patience to deal with the crone.

I walk back up and shut the basement door behind me. Miles wheels the woman to the far side of the kitchen, and she gives him a genuine smile.

"Would you like some coffee?" he asks.

"Yes," she replies. "Thank you. Anita picked good this time. You should have been the first ones to arrive."

When I catch Miles's eye, I motion him over. He jumps to my side without hesitation. "What're you doing?" I ask. "She doesn't need to like you for this to happen."

"You told me, and I quote, 'Make nice with the little guys.' What if she has information for us in the future? She sounds like she knows a few things."

I chortle to myself. I *did* tell him that. I guess he's serious about learning the ropes. I appreciate the dedication. "That's right," I say. "You keep doin' what you're doin'."

CHAPTER TWELVE

Jesus Christ. Time flies.

We transformed Juliet's house into an unwitting death trap filled with fatal gas. I'll have Brisko go over and clear the place out after a couple days. The man has brain cells to spare…. He's not doing anything with them.

But now it's close to 9:00 p.m. Where did the time go?

I turn my car onto the long street toward my flat, but Miles starts to fidget in the passenger seat. I glance over and he motions to the window.

"You said we could make one last stop before going home," he says.

That's right. I did. I let out a long sigh. "Fine. Where to?"

"The Applegate community in Gary, Indiana. It's not too far from here."

I hold back a scoff. It's nearly an hour away, but I don't make a fuss. I've been to the Applegate houses before—it's a gated community of upper middle-class assholes. What does he need there? What isn't he telling me? "Where're you taking me?"

"My mother's house."

"Hm."

I flip on the radio to some wordless music and light a cigarette. I like the night. I feel more comfortable in the darkness than the harsh revealing rays of the day. Everything is hidden. And out of sight. Maybe that means there are thugs lurking in the shadows, but if they can lurk, I can lurk too.

I start the long drive out and allow the music to quell my nerves.

"Did you ever graduate high school?" Miles asks, his gaze shifting from the evening scenery to me.

I roll the window down to allow the smoke to escape and shake my head. "No."

Nick's voice rings in my ears. *Uneducated*, he said. *A know-nothing uneducated street urchin.* I hadn't known he thought of me like that. It cuts, just like Miles's question. What do I care? I wouldn't have cared two weeks ago. Everything feels wrong lately.

"Have you ever considered getting your GED?"

"No."

"Why not?"

"People don't ask for my résumé these days. What does it matter?"

Miles shrugs. "I don't know. What do guys like us do when they retire?"

"Apparently they don't."

"Apparently?"

"We're not discussing this," I snap.

Silence comes between us. I regret that fact, but I can't voice my frustrations. Miles fidgets with his seat belt and returns his gaze to the scenery. I want to talk to him, if only to take my mind off Nick and his disregard for me, but I have nothing to discuss that wouldn't be frustrating.

The roads are empty and we travel without incident. I end up burning two cigarettes over the trek.

I turn the car into the secluded community and drive through the automatic gates. Lucky for us they open without need for a card or a buzzing in, but the guard behind the booth snaps a picture of my license plate. Miles tenses once we get onto the exclusive streets of the community.

"It's the fourth house down on Pebble Beach Drive," Miles says. "On the right."

The houses have well-sculpted topiary and mailboxes with names written along the side. No one house sticks out. They're all painted the same shade of white and accented with the same rock façade, no doubt the result of a bland homeowner's association. It's a place for the unadventurous to raise children.

I park the car in front of the driveway. For a second we do nothing but stare at the house. Despite the hour, the living room window is lit with the dim glow of a television.

My phone buzzes and I remove it from my pocket with a lifted eyebrow.

Jeremy.

I answer. "Pierce here."

"*Pierce*," Jeremy says, the quiet of the car carrying his voice until it echoes. "You told my father about the plan to kill Harlan? When I specifically told you not to? What did I say about the ears of the enemy?"

"I don't keep things from your father."

"And you told him about your *in with the police*? I knew he wouldn't want to risk doing that. Now you've squandered our opportunity! What were you thinking?"

"Jeremy. I don't keep things from your father."

"*My father*," he repeats, hate laced in his voice. "You better show *me* that same kind of devotion when it comes time."

"Of course." Whenever that happens.

Jeremy pauses for a moment, and I wonder if he's going to hang up. I can hear the man take a breath and murmur something, though I can't distinguish what he says. After a calming exhale he asks, "Have you thought any more about my offer?"

Miles gives me a sideways glance, and I hold back the urge to hang up the phone. "I made my position clear."

"I notice you didn't tell my father about *that*."

My mind mulls over the conversation, and I'm flooded with questions I can't ask. Did Nick tell Jeremy everything? He wouldn't do that. How does Jeremy know what we talked about, then? It was just me and Nick in the gym, after all.... Asking would only tip my suspicion. I doubt Jeremy can overthrow Nick, but that doesn't mean he hasn't hired enforcers to spy on him.... Perhaps Nick is right to be suspicious.

Jeremy doesn't give me long before he continues, "Keep it in mind, Pierce. I have a lot to offer in the way of promotion, so to speak."

He ends the conversation, and I jam my phone back into my pocket. I have a feeling in my gut that says this situation isn't going to disappear anytime soon. I need to think of a way to get Jeremy off my back before this turns into a full-blown problem.

"I'll be right back," Miles says as he steps out.

"I'm coming with."

I exit the vehicle and walk around to him. Miles shoves his hands into his pockets and shrugs. "Still don't trust me?"

"I left you alone with your family last time and look what happened."

"My mother isn't going to do anything."

"I don't know that. She could be a heinous bitch."

"No… my mother is everything my father isn't."

His voice is… odd. I can't place it. It's like he reveres his mother while simultaneously loathing her.

In truth I exited the car to hear what he had to say. Why speak to his mother? What's there to be gained? I don't know if it stems from my doubt—all I do know is that I'm curious. I want to know more, and I fear Miles might not be able to articulate all the subtle details I could gather from just watching the event unfold before me.

Miles walks up to the front door and rings the bell. Within seconds it opens to a man dressed in casual jeans and a T-shirt. He turns his gaze from Miles to me and hesitates for a moment, clearly at a loss for words.

"Can I help you?" he mutters.

The man is nothing impressive. He has the physique of a desk worker and the wide eyes of someone unaccustomed to surprise. His hair is parted so thoroughly the line of exposed skin has its own suntan.

"Andrew, is my mother home?" Miles asks.

"Miles?" the man says, giving us both a second once-over. "I didn't recognize you…."

"Is my mother home?"

"Yes. She's home. Who is this?" Andrew points to me.

I jut my chin forward in a reverse nod. "Call me Pierce." The man eyes my side, and I'm certain he's caught sight of my holster. "I'm a detective with the Noimore City Police."

"Is something wrong?"

"No. I'm here as a friend."

"What's going on, Andrew?" a woman calls out from within the house. "Is everything okay?"

Andrew steps aside and motions us in. "Uh, come in. We'll talk inside."

Miles and I walk in, this time with me following his lead. I don't know what's happening, and I'm content to watch unless something goes south.

The place is tasteful and cozy. The blue walls and white carpets give everything a feel of being clean. Nothing is out of place and nothing feels clustered. It's a house with everything—a coat rack, an umbrella bin, a couch, a TV, a recliner, a side table, a coffee table—but we travel through it quick and head straight to the kitchen.

A woman stands at the island with a young girl, age ten, perhaps, at her side. I know right away the woman is Miles's mother. She's Asian in heritage and beautiful, though my eyes shift over her with little interest. I can see where Miles gets his ageless smooth skin, honeyed complexion, and black hair.

"Miles?" she asks. "Is that you?"

When was the last time these two saw Miles? They ask if it's him like they haven't seen each other in years.

"Yeah," Miles intones. "It's me. Look, I need to speak with you. Is that okay?"

"Of course…."

Miles's mother motions for the little girl to join Andrew. The girl crosses the kitchen and glances up at me. Her gaze lingers on my face, and I don't flinch away from her stare.

"What happened to your eye?" she asks, unconcerned with proper etiquette.

"I got singed saving a little girl from a burning building," I reply.

"Wow."

She scampers away with a giggle, and I hear Andrew take her from the room, leaving me and Miles with his mother. She keeps her spot near the island, refusing to get any closer, and I hover near the shadows of the corner, hoping to blend in while they have their conversation.

"It looks like you're doing well," the woman says. She laces her fingers together and furrows her brow. I see tears well in her eyes, but again, she doesn't advance. "What're you doing here?"

Miles sighs. "I was hoping you could take Jayden in and send him to the same school you send Lacy to."

"No," she states.

"*Please*, Mom." Miles takes a step closer. "Listen. He's getting mixed in with all the wrong crowds and—"

"Which is why I refuse to take him. I won't have his evils coming to this house. I won't have your father here. I won't."

"He still has a chance to get better. He needs someone to watch him. He's your son."

Miles's mother turns away and glares at the countertop. "It's expensive. It's a private school. We don't have that kind of—"

"I'll pay for it," Miles interjects. "I'll give you everything for two years' worth of schooling right now."

His mother sits speechless, her lip quavering.

I don't know much about private schools, but I know they ain't cheap. If Miles intends to pay for two years, he's basically giving up the last of his money I gave him for helping me with Malloy. He'd go right back to being broke.

Miles steps up to the island and hangs his head. "Please take him. He won't listen to me and… I know he was upset when you left with only Lacy. I know he wants to live with you, even if he denies it."

"He's on drugs," she replies. "I won't have an addict near Lacy."

"I'll pay for rehab, then."

She turns her crying glare toward him. "How do you have all this money? Are you cooking stuff up with your father now too? Is that it?"

"No, Mom. I'm not doing that. Dad kicked me and Jayden out. Does it matter where I got the money if it's being used for good? Please just help Jayden."

"I knew it. I knew you would turn to drugs to solve your problems. That's just what your father would have done."

"It's not drugs. I promise."

"How can I be sure with you?" she snaps, accusation in her voice like she's talking to Miles's father instead of her twenty-year-old son. Miles shifts back, wounded by the statement. It probably doesn't help that earlier I didn't trust him much either. His defeated posture grates on me.

"Ma'am," I chime in, forcing the casual tone of my voice into that of an authoritative one. "Your son has been helping the detectives of the Noimore Police Department catch some unsavory criminals. We offer rewards to citizens with valuable information. I swear to you, as a detective on the force, he's doing good work."

Heh. It's not entirely a lie. Malloy *is* off the streets, after all. And he *was* a dangerous criminal.

Miles stares at me with a look of confusion and regret. His mother, on the other hand, rubs at her eyes and stares at her son as though seeing him for the first time since we got here.

"You're helping the police?" she whispers.

Miles doesn't answer. She doesn't need confirmation, though. She walks over and wraps her arms around his neck. For a moment they embrace before she breaks the connection.

"You look so good," she says, holding him at arm's length. "So manly. So professional. I should've seen it before. You're really turning your life around."

He nods. I can practically see the lump in his throat brought about by the lie. Does it matter if the lie is being used for good? Miles doesn't say anything. His mother goes into another round of silent crying. She pulls him in for a second hug, and this time he returns it.

I turn away. For some reason this moment feels personal—like I'm sullying something special with my presence. I walk out of the kitchen and into the living room. Andrew and the little girl have gone to the back of the house. I'm alone and I stand awkwardly by the front door, on the verge of going back to the car.

Miles said his brother was hurt by their mother's choice to take only their sister…. It's clear to me that Miles felt betrayed as well. The look on his face when his mother hugged him…. This is the kind of life he wants. This is the kind of life he should have had if family circumstances had been different.

I chortle to myself, half lost in musings. My mother is seated firmly in prison and my father killed himself in a drunk driving "accident." When I hit the streets, I never thought *what if my parents had just stayed together*. I imagine Miles must wonder what it would be like if his mother had just kept him. The thoughts get me feeling icy again.

"Pierce?"

"What?" I ask, turning around.

Miles, standing next to me with a melancholy expression, motions to the door.

I nod. We exit the house and wander back to the car.

"Let's go home," I say.

Miles perks up as he slides into the passenger seat and buckles himself in. "Home?"

"Yeah. You live at my flat now, right? Then we're going home."

He half smiles to himself. "Right. Home."

I UNLOCK the front door and we enter in silence. My apartment is cool and still despite the life and activity outside, but I like it that way. I take off my coat and hang it on the hook by the door. Miles does the same, just as quiet as he has been the entire ride back.

I stop in the middle of the entrance hall and turn to him. "So you're gonna pay for your brother's school and rehab?"

"Yeah," Miles intones, never glancing over to me. "With the money you gave me."

"You should keep some of it for yourself."

"Why? I'm working with you now, right? I'll get paid from other jobs, and… and that'll be enough."

"Don't you want a house or something? Or a car? Or college classes?"

"College?" he repeats, turning to me. "Why would I take college classes? We don't have résumés, right? No retirement? What's the point?"

"You should just keep some of the damn money for yourself," I say, waving a hand in anger as I storm into the kitchen. "If you *give and give and give*, people will *take and take and take*. For fuck's sake, kid, I thought you had learned that lesson already."

Miles follows me into the kitchen, and I flip on the overhead light. My anger from the day's activities is mounting. I felt a little better after my excursion with Miles, but that didn't solve the underlying problem.

I hate my life.

I didn't want to admit it, but the more I analyze, the more I realize I'm just tired. I've done the same thing for twenty years, and I know it's going nowhere. Actually, I take that back. It's going straight to the grave. What's the point? The days are the same, the jobs are the same— or worse—and even if the money is good, what am I doing with it? I have no long-term plans or goals….

I feel empty.

Miles ambles over to my side. I pull myself out of my own thoughts and sigh.

"Just keep some money," I say. "You should do something for yourself every once in a while. You deserve to be happy."

I don't know what it was I said, but Miles looks me in the eye like he's realized something. I cock an eyebrow, but he doesn't elaborate. He just stares.

Before I can ask what he's doing, Miles closes the distance between us and wraps his arms around my torso. With gentle movements he brushes his lips against mine and kisses me. Not with lust or need or hunger—he's not even hard. He kisses me like lovers kiss, taking his time and reaching a hand up to stroke the base of my hair.

I push him away. "Stop."

Flushed and looking hurt, he shakes his head. "What's wrong?"

"Don't."

"Don't what?"

"You can't do *this*. You can't wear your heart on your sleeve. You can't."

"Why?" Miles asks, glancing around. "It's not like anyone else is here. It's just us."

"They'll use it against you."

"They? Who're *they*?"

I turn away and shake my head. "Everyone, all right? Everyone will use it against you. Don't go around givin' your affection away like you do your damn money. Keep it to yourself and you'll be better for it."

Miles grabs my arm and forces me back around. I jerk free from his grip and glare, but he meets me with a glare in kind. For a moment we say nothing. After a long minute, Miles relaxes and runs a hand up my chest.

"No one ever tells me to save my money," he whispers. "No one ever tells me to do things for *me*. They always want me to do things *for them*."

"What's your point?" I ask, my tone more callous than I wanted.

"I feel like… you're looking out for me. I trust you, Pierce. I want to stay with you."

"Don't say things like that. It'll get you in trouble."

"You keep saying that, but we're all alone."

"If you let it start here, it'll get out someday. It'll come back to haunt us."

Miles forces a laugh as he wraps his arms around my neck and pulls me close. I'm moments from pushing him away again, but he squeezes tight and keeps his face buried in my neck. "Nobody has to know," he whispers. "Or at least… let me pretend when we're alone."

His last bit cuts me. I grit my teeth and wrap a single arm around to rub along his spine. I know, in my gut, this is wrong. It's not wrong because I don't feel anything—it's wrong because I know how *this* plays out in the Vice family. Nick almost had me shoot Miles earlier today. The deeper we get into this, the more likely it is I'll have conflicts in the future. It's a slippery slope but….

Miles tightens his hold with each fleeting graze of my fingertips. I can tell he wants me to return his affection. I can feel it in his accelerated heart rate and the way he digs his nails into my skin.

Nobody in his life wants him. Not his mother or his father or his brother. Even the people on the streets want him dead. He's so kindhearted and naïve, I suspect he thinks something is wrong with *him* rather than the other way around. He couldn't be further from the truth.

"You don't have to pretend," I murmur, pulling him in with both arms.

Miles tenses for a second and holds his breath. After a moment he lifts his head and presses his mouth against mine, the resulting kiss one of emotional need rather than physical. Against my better judgment, I allow the scene to continue. When he strokes my bottom lip with his tongue, I shudder. I'm hot from pent-up emotions and anxious because of the situation.

I've never tried to make something like this work. I've never felt like I was simultaneously making a mistake while at the same time enjoying every second of it.

I'm sure I'll regret everything in the morning, but for now I relax into the embrace and enjoy the way Miles tastes as he presses against me.

CHAPTER THIRTEEN

THE DARKNESS blankets me and the cool night air is a comfort against my skin, but I can't seem to sleep. Miles shivers and scoots deeper into my embrace. I tuck my nose into his short hair and inhale. I like his scent.

My phone beeps and I let out a low groan. Flipping over, I grab it off the nightstand and click on the screen. The brightness catches me off guard, and I squint past the light to read my messages.

I have thirty-two from Anita, three from Jeremy, two from an advertising number, and four from random associates looking for people who've gone missing. I blink twice and read a few.

Eh. Same thing. Different night.

Anita's still upset I haven't found Rodger. Jeremy's asking about the explosives…. I guess that's new. I've been gathering the shit he's asked for, and I know the Nightquarter Café tunnel, but the stuff isn't fit into place yet. I'll contact him later. And the others can wait. I need to sleep.

I return my phone to the nightstand and roll back into my initial position, wrapping my arm over Miles. He stirs and lifts his head off the pillow. "Any word on my brother?" he asks through his grogginess.

"Not yet," I reply.

Miles rests back into place.

It's been three weeks since I asked my street guys to keep a lookout for a younger Asian kid looking for a hit. I thought they would see something by now, but clearly Jayden has skipped town, or else he's gettin' his fix somewhere else. A small piece of me worries he's supplied by the Cobras directly.

A day hasn't gone by that Miles didn't ask about him.

Another beep from my phone, and I sigh. Turning over, I pick it up and glance at the screen. It's another message, this one from Big Man Vice himself. I scroll through it.

The text reads: *Where is Rodger? Why haven't you found him yet? Get off your lazy ass and do something!*

Nick doesn't send texts. Anita must have used his phone, or else he gave her permission to send a message.

I sigh. Her persistence is enough to wear anyone down. If I can't find Rodger, I doubt the Cobras can—he's not in danger yet. The phone buzzes in my grasp, and I glare down at the screen.

Anita writes: *If you don't find him soon I'll be sending men over to knock your priorities into line.*

With gritted teeth I chuck my phone across the room and it hits the far wall. Fuck her. I haven't worked for two decades to be threatened into compliance. I've done everything she wants—where does she get off?

"What's wrong?" Miles asks, propping himself up on an elbow.

"Nothing. Go back to sleep."

"Did you just throw your phone?"

"Yes."

"Yeah, really sounds like *nothing*," he quips.

I snort. "Anita's ridin' my ass to find her son."

"She's been doing that forever. Why throw your phone now?"

"She's got no respect. She thinks she can intimidate me into working hard—like I'm not working hard already—it fuckin' pisses me off."

Miles lets out a sigh and relaxes back onto the bed. I pull him close and enjoy his warmth. His presence calms my anger. He must know it because he lets me hold him like a friggin' teddy bear. I laugh to myself at the thought, but I don't voice it. I doubt he wants to hear my sleep-deprived musings.

"You okay?" he asks in a low and quiet voice.

"Yeah," I reply. "Why?"

"You seem like you're in an odd mood."

"I'm done with this job," I say, more earnest than I want.

"Whadda ya mean?"

"Forget it."

Miles goes silent. I don't want to say anything, but I've made up my mind. I'm not some punk lackey who needs permission to leave. After I kill Harlan, I'm going to take everything I have and skip town. Permanently. Two decades of my life is worth everything I've been given—at least I think so. Maybe Nick will disagree, but he doesn't think of me as an equal.

"Are you thinking about working somewhere else?" Miles asks.

"I don't know."

That's not true. I know what I want. I've been saving my money for years now. I have a small fortune, and I think Miles can do more good with it than I can. I'll give him half, take the rest for myself, and disappear into a small town out West, in North Dakota. I know Miles wants to repay me for my "kindness," but I'd rather him not live like me—his life circumstances mirror mine to an unsettling degree, and if I hate my life now, how will Miles feel twenty years in?

He thinks he owes me a debt, but I'll release him from his obligations and we'll go our separate ways, just as it should be. Miles's pride won't allow him to agree with the plan, which is why I'll keep it to myself.

"Well, hypothetically speaking, maybe you could become a detective with some police department," he says.

"*Hypothetically speaking*, I'm too old. Most cops don't start their career after the age of thirty-five. Besides, it'd be a little hypocritical."

"You could be a private investigator, then."

I catch my breath in realization. I had never considered that idea before. Private investigators are self-made men in a lot of ways. They use their streetwise in exchange for money—either trailing unfaithful spouses or helping attorneys gather evidence for their trials. It might actually be a legitimate occupation I could handle.

"Your suggestions are inspired sometimes," I say, honest in my comment.

Miles chuckles. "Should I call you *gumshoe* from now on?"

"It was a hypothetical situation. Don't get married to the idea."

He continues to chuckle as he slips closer to sleep.

RUMRUNNER TUNNELS are narrow as fuck. It's a good thing I'm not claustrophobic.

The brick and wood all around me reeks of rot and decay. I fit the last of the explosives into place and wipe sweat from my face. The tunnel has the airflow of a coffin. I exhale and crawl out backward, relishing the freedom.

Jeremy thought of everything. The rumrunner tunnel ends at the Nightquarter Café, but it begins in an old run-down laundromat. Jeremy purchased the property months ago and closed it down for "renovations." I'm the only one in the building, ensuring no one sees me work, and I mill about the storage room in an undershirt and old slacks. The false door that hides the tunnel amuses me, simply because I haven't seen one so well hidden before.

I dust myself off and stretch. The explosives line the end of the tunnel near the café, but I had to run the triggering wires from one end to the other. The prep and work took longer than I expected—we only have a week and half before the main event—but at least it wasn't rats in a goddamn basement. I turn and stare at the door to the tunnel. I still need to mount the wires to the wall and string them to the other side of the room—anything to distance the person triggering the bombs from the explosion.

The front door rings as it opens. I tense but continue with my work, grabbing a spool of wire and unraveling an arm's length worth.

"Pierce?" Miles calls out.

I relax. I figured it was it him—since he's the only other man with a key—but you never know. Maybe it was a mugger looking for an easy target.

"In here," I reply.

I affix the wire to the trigger and walk it up the wall near the door, mounting the wire with curved tacks. Miles walks in and examines my work. He tucks his hands into his pockets and leans against the far wall, his shoulders slumped.

"Didn't see him?" I ask.

"No. I didn't."

"Maybe he left town."

"I doubt it. Where would he go?"

I keep quiet. I don't know Miles's brother. He could be anywhere, which is why I think it's foolish that Miles wants to drive around looking for him. I know he's desperate at this point, but some things in life just aren't worth worrying about.

"What're you doing?" he asks.

I reach up and secure the wire to the top of the tunnel door. "I'm finishing this up. I'll be done shortly."

My phone buzzes in my pants pocket. I'm not done with the wires, and I'm content to let it go to voice mail, but Miles walks over and slides his hand into my pocket, caressing more of me than necessary to grab my phone. I lift an eyebrow as he flashes me the cracked screen. It's an old fling of mine—Donny McCoy—and I wonder why he's calling.

"Answer it and hand it over," I command.

Miles complies. He answers the call and places it between my shoulder and ear. I continue to affix the wires.

"What is it?"

"Pierce?" Donny asks with a hint of amusement in his voice. "You said you were looking for Rodger, right? That we should give you a call if we found him?"

"Yeah," I say. "I did. What of it?"

"I saw him. I know where he's staying, and you won't believe it."

"Out with it. I need to drag him back to his father."

Miles situates himself behind me and slips his hands back into my pockets, kneading the top of my thighs. I'm covered in dirt and sweat, but Miles leans against me regardless, his hot breath on the back of my neck.

Donny chuckles. "He's at this gated house with a woman. I think it's also a church or somethin'. A bunch of weirdos run the place and wouldn't let me in. You want me to break into the place and scope it out?"

"No," I say. "Tell me where you are. I'll handle it."

"I'm at the corner of Poppy Cotton and Merrymore. You know the area? Near the country club?"

I curse under my breath. I must've passed that area of the city fifty times by now. How did I never catch sight of Rodger? Fuck me.

"I'll be right there," I mutter.

"All right."

The conversation ends. With my hands preoccupied, I leave the phone trapped between my arm and head. My work slows the more Miles grips my cock. I close my eyes and tilt my head back, enjoying the way he breathes onto the nape of my neck. Miles removes one hand and slides it down the back of my pants, tracing the cleft of my ass. I tense and jerk back, pushing him away with my shoulder.

"*Stop*," I snap. "I'm not into that."

"You sure? You got pretty hard when I did it."

I drop the wires and my phone as I turn on my heel. Miles flinches back with a half smile. I glare.

"It doesn't feel good for you?" Miles asks, his tone and posture nonconfrontational. "I mean, it hurts a little for me at the start, but once we get into it…. It feels good. Real good."

I pick up my phone—the screen has another crack in it, but I don't care—and gather the wires with a snort. I know he enjoys it. Hell, I'm sure our neighbors know he enjoys it.

Miles shrugs. "Have you ever tried it before?"

Yeah, I've played bottom. And Miles is right—after the initial pain there's a physical pleasure to playing bitch that's unique to the experience—but I don't enjoy it for outside reasons. It's all psychological. I feel uncomfortable with the idea of submitting to another man. It's hard to articulate, but it's like I'm relinquishing control, and I don't truly trust anyone anymore. Even my exception for Nick has become suspect.

"I don't feel like talkin' about it," I say, tossing the wires to the corner. "Besides, we've got work to do. C'mon. Back to the car."

Miles nods and heads for the front. I pull my jacket over my sullied clothes and follow after. The laundromat sits empty with a hundred machines dark and unused stacked in rows throughout the front room. I exit and lock the door behind me, glancing over my shoulder the entire time. It's imperative no one knows what Miles and I are doing, lest the plan become leaked to the Cobras. Once everything is secure, I walk to my car and take my place in the driver's seat.

My phone buzzes again, and I wish I had just destroyed the damn thing. I snatch it from my pocket and answer without looking.

"*What is it?*" I growl.

"Pierce," Jeremy replies.

I sigh as I pull the car out and speed down the road. Jeremy is the last man I want to talk to. "Jeremy. I didn't think it would be you. What can I do for you?"

"What's the progress on the tunnels?"

"They're almost done. I'll return to them later tonight."

"Why not finish them now?" he asks in a tone of irritation.

"Your brother showed up," I reply. "I need to go pick him up and bring him home. He's been out past his curfew, and you know how your mother gets."

Jeremy is silent for second before asking, in a voice more hopeful than before, "You found Rodger?"

"Yeah."

"Where?"

"The corner of Poppy Cotton and Merrymore. That posh area near the club."

"Hm. Well, thank you, Pierce. Call me when you're done with the tunnel. I need to know—we don't have much time left until Harlan's game."

He ends the call and I toss my phone onto the backseat. Now that I've decided to leave, everything seems a little less important than it did a few months ago. I relax back against my seat and smile to myself. It's a load off.

"You look happy," Miles says.

"Tell me," I say, ignoring his comment, "what would you do with five hundred thousand dollars?"

He lifts an eyebrow and shrugs. "Uh, I don't know. Get my brother the best help money can buy."

Of course that's what he'd say. "And after that?"

"Maybe get a house."

"I could see that. You should get it some place nice. Maybe the West Coast."

Miles stares at me for a moment, his expression unreadable. I return his stare, but he doesn't say anything. Maybe he knows my plan, maybe he doesn't. Either way, now when I imagine what he'll do after we part ways I'll have a basic idea.

The ride isn't long. It's an odd time of day—still morning, but long after breakfast and too soon for lunch. Everyone is at work or busy. I zip along the roads and make it to the exclusive part of town in record time. I want to wrap up everything before I go, and Rodger is one such thing I need to cross off my list.

I narrow my eyes as I get closer to my destination. Merrymore Street is bizarre compared to the ones around it. It's covered in trees and there are tall iron fences around every piece of property. Even Miles shifts nervously in his seat as we continue down the road. Everything is muted—the sounds, the people, the animals. The place has a natural secrecy to it.

I spot Donny on the corner of Poppy Cotton, and I pull my car alongside him. He's leaning against his blue Chevy truck with a grin and a bottle of beer. Unlike Nick's other enforcers, he's got a real problem with following rules or conforming to the norm. He wears jeans and a T-shirt whenever he's out on assignment, and his boots look like something a cowboy would sport in the 1700s. I like it—that's why I fucked him a few years back as part of my daily routine—but it gets Nick mad.

"Donny," I say, exiting my car.

"Pierce," he replies, his grin widening into a full-blown smile. "What took you so long?"

"Does it matter? I'm here now. Where's Rodger?"

He throws back his bottle and finishes his drink as Miles exits the vehicle. Donny gives him the once-over. "He's a little small for your tastes, isn't he?"

Donny stands six inches taller than either me or Miles—and he's got enough muscles to spare for the both of us. I give Miles a sideways glance before returning my attention to Donny. "I said, *where's Rodger* not *let's chitchat about bullshit.*"

Donny chuckles. "I missed your no-fucks-given attitude, Pierce. Jail isn't as exciting as the streets. I'm gonna ask Big Man Vice to pair us together again in the future." He nods to Miles. "Maybe we could make it a three-way."

Before I repeat myself for a third goddamn time, Donny tosses me a pamphlet. I open it up and glare down at the pictures. Is it for some sort of church? Everyone is gathered in circles and praying to a pillar in the center. Everyone is disturbingly happy in each photograph, like they're high as fuck or being blackmailed into such appearance—no one is that jovial without outside influence.

The pamphlet is titled *The Pillars of Virtue.*

The first paragraph on the first page reads:

And it came to pass as he prayed unto the Lord, there came a pillar of virtue; and he saw and heard much; and because of the things that he saw and heard, he did quake and tremble. And he cast himself upon his bed, being overcome with the things that he had seen.

Miles leans in close and stares. "What is it?"

"It's the literary equivalent to a flaccid cock," I quip. "No substance. I bet there's some sort of catch too. Like you can only see virtue once you've handed all your money over to the fat asshole in charge."

"The picture of the fat asshole is on the back," Donny chimes in.

I flip the pamphlet over and, sure enough, some orange motherfucker in a pope costume is there smiling back at me. I have no idea what these people are selling—salvation?—but I'm not buying.

"Where's the church?" I ask.

Donny points to the building set back on the corner lot. It's surrounded by tall bushes and trees, keeping it hidden despite the time of day, and I can already see a myriad of problems ahead of me. The property itself is large enough for three compounds, and I suspect there are multiple buildings around in places I can't see.

"There're men at the gate," Donny says. "I tried to get in but they wouldn't have any of it."

"We'll see about that." I pocket the pamphlet and mull over the information. If Rodger is inside, and it's likely he is, I'm gonna need to get in and look around. But how?

Donny tosses his empty bottle onto the bed of his truck before pulling a cold one out of the cooler he has strapped down inside. He twists off the top and offers it to Miles, who declines with a shake of his head.

"Whadda ya say, kid?" Donny asks. "Pierce and I had a lot of fun back in the day. You wanna get in the middle?"

"Whatever Pierce wants," Miles murmurs.

The comment catches me off guard and gets me hot. I didn't know he was submitting so thoroughly to me—then again, he seems to enjoy having someone else run things. He's eager to please and not so eager to call the shots.

Donny smiles and takes a step closer to Miles. "Whoa. Seems Pierce has you trained good. How long you been under him?" He reaches out to touch him, but I turn on my heel and shove Donny back, spilling some of his beer.

"Keep it in your pants," I say, restraining my rage. "I'm not here for this. I'm here for Rodger. Either think of a way to get us on the property or get out of here."

"Sure," Donny replies, wiping off the spilled liquid. "Okay. I'll keep my hands to myself. Just let me know what you want me to do." He saunters back over to his truck and leans against it.

I walk a few hundred feet up the block to get a better look at the property. Miles shadows my steps, not saying a word, but his gaze is glued to our target. There are cameras around on the black iron fence, and men circle the palatial estate wearing robes. I doubt they have weapons, but if they do, they'd be well hidden.

I glance over at Miles. He looks unperturbed and focuses on our target until he notices my staring. He rubs at his neck and cocks an eyebrow.

There's no denying that Miles is good-looking—it's no wonder Donny honed in on him—especially in his new suit of confidence. I find myself still worked up from Miles's earlier remark. "Don't let him touch you," I command. "If he does, tell me. I'll handle it."

Miles offers me a one-sided smile. "It sounded like you two were a thing before. I'm sure it's an interesting story."

"We had our fun. Now I'm not in the mood for sharing. That's the end of the story."

"All right."

His willingness to do what I tell him is exciting in a primal way, but at the same time it irritates me. What if he's just telling me what I want to hear? I want to know more of his thoughts on the situation. I turn back to him. "Do you want to fuck him?"

"Donny?" Miles asks.

"Don't play stupid," I snap. "Who else am I talking about?"

He scratches at the back of his head and avoids looking at me straight on—a habit I thought he had kicked. "He's attractive, and I've only ever been with… one person…." He shakes away his nervousness and returns his gaze to meet mine. "But I'm with you. I don't want any experience so much that I'd jeopardize that."

"That doesn't mean you should do everything I say without question."

"Is that what you think I do?"

I turn away and glower at the scenery. Miles has been the one pushing our "relationship" in a direction I don't normally go. He's the one who wanted to make it more intimate—sleeping together, kissing—all the stuff I try to avoid. I guess he's pretty vocal when he wants to be.

I shake my head. "No. You speak up when you want something."

"Yeah, well, I didn't speak up this time so what does that mean?"

"Smartass," I drawl.

Miles glances back at Donny and then to me. "He was the bottom?"

"Yeah."

"But he's pretty big. Like, bulky. Ripped."

"That's how I like 'em."

Miles turns his attention down to his wiry frame. Before he can interpret anything as an insult or a suggestion, I point to the entrance gate at the front of the property. "Look. Stop worrying about this and help me think of a way to get in."

"Do we need to go in through the front?" Miles asks.

"No."

"Then why not go in through the back while they're all distracted?"

"Distracted by what?"

Miles gestures to Donny with a devious smirk.

CHAPTER FOURTEEN

MILES IS more creative than I realized. Maybe there's something to this *high school diploma* thing after all.

Donny rams his pickup truck into the front gate going full tilt. He breaks the iron bars and sideswipes a decorative post, almost hitting a man with the splinters, but that doesn't slow him. He swirls into donuts, digging his tires into the grass and kicking up flowers. I can hear him whooping from the other side of the property. He enjoys wrecking things—it made it easy for him to fall into the career of mob muscle.

Men and women in white robes shuffle to the front, their arms up and their voices incoherent in their yelling. While they're busy I grab the top of the iron fence. With some struggle I pull myself up and kick a leg over the black fence points. Miles mimics my motions with ease. We land on the grass and crouch-run over to the main building. Just as I suspected, there are other buildings on the property, but I decide to start with the largest one first.

The "house" is one part church, one part communal area. It's two stories and painted dark blue with old colonial architecture. We run up to the back door and, to my luck, it's unlocked. Miles and I slip in during the commotion. Donny isn't going to stop anytime soon.

The first room is a kitchen—clean and filled with the aroma of cooked beef. It's set up for mass production, much like a restaurant, and I weave between countertops until I pass through to the next room.

I stop when I enter the hall.

The entire place is covered from floor to ceiling in artwork—which is saying something, considering the mammoth size of the building. It's straight up gaudy and not noteworthy in skill or color palette. The paintings range from landscapes to portraits… it's eclectic.

I hear people running before I see them, and Miles and I round a corner to allow them by without confrontation. I should just coldcock everyone until we run across someone willing to tell us where Rodger is, but stealth isn't a bad option either.

A group of women clad in robes runs up the stairs muttering something about going to their rooms. I motion to Miles, and he picks up on it as well. The upstairs has the dorms. There's a good chance Rodger is in one of them.

Miles jumps up the stairs two at a time, and I trail after, pulling my gun and watching for anyone who might try and stop us. I get a better look at the pictures on the wall, and I realize they all have something to do with religion or religious imagery, though not in a positive way: a lot of death, starvation, and burning stakes. The place is well furnished, though—I suspect this "church" has money to spare.

"What's going on?" I hear a man ask.

I leap to the top of the stairs and, to my relief, spot Rodger Vice, the oldest of Nick's children. He's the spitting image of his father if Nick were thirty years younger—black hair, broad shoulders, clean-shaven, and tall enough to be a model. He's dressed in a robe tie-dyed all the colors of the rainbow, the bright swirls detracting from his natural appearance.

"*Pierce?*" he asks. "Is that you?"

Miles steps aside and allows me to take the lead. I walk over, holster my gun, and nod to Miles. He picks up on my nonverbal communication and pulls his own gun, taking the role of guard.

I step up to Rodger and shake my head. "What're you doing here?"

"I'm glad you're here, actually. I've wanted to go for a few days, but I haven't had the motivation. Seeing you reminds me what I'm missing back home." He turns with a dramatic swoosh of his arm and flounces to a door at the end of the hallway. Without another word he dives in and motions for me to follow. I roll my eyes and pursue him, but there's a piece of me that regrets ever taking this assignment.

I enter the bedroom and Miles ducks in seconds after. It's just as gaudy as the hallway, perhaps worse. The art is wall-sized, and I wonder how they got it into Rodger's room in the first place. The brightness and clash of colors hurts my one good eye. At least he has a decent-sized bed, but even then it's a room I wouldn't pay money to stay in.

"Oh my," Rodger says, examining me and Miles. "I see no one made you shed your mortal holdings before entering the house. That's a sin, Pierce. They take that seriously here."

"I don't care," I reply. "I didn't come here for them. I came here for you. What're you even doing? Let's go."

"First I need my things."

He saunters over to the dresser and picks through the contents one at a time. I grit my teeth to hold back a whole host of choice words. Does it look like my time is free? With my heart rate rising, I pull a cigarette from my jacket and light it up. I've cut back in the last few days, but I still purchase a pack every week, sometimes more. At moments like this I wonder why I even bother trying to quit. I need *something* to dull the stupidity around me.

Rodger frowns at his wardrobe and walks over to the attached bathroom door.

"Please enjoy the art," he says as he enters the bathroom. "It was all painted by our Elder's daughter. So beautiful. So powerful. So *bold.*" He balls his hand into a fist and then bursts it open with wavy fingers before disappearing.

Silence fills the bedroom.

With a single chuckle Miles turns to me. "That guy puts the *fart* in *artsy-fartsy.*"

I laugh so hard I inhale a part of my damn cigarette. I cough up ash as I steady myself, but the sentiment rings true. Rodger has always been an odd kid. I don't think he fits in with the Vice family aesthetics, so to speak, and unlike his siblings, he's never found something he's good at.

The sound of running fills the hallway. I lift an eyebrow and Miles shrugs. He leaves the bedroom with his gun at the ready, and I wait for Rodger to finish whatever business he has in the bathroom.

A few minutes pass and I scratch my stomach, feeling like a useless blob. What the hell is taking him so long? He better not be yankin' it in there, or so help me I'll—

The bedroom door opens and Miles steps through with a look of panic. "Pierce, we have problems."

"We always have problems," I say. "What is it this time?"

"I thought everyone was panicking because of Donny, but there are Cobras here. They're fighting with some of the church guys downstairs. They brought guns."

There're Cobras here? When did that happen? I didn't see anyone when we first drove up....

I walk over to the bedroom door and crane my head out into the hall. Robed individuals hustle into their rooms and lock the doors. Vague hints of yelling echo their way up the stairs, and I hear the distinct stomp of boots heading our way. I pull my gun and duck back into the bedroom.

"How many were there?" I ask, my voice low.

"There were eight downstairs," Miles whispers. "And a few guys outside when I glanced out the window. I think they're circling the building."

Shit. I didn't know the Cobras were so close to finding Rodger. Do they know that Miles and I are here as well? The element of surprise might be the only tool we have before getting swarmed.

I crush my cigarette underfoot as the bathroom door opens. Rodger steps out and I momentarily lose my words upon catching sight of him.

He's a different man when wearing a suit—even if it's a wrinkled suit without a tie. I stare, although *now* isn't the time to get hot and ready to go. Rodger's striking resemblance to his father is uncanny, and it brings back a whole host of lurid fantasies I thought long forgotten.

Miles elbows me in the arm. "What're we doing?"

"We're… leaving this room," I say, ripping my gaze off Rodger. "It's the first place they'll check."

"Where did you get that suit?" Miles asks, motioning to Rodger.

He pats himself. "I kept it in secret after they admitted me to the inner sanctum of pillars. There are some things in life a man can't part with."

"Did you happen to keep a gun?"

"*A gun?* Pah. Of course not. I have others to do the shooting for me. I need to be concerned with greater things in life."

Miles gives me an odd glance before nodding to Rodger, who joins us with a smile. Unlike Nick and Guinevere, who both hold themselves like the blood of kings courses through their body, Rodger braces his weight on his bent legs and lifts his eyebrows, striking a very relaxed pose. It's clear he doesn't understand the urgency or danger of the situation.

"I can't believe you tossed your smoke on the floor," he says. "This is a historic building. It's over a hundred years old. Could you imagine a fire? What a travesty."

I grab him by the collar and shove him out the door. "Keep it to yourself," I snap. "We're leaving and you need to stay quiet. Thugs are here to bury a bullet in your head."

"Tsk. Fine, we'll go, but do you need to be so gruff?"

Miles enters the hall and opens the door across the way. I push Rodger in, unconcerned with his bitching and flailing. Miles locks the door, and I hear a gaggle of people storm the second story. We don't have much time.

I spot a window and run over to it. There are small roof ledges built into the first story under most second-story windows, but will they hold our weight? I lift the window and lean out onto the sill. The men circling the house down below don't catch sight of me. I step back into the room and mull over my options.

We aren't far from Vice family holdings. I should call for backup.

I reach into my pocket and freeze. My cell phone is sitting on the backseat of my car. I turn to Miles. "You have your phone?"

"I still don't have a phone," he says. "Remember?"

Goddammit. That's my fault.

With a frown I turn to Rodger. "Do you have a phone?"

"I gave away all earthly possessions when I joined the Pillars of Virtue," he replies.

"Except for the suit," Miles says. "Because you couldn't part with it."

"Exactly. Everything else is just a distraction I had to purge from my life. You won't believe how enlightening the last few months of my life have been. All stress has disappeared and—"

"Do you, or do you not, have a cell phone?" I interject.

He frowns. "I do not."

Jesus fucking Christ. I shake my head and run a hand over my face. Of course the fruit loop gave away his cell phone—what was I expecting?

"Is there a phone anywhere here?" I ask, my volume a little louder than it should be.

"In the Elder's office."

A bang on the bedroom door causes me to tense. I keep my handgun close and gesture to the window with a finger over my lips. There isn't any more time.

Rodger goes out first, small grunts of displeasure escaping him with each move and step. Miles follows out after, quick to grab Rodger before he falls like an idiot. I slip onto the roof last and shut the window before balancing out across the shingles. It's more than a ten-foot fall to the ground, and thugs are waiting in groups around the property.

We shamble around the outside of the building, careful to stay in the shade cast by the nearby trees, lest we draw unwanted attention. Once we round the corner, I gesture to a window. Miles claws his way over and opens it up, helping Rodger the entire way. I join them and half stumble inside.

It's a study—furnished like a normal house instead of an acid-trip museum—complete with a desk, three bookshelves, and an old-fashioned vinyl player. The place looks ransacked. Books litter the floor, papers are strewn about all over, and the desk chair sits on its side in the corner. The gangbangers must've searched the room already.

"Where's the Elder's office?" I ask.

Rodger points to the door. "Out there and down the stairs. It's the far room on the first floor, but we don't have permission to go there."

"My boot up the Elder's ass is the only permission we need."

"I'm not sure if I should use the word *droll* or *gauche* when describing you, Pierce, but I know it's one or the other."

"Would you keep it down?" Miles says with an edge in his voice. "We need to listen."

I let out a single chuckle. Rodger even gets under Miles's skin. At least it isn't just me.

"There's a wine cellar with two exits," Rodger says, ignoring Miles's command. "And there's a door to the cellar in the Elder's office. We could go outside that way. It'd take us close to the garage."

Eh. It's as good a plan as any. I give Miles a curt nod and he returns it. We understand what needs to be done, and we take opposite sides of the door. Once things get quiet, we exit and cover each other's backs. The stairs are close. I go down first and motion for the other two to follow.

Gunshots ring in my ears as we reach the first story. A Cobras gunman is on the far side of the front room, crouching behind a couch and haphazardly firing in our direction without leaning his head out of cover. I didn't see him—I blame my bad eye—but now the plans have changed.

"Run," I command as I shoot at the punk trying to kill me.

Miles grabs Rodger and manhandles him down the hall. I shoot a few holes through the upholstery and hear a grunt echo in the front room. Jogging after Miles, I know we'll be surrounded in a matter of minutes—.45 handguns have a bang that carries.

Before we reach the Elder's office, we're assaulted by four guys wearing bulletproof vests. Miles and I jump into a sitting room, but Rodger slips into the room across from ours and keeps going, despite not being armed.

Where the fuck is he going? Why can't he just listen to what I'm telling him?

"What're we going to do?" Miles asks, his arm over his head as another round of bullets pelts the doorframe in front of us.

I shake my head. We need to get Rodger out of here, but we also need to stay alive. The hail of shots stops, and I hear the familiar sound of reloading. I tuck and roll across the narrow hall into the other room and Miles leaps after. A few gunmen shoot and one clips Miles's slacks, the bullet grazing his calf. He groans and limps but straightens himself quick before getting to my side.

"You okay?" I ask, my tone betraying none of my panicked emotions.

"Yeah," he breathes, nodding. "I'm fine. Let's go."

I nod and we continue on.

The house is a maze. Every room has three doors, and I swear there are two major hallways that appear to be identical, right down to the art on the walls. This is to our advantage—the gunners following us take it slower.

We enter a large study and I know in my gut it's the Elder's office. To my horror we're not the first ones to make it here.

Ten Cobras thugs are in the room waiting—one of which is Santiago—and they're holding automatic rifles and spray-n-pray Uzi submachine guns. My .45 handgun doesn't compare. They heft the weapons, and I'm certain this is the moment where I get my one-way ticket to hell, but no one fires.

"Drop your guns," Santiago commands.

I exchange a sideways glance with Miles, and we both comply. Our guns hit the wood floor with a heavy clunk. Rodger is nowhere to be seen. Did he make it outside? Did he make it to the wine cellar before anyone else made it to the office? There are a few cultists cowering in the corner, but they're not my concern—I can't even get *myself* out of this situation.

"Get your hands up."

I raise my hands. Miles follows my lead. One of the Cobras walks over with two pairs of handcuffs and, for a brief moment, I wonder if they're undercover cops. The guy cuffing me smells of booze and smoke, however, dispelling my theory before it becomes a plausible explanation. How did the Cobras know to get here so fast? Miles and I barely had time to do anything before they descended upon us.

The guy rips off my jacket and holster before torquing my arms and cuffing me tight.

I want to tell them that the Vice family doesn't pay ransom for enforcers, but that would only provoke them to shoot us both now. I wouldn't mind if they were just shooting me—my lack of giving a damn for the past few days has given me an apathetic disposition—but I can't stand the thought of them shooting Miles. I keep my mouth shut and ponder our situation.

Why keep us alive at all? Maybe they're going to question me like I questioned Malloy. I guess a river grave is as good as the gutter.

Santiago walks forward. He's the largest guy in the room, and he stands with all the brute intimidation one person could possibly have. Despite me shooting him—and Miles stabbing him—the man doesn't show any hint of slowing down. Sure, his right arm is stiff and bandaged, but I don't doubt he can use it. I should have aimed for bone.

"Where's Rodger Vice?" he asks, his voice just as deep and baritone as one would expect from a throat shaped like a bulging bicep.

"If I knew, I would have found him already," I quip, glancing around. "But I lost him during the commotion. I guess we're both out of luck."

Santiago chuckles. I smirk. He punches me in the gut with the force of a wrecking ball. I double over and hit the floor on my knees, sending a second wave of shock and pain through my paralyzed system. With a shudder I cough, my spittle laced with blood. It takes a full thirty seconds before I can take in air. I'll be feeling this for a week.

Santiago effortlessly drags me up by my shoulder, digging his fingers into my flesh. With my arms behind my back, I'm open to his brutality, but I can't find the breath needed to offer a protest.

"We don't know where Rodger is," Miles interjects.

Two Cobras grab his arms and pull him back, keeping him from the confrontation. I wish he wouldn't get involved. He's lucky Santiago isn't taking his revenge for a stabbing.

Miles shakes his head and jerks against the guys holding him. "It's true! I swear! Rodger ran off during the fighting. We were chasing him. He might still be nearby!"

The thugs exchange glances. Obviously none of them is the leader of this operation—they turn with questioning stares and hesitant motions. I'm certain their orders were *guard the Elder's room*, and now that they're presented with a logical course of action, they're confused because they can't think for themselves. Fuckin' sheep.

Santiago must have all the brawn *and* brains because he glares at the four closest to the door. "Well? You heard him. Search the area. The rest of us can handle these two."

The four funnel out.

I take in a ragged breath and find my footing. My knees are on fire, and the urge to vomit is powerful. Santiago brushes my shoulder off. "It's just business," he says. "You understand."

"Yeah," I rasp. "*Business.*"

"You got any other guns on you?"

I shake my head but gesture with my eyes down to my belt. "I have a few extra clips. That's it."

"What about your boy toy?"

"He's got the same."

Santiago reaches for my belt, and I tense, preparing for another sudden blow to the body. It never comes. Instead he takes my ammo and motions to the far door.

"You're coming with us, Pierce."

I turn my gaze to Miles. I know if I leave him alone with a group of Cobras, they'll kill him.

"He's coming too," Santiago says. "Now get moving before I need to beat some compliance into you."

CHAPTER FIFTEEN

"Did you kill Malloy?"

I don't answer.

The apartment storage room is larger than most I've seen. Boxes line the walls and chairs are stacked in the corners, but there's still room for a small forklift, an industrial chain, and five grown men. The carpet is stained black from blood, and I know, despite *some* things being stored here, that the main purpose of the room is to beat answers from barely conscious bodies.

Two Cobras thugs hold Miles while Santiago keeps his powerful grip on my shirt, the fluorescent lighting shining off his bald head. The dim atmosphere and punch to my gut leave me feeling dizzy and drained. They took us from the cult church to this apartment building, but I don't exactly know where we are. I guess it doesn't matter. I don't expect to leave.

"You should beat the fuck out of his toy," one thug says, holding up Miles's arm.

The other guy laughs and shakes his head. "Nah, you should cut off his dick—that's what that pedo deserves."

Santiago chortles as he pulls me near. I brace myself for the inevitable, but Santiago doesn't look like he's in a rush. Damn. This'll be terrible. I'd rather an inexperienced lummox like Brisko beat me to death than someone who's going to take their time. I close my eyes and try to prepare myself mentally.

Drawing me close, Santiago mutters, "You didn't kill me back at the card club."

I glance up at him. "No," I reply. "I wasn't there for you."

"I'll let you pick," he says in a frank and emotionless tone. "I'm either gonna question you or I'm gonna question the kid. Which is it?"

Heh. I see. He thinks he's doing me a favor by offering to question Miles instead—I guess it would save me one final beating, but I can't stand the thought of watching.

I shake my head. "Question me. Leave the kid out of it."

My answer must take Santiago by surprise because he hesitates, but only for a moment. "If that's what you want."

He drags me back to the forklift and wrenches my handcuffed arms over my head to hang me from the prong. It's tall enough that I have to stand on my tiptoes to prevent the metal of the cuffs from cutting into my wrists. I stare at the blood-soaked floor as Santiago rotates his head and cracks his knuckles. His bandaged arm doesn't move as well as the other, and he avoids using it.

The peanut gallery gets giddy, and both men holding Miles offer their comments.

"This'll be classic. We should take pictures."

"I can't wait until Harlan hears we killed *Nicholas Pierce*."

"No one is killing him," Santiago says. "Orders from the top."

Both men groan, but I glance up with a smirk. "Amateur move," I mutter, keeping my voice low so that only Santiago will hear. "You never admit to your victim that you're not gonna kill him. It gives them hope for holding out."

"Does it?" he whispers with a laugh. "Because I didn't get any orders relating to your toy."

I narrow my eyes into a glare as I realize I've tipped my hand. He knows I don't want any harm to come to Miles—I picked myself to get a beating rather than the kid—which means he's going to hold that against me. Fuck. He's got me by the balls. It's a no-win situation.

Then again, my mind grinds to a halt on the fact that someone in the Cobras doesn't want me dead. Why? Maybe it's because they want to do it themselves....

"Did you kill Malloy?" Santiago asks, ripping me from my thoughts.

"You know I did," I reply. "Why bother asking?"

"We haven't found his body. You never know for sure until then."

"Yeah, well, I threw him in the river while he cried like the bitch he was."

"Fine. I didn't like him much anyway. Now, tell me, where's Rodger gonna go?"

I shake my head. "Why're you so concerned about Rodger? He's barely involved in reality, let alone gang politics."

"That's the wrong answer."

Santiago busts me good in the side. I yelp and whimper, unable to curl my body around the injury. He hits like he's aiming to get to my heart through my stomach—he says he's not going to kill me, but I may die regardless if he keeps that up. Even with his off-arm, he's a force unto himself. With gasps for air, I wait for another hit. It doesn't come. Santiago lets me recover a bit…. He's done this before.

"Where's Rodger gonna go?" he repeats.

"I don't know," I answer, earnest in every regard. It took me forever to find him in the first place. He could be anywhere. I didn't even get the chance to talk to him about his future plans or the fact I was supposed to take him to the airport so he could ditch town. I'm at a loss in regards to his whereabouts, no matter how hard Santiago hits me.

Perhaps he can tell I'm truthful—he seems to take the information and contemplate other questions.

"Where's Guinevere?"

What? Why would he be asking about Guinevere? Why're they so concerned with the Vice kids? Especially the two who are the least involved?

"Don't you mean, where's *Jeremy*?" I ask.

Santiago rotates his shoulder and strikes me hard across the left side of my head. He busts the skin open over part of my eye socket and blood weeps in streams down my face, neck, and chest. I'd be worried about my eye if he had struck the right side, but my cataract eye doesn't do anything for me anyway. I might go blind on that side, but I expected it to happen at some point.

With the room spinning, I hang my head and attempt to gather my thoughts. Santiago hits me again, this time at the base of my ribs. Agony flares through my gut and into my spine. My vision goes black, and I attempt to count my breaths. Everything hurts. I can't think straight. Hot blood dribbles across my mouth. The urge to vomit is strong.

Santiago says something, but I can't distinguish the words from the white noise buzzing in my ears. He starts yelling and I go limp—my full weight suspended on my wrists.

"—that it?" I hear him ask, his voice fading into my consciousness. "Out already?"

I crane my head up and stare with my one good eye. "I'm still here...." I take in a deep breath and regret it. Inhaling is painful. "You might as well finish it," I drawl. "I don't know where the damn kids are… and I need the rest anyway." I spit blood onto his T-shirt and jeans, half doing it to provoke him and half doing it to get the copper taste out of my mouth.

Santiago offers me a smile before turning to the other two goons. "Take his toy and secure him with the others. I'll take care of this myself."

The thugs, dejected, turn on their heel and take Miles along with them. For a moment Miles struggles, but they overpower him and continue. I'm glad—there's no reason Miles should get involved in the situation—and once the door shuts I feel myself relax despite the ongoing ache radiating from my injured ribs, organs, and face.

Santiago reaches into my pants pocket, and I grit my teeth.

What the hell?

My heart rate returns to normal the moment he withdraws my cigarettes and lighter. He pulls out a single stick and places it between my bloody lips. I offer a restrained smile as he clicks on the lighter and holds it out. With unsteady movements I lean forward and inhale.

The familiar taste and pleasure eases my pain. Maybe he's doing this to make the next punch hurt even more, but I don't care. I savor the tobacco and exhale smoke through my nose.

For an extended moment, we sit in peace. I regain enough of my strength to stand back on my tiptoes and take the weight off my wrists. Using my lips I rearrange the cigarette and glance up at the other man.

"What is this?" I ask, my voice just above a whisper.

"You didn't kill Caesar or Rio," Santiago states. "You could've. It wouldn't have taken much."

That's all he says, and I give him a halfhearted nod. The two guys in the bathroom of the card club got lucky—I didn't feel like wasting them even though I should have. I guess it's to my good fortune, but now I know why Santiago sent the others away. He doesn't wanna look soft. He had to throw a few punches while everyone watched so they'd think I'd get it worse once they left.

He returns the cigarettes and lighter to my pants pocket. I like Santiago. He's a good man.

After a couple seconds, he motions to my left eye. "What's up with your thing?"

I force a single laugh. "My body hates me. Maybe it's hereditary."

"It's not a scar?"

"Nah."

"My boys on the street say Big Man Vice took a piece of your eye for failing him big."

"Your boys on the street make up bullshit because they've got too much free time on their hands."

He relaxes a bit and chuckles.

"Why aren't they going to kill me?" I ask, hoping the man will have loose lips.

Santiago shrugs.

I guess I'm out of luck. "Thanks for this," I say. Miles has rubbed off on me. Thanking people always felt cheap before—now I associate it with his good nature.

"I can't wait till this turf war is over," Santiago says with a heavy sigh. "Then we can all start doin' real business."

I nod along with the statement but stop once the words sink in. He wants the turf war to be over… so we can *all* start doing business? If the turf war ends, doesn't that mean one of the competing factions got the shaft? We can't *all* do business if one side is dead.

Despite the contradiction in his statement, I remain silent. Maybe he's speaking generally, or maybe he knows things I don't. Either way, arguing with the man is low on my agenda. Instead I enjoy his quiet company and nurse my cigarette until I get down to the butt. Santiago pulls it from my mouth and stomps it out.

"Time's up," he says. "You're gettin' locked up with the others."

"You gonna punch me one more time for good measure?"

"Yeah. And rip up your shirt a little."

"This is an expensive shirt."

"It's already got blood on it."

I force an awkward shrug. "Fair enough. Get it over with quick."

Santiago telegraphs a heavy swing. "I suggest you lean into it."

SANTIAGO HIT me so hard I forgot cursive.

I wake with a pounding in my head worse than any hangover I've experienced, and my lips stick together with dried blood. With each passing moment, I realize more and more of my body is on fire—everything hurts and even the slightest of movements triggers a domino effect of agony. I groan and shift around in my seat. I'm tied to a chair with coarse rope, my hands behind my back and my head unsupported.

My neck has a crick in it that runs as deep as Lake Superior. I straighten my back and stare out ahead of me. I'm in a room, a smaller space with old electronics, desks, and empty boxes. The dim lighting is terrible for my vision, but I overlook that the moment I realize I can still see from my right eye. Santiago may have punched me hard, but he didn't completely mangle my sight. It gives me a small bit of relief despite my situation.

The windows have thick blankets hanging from the curtain rods, blocking out the natural light. It makes it hard to know where I am in the city.

"Pierce?"

I perk up at the sound of Miles's voice. "Yeah?" I say, my throat sore.

"Are you okay?"

"I've had better days."

Someone grips my hand and squeezes down. I stiffen and force myself to take stock of the area. Miles is tied to a chair behind mine, our backs to each other, and our hands secure in the same location. He strokes my knuckles with his own, but neither of us can turn out of our chair due to the restraints.

I spot Donny on the other side of the room. He's handcuffed to a desk with half his face busted up and a hole in his arm—most likely a stabbing, but I'm not close enough to say for sure. He takes in long, deep breaths as he situates himself up against the wall. I'd say he looks a mess, but it'd be hypocritical, considering the state I'm in.

The door to the room busts open, and I jerk my attention toward it, regretting the movement mere fractions of a second after. I soldier through the pain to get an eyeful of the newcomer.

"*Jayden*," Miles gasps. "What're you doing here?"

Miles's brother walks into the room with a newfound swagger he didn't have the last time I saw him. He also has a dreamy quality to his eyes, like he's not focusing correctly, and even in my fucked-up state, I can tell he's high. Jayden crosses his arms over his chest and juts his head up high.

"Well, what do we have here?" he says. "The guys were right. You *did* come along with Pedo-Enforcer."

Three muscle-bound meatheads lumber into the cramped room after Jayden. They don't leave the proximity of the door, but they make their presence known with a tap to their knuckles and the jingle of wallet chains. I don't recognize any of them, but I suspect they're low on the totem pole if their assignment involves working with Jayden. Most of them look high as well—they're goons of the worst kind, easily controlled by substances and lacking any real skill.

"Jayden, what's going on?" Miles asks.

Jayden ambles over, his stride wide and his smile wider—the look doesn't suit him. He's the kind of guy who revels in whatever little power he's given, and it comes off as a pretentious attempt to be a tyrant. I'd laugh, but I think I'm physically incapable at the moment.

"Things are different now, Miles," Jayden says. "Surprised to see me?"

"Where have you been? I've looked all over for you."

"Why? So you could take me back to Mom?"

"Listen, I think—"

"*No, you listen!*" Jayden draws a gun from a side holster, and the Cobras in the room chortle at the confrontation. "I don't want you to help me, got it? I can take care of myself." He waves the handgun around with a weak grip and an unsteady wrist. I doubt he knows what he's doing.

Miles sighs.

Jayden uses his other hand to pull his cell phone out of his pocket. With a giddy laugh, he shuffles through the contents and then flashes the screen at Miles. I get a fleeting look and see a handful of the pictures on display. They're not pleasant—a half-second glance and I could see blood in every photo—but I recognize the area in the background.

The Little Trees Trailer Village… where their father and half brother, Lawrence, make their home.

"You keep telling me *stay in school* and *go back to Mom*, but what good will that do me, huh?" Jayden asks, his question rhetorical and his tone condescending. "Who gives a fuck about school? School didn't help me get back at Dad and Lawrence for all the terrible shit they gave us. But now look! *C'mon!* Get a good look!"

Miles remains quiet as he turns away from the phone. I can't see his face, but in my mind's eye I see him upset by the imagery. He's never been one for overt violence and heavy brutality. He's got too much empathy for that.

"The Cobras did that," Jayden says, holding his gun sideways like a "gangster" and pointing it down at Miles. "Why aren't you looking?"

"Jayden… how could you?"

"They deserved it! C'mon, look!"

He plays a video clip, this time zooming in on his gut-heavy father and out-of-control half brother. Lawrence, though large and fighting like an untrained junkyard dog, is beaten by a group of men until he hits the ground. They stomp on him afterward, laughing the entire time until finally exhausting themselves.

Jayden smiles. "We busted up Dad's house and took all the drugs he's been cookin'. We hit him hard and where it hurts." He ends the video and tucks his cell phone away. He's the literal definition of smug as he says, "They're not gonna fuck with me anymore, Miles. Not me. Not ever again. Don't you get it? I have everything I want."

"Really?" Miles asks. "Don't you realize you've turned into Dad? Is that really everything you wanted? To be just like him?"

Jayden catches his breath on his next word and goes silent. The audience of Cobras sits idle, watching the spectacle with keen eyes. I suspect they want to see someone get hurt bad—especially someone who can't defend themselves—but I don't know for sure. Their grins are a little too sadistic to be waiting around to help someone, that's for sure.

All *I* want is for everyone to be quiet. Every word yelled is another word drilled into my head, thanks to my splitting headache. I swear I can feel the reverberations of the slightest noise right down to my spine.

"Y-ya know what?" Jayden says, regaining his voice. "Fuck you, Miles. You're just some doormat who doesn't get anything from life. No one wants you. No one wants your shitty life advice that even *you* don't take. You think you know what's best for me? You're just trying to hold me back!"

I know the words hurt Miles, even if he doesn't admit it through his actions.

I lace my fingers between his. No matter what anyone says, I have his back. I want him. If everyone else is too fucking stupid to see his worth, it's their problem, not mine.

Miles curls his fingers around mine and remains quiet.

"What?" Jayden asks. He throws his arms up wide and postures like a punk. "You got nothin' to say? Of course not."

"Are you done?" I ask, cutting into the conversation and eliciting chuckles from the men by the door. "We get it. You've got a short-man's complex and unresolved daddy issues. We've all got troubles, kid. You ain't special."

Jayden shifts his full attention to me, even going so far as to walk around to the front of my chair and wave his gun in my face.

"*What's that?*" he asks, his words slurred with emotion and exaggerated through drugs. "Look who's handcuffed now. Look who's gonna get what's coming to him."

"It's a small convoluted world," I quip.

"I don't gotta take anything from you."

He smashes his heavy handgun into the side of my face. I lose a second or two of reality before regaining my composure. Everything spins. I'm pretty sure the words *Colt Rail Gun* are imprinted on my cheek, but I don't give a shit. Dazed and light-headed, I offer the kid a smirk.

"Maybe you should get one of your buddies to handle this—ya know, just like you did with all your other problems."

He hits me again, this time twice as hard and three times as reckless. I feel a tooth go loose as blood gushes from my broken gums and lip, but I spit out what I can and ignore it. I'm numb from the pain and on the verge of full-blown shock. Anything to get him away from Miles—this kid isn't worth all the effort and trouble Miles has offered, and I'll be damned before I see Jayden hurt him further.

Jayden points his gun at my forehead, and I close my eyes. I don't doubt he'll pull the trigger.

I hear the sounds of a scuffle and open my eyes to see the Cobras thugs fighting amongst each other. They rip the gun from Jayden's hand and push him back.

"What did we say?" one guy shouts. "No one's supposed to shoot him."

"He's a creep and *child molester*!" Jayden yells. "Kill this sack of shit! *Kill him!*"

The other guys shake their heads and point to the door. "Get out. He's supposed to be alive for Diver. You're not helping anything."

"What about my brother?"

"What about him? You wanna shoot him instead?"

Through my pain I ice over. Would Jayden shoot Miles? He's not thinking straight. I don't know what he's on, but it's enough to mess with his head. He *could* reason himself into the situation—all addicts have their own twisted logic that makes zero sense to the sober.

"I want him in the Cobras," Jayden says.

My body settles back into its state of torment as I realize the situation won't turn messy. The Cobra thugs shrug and continue to shove Jayden toward the door, even as he gestures to his brother.

"You know the rules," one guy says. "Take it up with Diver."

"He's my brother. He should be in the Cobras."

"We heard you. *Take it up with Diver.*"

They exit the room, slamming the door behind them once everyone is out. It's just me, Miles, Donny, and a whole host of discarded junk. I'm incapable of formulating a plan—Donny and I are half beaten to death anyway—and I wonder what this *Diver* guy has to say to me.

Diver?

The name rings a bell, but my brain is scrambled from the myriad of blows to the head. I focus on my lap and concentrate. Behind me Miles struggles with the restraints, but I push all distractions from my mind.

Diver....

I remember and smile to myself. Malloy mentioned the name in the middle of our interrogation. Diver is the man who receives all the insider information from the Vice family turncoat. Which is how they knew where Mikey would be the night of his murder....

The more I ponder the situation, the more I realize a lot of crazy bullshit is starting to add up. The Vice family and the Cobras have been exchanging blows at a rapid rate. It's not just someone in the Vice family feeding information—it's like there's someone in the Cobras who's *also* leaking info. But why? Are the two informants independent of each other, or are they both working to destroy the organizations from within?

My head can't keep facts and figures straight. Now isn't the time to ask it to compute a bunch of new information. I'm surprised I'm still conscious.

"They're gonna shoot us all execution style," Donny says from the corner of the room. "You know how these punks get. They'll throw our bodies in the lake. That's what they did to a handful of other Vice family enforcers they got a few weeks back."

Miles doesn't reply. Instead, he continues to fiddle with his handcuffs. I don't know what he's doing, but perhaps he's trying to escape? But then what? I don't even know where we are. It would be suicide to try and fight our way out. We have no firearms, and we're in the heart of a Cobras hideout.

With a long groan of pain, Miles jerks his arm around. I want to crane my head back, but I can't will myself to do so through the agony.

"What're you doing?" I ask.

Miles ignores my question. He sucks in a breath through his teeth as he twists and squirms in his chair. After another grunt I feel some of the restraints get tight and then loosen.

"*There*," he says through a heavy sigh. "We need to get outta here."

CHAPTER SIXTEEN

MILES SLIPS from the last of his restraints and stands up. I turn halfway to see him undoing the rough rope around my arms.

"How did you get out?" I ask.

His handcuffs dangle from one wrist and the other is raw and damaged. Miles squeezed his narrow hand through the metal ring, using blood as lubricant by the looks of it. That's a difficult ordeal—I don't know many guys who could do it without ripping off their thumb—but Miles went through the process like he had done it before.

The ropes go slack, and I take a moment to gather my strength. I don't recover like I used to. My body screams at me—telling me to lie down and recuperate—but that's not an option.

Before I stand, Miles walks around and gives me the once-over. With a furrowed brow he runs a hand up my neck and rubs a finger across my chin, clearing away blood. I don't resist when he leans down and locks his mouth with mine. Now isn't the time… but we might not get another chance. His forceful motions sting—he pulls me in deeper with a hand gripping the back of my neck—and I grimace when he pulls away.

"I'm sorry," he breathes.

"Don't be. I like the taste of you more than I like the taste of blood."

"Can you stand?"

"We'll find out."

Miles replies with a curt nod and turns his attention to Donny. While the two fiddle with Donny's restraints, I push up from my chair and wobble to my feet. Nothing makes you feel old like struggling against gravity. I grab my head and try to stop the spinning, but I know it's futile. I can walk, and I half stumble over to the windows.

I need to know where we are.

Peeking past the heavy blankets, I glance outside. I suspect it's late afternoon, and once my vision adjusts, I take in a few key landmarks.

We're in the projects—subsidized apartment complexes built one after another in the same area. They're notorious for having more problems than a season of *Judge Judy*, and I'm not surprised the Cobras would call one building home.

Miles rummages around in the contents of the room, careful to keep the volume down. There're thugs all over the place, and drawing any unnecessary attention could end our escape. I appreciate that Miles learns quick and takes my advice to heart. Some flings of mine—I shoot Donny a sideways glance—could never seem to remember the basic rules of the game.

Before I step away from the window, I spot another interesting detail. The police are outside but… they're not here to do their job. They chat with a few Cobras, laughing and pointing to a run-down apartment complex down the road. It's the kind of casual relationship that makes me suspect there are dirty cops on the force.

"Miles," I say. "Come look at this."

He frees Donny from his handcuffs, thanks to a few thin metal pieces of a discarded computer, and rids himself of his own dangling pair. Miles pats off the other man and jumps to my side, a questioning look on his face. I motion to the window. He glances through the narrow sliver of space I've opened to the outside.

"Cops?" he asks. "Do you think we could run out and ask for help?"

"Keep watching."

Miles narrows his eyes. "They're cooperating."

"Right."

"I didn't know Cobras had allies in the Noimore Police Department."

"Didn't you say the detectives asked you to hunt down Nick's enforcers?"

Miles nods.

Damn. Something *is* going on. Something big. But are all the cops in on this? I think back to the handful I know. Detective Ambers isn't like that. She'd never turn dirty for some street punks…. Would she?

"Which detectives asked you to bring guys like me in?" I ask.

"The lead detective. He said his name was Detective Strout?"

"Not Detective Ambers?"

"No. Not her. She didn't make deals like that. Every time I talk to her, she mentions I should stop calling in tips…. That being an informant for the police is risky."

I chuckle. "Smart woman."

But that means not *all* the cops are in on this. I almost wish I had a phone so I could take pictures. It would be advantageous to know which cops are good and which are going to stab me in the back. Then again, I don't want anything to do with the cops, so avoiding them all is my best solution.

"How're we going to get out of here?" Donny asks. He leans against the far wall, his condition as bad as mine, but he's a decade younger. He'll survive.

Miles turns to me for the answer. I shake my head.

"We don't have many options," I say, returning the blanket to its original position.

"Do you think there are guys outside the door?" Miles asks.

"Yeah. At least one. Maybe two. They'll be there until Diver gets here. I'm willing to bet the door's locked too, but we shouldn't risk checking."

Miles goes silent as he mulls over the information. I reach into my pants pocket and pull out my cigarettes and lighter—a motion of habit—but I stop the moment I realize what I have. Santiago should've taken everything from me. I'm struck by an idea.

"Get some of those boxes," I command. "Donny, you able to throw a punch?"

He shakes his head. "I'm dizzy, but maybe." He rotates his arms and flexes.

Peppy son of a bitch. I envy his fortitude.

Miles complies with my order and does so in a quick fashion. It's a good thing one of us isn't half limping to the grave or else we'd be in big trouble. Once he has a decent pile, he turns to me with a lifted eyebrow.

"What're we doing?"

I toss him the lighter. "Light it up. We'll get some smoke blowing and get the drop on the guys who enter to investigate."

"What about the fire alarm?"

"I'm banking on it. Maybe in the commotion, we'll be able to duck out of here."

Miles hardens his expression and stares at me for a long moment. He's about to ask for something unreasonable. But what? I grit my teeth.

I know. He wants to save his scumbag brother. I can't believe he's still worried about that little stain on humanity.

"I want to take Jayden," he says, confirming all my deductions.

"Leave him," I reply. "He doesn't want your help."

Miles glares down at the floor, visibly conflicted by some argument raging in his mind. I don't know what fuels Miles's need to help his brother, and I probably never will. As far as I'm concerned, Jayden's a grown-ass man with his own grown-ass problems. Shouldering all the extra responsibility of correcting someone else's life is more than Miles owes any of his siblings. I admire the dedication and willingness to accept the challenge, but right now it jeopardizes everything. We might all get shot thanks to Jayden's douche-baggery.

"I'll go, then," Miles says. "You and Donny can make for the exit."

"You would risk everything to get him out of here?"

"I can't leave him."

I roll my eyes and rake my fingers through my hair. I can't believe Miles is *this* adamant. He must know this is suicide. He must know he can't do this alone.

I grab him by the shirt and force his attention to me. "We don't split up. I'll help you get your brother, but this is the last time. After this he makes his own choices and suffers the consequences, understand? You can't save him forever."

Miles nods in a slow and deliberate manner. "I understand. Thank you, Pierce."

I release him and exhale. Donny glances between the two of us with a look of realization in his eyes, but he doesn't voice his discovery. Instead he clears his throat and motions to the boxes. Miles turns and lights the pile on fire as he scoots it closer to the door.

While the tiny flames lick at the cardboard, I glance around to find an impromptu weapon. Anything will do, so long as it's heavy. Miles and Donny have the same idea. The junk gathered in the corners is mostly small and flimsy, but I find a sturdy lamp with a thick metal body, and Miles takes the leg to a busted aluminum patio chair.

I motion him over, and we exchange objects. I need the lighter one.

Donny comes up empty-handed and instead takes a spare box to fan the fire. It spreads throughout the cardboard, and smoke gathers above it. With heavy gusts of air, the smoke filters under the door. Miles and I get on either side of the doorframe. I want to help out in the fighting, but I know I have one good hit in me and then I'm out.

Sure enough, the door unlocks and opens. Miles swings first and connects with the man's face, breaking his nose in an explosion of blood and a sick crunch of bone. The man stumbles back, blind, and I follow up the assault with another bash to the head. He collapses to the ground with a heavy thud.

The fire alarm pierces the still atmosphere of the apartment complex with its incessant ringing.

Adrenaline pumps into my system, soothing my pain like a powerful drug. I'm stiff and weak, but at least I'll be able to get through the discomfort. All I can do now is hope the feeling lasts until we've made our way out of the apartment.

We enter the hall and Donny veers left. "I'm going," he says. "You two can find whoever you're looking for on your own."

I motion him to leave. I didn't think he would want to stay—most men aren't as altruistic as Miles. Donny gives me one final nod before taking off down the corridor.

I take a look around and sigh. The hall is short. To the left is the living room, and to the right is the front door leading deeper into the complex. I catch sight of Donny opening the window in the living room and leaping out. We're on the first story and going out seems like the best plan, considering the number of people who live in the projects. Donny looks like an escapee from Guantanamo Bay, but I'm sure that's not the craziest thing the people in this area have seen today.

Miles heads right. I follow, cursing Jayden's existence under my breath.

We enter the main hall, and my nose is accosted with the odors of filth. A few druggie bums mill about as they come down from a high. They give us odd glances as we hustle by, and I take note of the graffiti on the walls instead of paintings or decorations. One man, dressed in a hat and decent shirt, is half asleep at the foot of a locked door. I stop in front of him and brandish my silver chair leg. He cringes.

"Give me your hat and shirt," I shout over the alarm.

He nods, his face set in a permanent daze, and sheds his clothing. I toss my ripped and bloody shirt at his feet before pulling on his clothes. Now I don't look like such an obvious target. Miles approves of the change and strips himself of his outer shirt, leaving him with just a tank top and slacks. The high-class wardrobe of the Vice family is not shared among the gangbangers of the Cobras.

Miles motions to the lobby.

I limp after him and suppress the need to vomit. I'm guessing I suffered a mild concussion, but I'm no medical expert. All I want is to lie down. I wonder how often those exact thoughts are the last thing someone thinks before they die.

Miles halts before crossing the threshold of the larger room. I stop behind him and take in the scene. A few younger men and a couple of tween women are glancing up at the ceiling. They all have snake tattoos visible somewhere on their person, and I'm guessing everyone who lives in this apartment is associated with the Cobras on some level, but they don't appear to be the normal thugs. They're dressed in casual clothing and don't have any firearms.

"What's that noise?" one girl asks.

A man shrugs. "I don't know. The fire alarm?"

"Do you see a fire?"

"No."

"Why's it going off, then?"

This isn't the mass exodus I had imagined, but I guess *not giving a damn about anything* is an acceptable response as well.

"Get one of their phones," I whisper.

They've all got one, and they pass them around to show off pictures or potential text messages. The smoke in the room and their need to laugh over the sounds of the alarm tell me they're buzzed enough not to notice a phone disappearing for a few moments.

Miles places his dented lamp on the ground and walks out with a confused look on his face. "What's going on?" he asks.

The men and women of the lobby answer him with a collective shrug. They accept Miles's presence and return to their activities without further question. I guess they think of him as one of their own, considering his age. I suspect I wouldn't have blended as well.

Miles swipes one of the closer phones and walks back around the corner. I take it and stare at the pink bunny wallpaper, my mind blanking.

Who am I gonna call?

I'm certain someone in the Vice family circle is a traitor and working with the Cobras. I could call Nick—there's no way *he's* the traitor—but it's not like he's going to personally come and help me get out of here. Plus, he might order me to keep or kill Jayden if he learns of the specifics.

Who else is there? Guinevere is gone. Most of my associates aren't around. Donny isn't an option because he already left. I shake my head as I reach the bottom of my trustworthy list and find myself contemplating names like Brisko or Jeremy. If I call Jeremy, he's gonna want compensation, which leaves me with few alternatives.

I dial Brisko and pray his low-IQ persona isn't a shtick to hide his turncoat agenda.

"Hello?" Brisko answers, confusion in his voice.

"Brisko. It's Pierce. I need you in the downtown projects now."

"Pierce? This a new number? What's that ringing I hear?"

"Did you hear me, Brisko? Never mind everything else."

I wait. He breathes through his mouth, exhaling on the phone's mic in irritating bursts.

"Okay," he finally replies. "I'll get in my car and be there."

"Take Forty-Third Street. I'll meet you there, understand?"

"Yeah."

I hang up. We have a ride out of this scumhole, and someone knows where we are. All we need now is Jayden....

Miles takes the phone back and drops it off on the table in the lobby. The girl who lost it snatches it up and pokes at the screen. Everyone glances up the moment they hear the sound of fire engines drawing near. The alarm will be off soon. I motion for Miles to return.

"We should hurry," I say.

He heads to the stairs, and I walk to the elevator. We meet back up on the second story.

There are more people here than on the first story. Men, women, hookers, a fair number of teenagers—the place is an odd collection of individuals. Unlike the tweens downstairs, they watch the streets through windows and balconies, keeping steady eyes on the disturbance down below.

The Cobras aren't known for their order and sophistication. Miles and I walk among the residents of the apartment without hassle. I doubt many of them know who we are, but just in case, I keep the hat brim low on my face. Occasionally blood drips down onto my new shirt, but it's a drab thing that absorbs color.

The alarms cease. I suspect we won't have the cover of confusion any longer.

We make our way through the square-shaped hallway, all around the building, and a piece of me wonders if Jayden is even here anymore. I'm ready to tell Miles we need to leave when I hear Jayden's distinct voice ringing from an open apartment door.

"—and then, he, uh, doubles over, right?"

A round of laughter follows his words.

"It was crazy! Just one blow! You should have been there!"

The laughter that continues is a cacophony of mingling voices, emotions, and hysteria. They're drunk, high, or a combination of both. Nothing else explains the boisterous tones of the chuckling hyenas. It's a good thing this place wasn't *actually* on fire. They might've all laughed themselves to the grave.

Miles turns to me and I shrug. There must be at least ten men inside the apartment with Jayden. We're not breaking in and kidnapping anyone in that situation. What does Miles want me to do? I'm no miracle worker.

Through my pounding headache, I take stock of the people around us. One woman—a streetwalker if I ever saw one—is attempting to bum a cigarette off a man down the hall. I motion her over by flashing my full pack. She makes her way to my side and smiles, though the bags under her eyes tell me she's fatigued.

"You got a smoke?" she asks.

"I'll give you the whole pack if you do me a favor," I say.

She glares and folds her arms over her chest. "I'm not workin' right now. And it's more expensive than a pack anyway."

"I want you to call some guy outta this room and nothing more. Get his attention and get him out here. Done deal."

She stares at the open door and returns her gaze to me. "That's it? All the smokes are mine?"

"All of them."

"Fine. What name am I callin'?"

I turn to Miles and pull him close.

"Tell him they let you out," I say, keeping my voice low. "Tell him you want to talk about joining the Cobras. How you think he's right. How you liked that he roughed up your father and brother. But tell him you want to talk outside. I'll be waiting."

Miles nods, but he fidgets with his hands and jams them in his pockets like he can't decide on something.

I don't know if it's the best idea I've ever had, but Jayden is a dumb fuck. He's also not thinking straight. If Miles manages this, we can get outside and away from the others, which is the only way we'll pull this "kidnapping" off.

"Okay," he says. "I'll meet you at the back side of the building."

He leans in close and I stop him cold. "*Not here*," I growl. "Never in front of people like this." They're the enemy.

Miles takes a step back. "Right. Sorry. I'll handle this."

"Good."

CHAPTER SEVENTEEN

THE HOVEL of an apartment complex is nicer from the outside. No graffiti, no trash piles or rooms stuffed to the brim with garbage. It's a pleasant sight if you give it a fleeting glance.

I wait out around back, missing my cigarettes and feeling the itch to flee the area. What's taking Miles so long? He should've been right behind me. I try to relax, but I know what'll happen if he doesn't show up in the next five minutes. I'm going to march back in and get tied down all over again, this time in a more secure location with broken kneecaps. I don't look forward to it.

The cops chase the firefighters away after they do some hasty investigations. No one stands to gain anything from allowing the authorities to rummage through the place. It's a hive of drugs, scum, and illicit activities, giving this entire neighborhood its bad reputation even though I can see other apartment complexes just trying to make their way in life without trouble.

"We got a problem, Diver," a man says, his voice demanding my attention.

I walk to the corner of the building and crane my head around. I spot the men talking—they're gruffer than the rest and more organized to boot.

"What happened?"

The man speaking—the man I assume is Diver—isn't what I thought he'd be. Unlike the others, who could throw down in a fight at a moment's notice, Diver is missing his left arm. Sure, he's muscular, but it takes away from the imposing aura to have a phantom limb.

I've seen guys without an arm before.

Heroin use. It's always heroin use.

One night they'll shoot up and miss their vein—next day they'll have an infection that swells their hand and oozes pus from the needle mark. If you don't get it treated, the infection gets worse until, at the final stages, the doctors have to amputate. I'd bet money it happened to Diver. I'm surprised he's still an important member of the Cobras' hierarchy, considering most druggies with one arm aren't respected much on the streets.

I don't catch any more of the conversation, however. They go to talking low and quick. I suspect they're telling Diver the bad news about my escape.

I duck back around the building and attempt to blend in with the surroundings. Hiding in plain sight is often the best way to go about not getting caught. No one's going to look for me leaning against the outside of the apartment complex. They'll scour the darkest nooks and crannies before they try searching the groups of hobos out front.

The crunch of feet on gravel gets me tense. I bunch up my shoulders close to my sore neck and I tip my hat to cover most of my face.

To my relief, Miles and his brother are the ones to round the far corner. They're in a heated discussion, but they don't appear to be fighting. That's good. Now isn't the time for arguing. Miles should be saying whatever he needs to say in order to get his brother away from the others.

They walk along the narrow alley between buildings, their attention focused on each other. I don't even know if Miles has spotted me yet, but I yank off my belt and prepare myself for a struggle. I'm in no mood to brawl, but it can't be helped.

The moment they draw near, I lunge and wrap the leather strap around Jayden's neck. He jabs his elbow back without warning, catching me in my bruised gut. I let go of the belt, but Miles is quick on the uptake and wrestles with his confused brother, betrayal on Jayden's face as clear as the sun in the sky.

I attempt to restrain Jayden, but my efforts earn me a kick to the side and a boot to the inner thigh. I stumble back, reaching for my .45 and realizing I don't have it.

I feel naked without my gun.

Miles's grip holds firm as he wrenches his brother back by the neck. It's an odd form of affection to choke another man out "for his own good," and the thought causes me to chuckle. After a handful of stressful seconds, Jayden falls limp in his brother's arms.

"We're not gonna have much time," I say. "A few minutes at the most before he wakes."

Coated in sweat, Miles gulps down air and nods. "How're we going to get him to the street?"

"I don't know. I get his feet, you get his arms?"

My body is killing me. The thought of carrying this kid two blocks is a nightmare.

"We're gonna get a lot of unwanted attention carrying an unconscious body," Miles says with a sardonic expression etched into his exhausted features.

"Look. I'm out of ideas. You got anything?"

Miles glances around. His eyes go wide when he spots the large trash bins on the side of the road. He jogs out to one and wheels it back, nonchalant, before dumping the contents out in the alley. I give him a questioning stare, and Miles motions for me to lift Jayden and dump him inside.

I let out a genuine laugh. I love the idea of throwing this kid into a trash can.

With a grunt and huff, I heft the kid up and over. He falls to the bottom of the grimy bin with a thunk. I grab some of the loose trash bags and throw them over top of his body. I do it in part because I hate his guts, but also to disguise the fact he's there, should anyone look inside. Once situated, we wheel the trash can out of the alley and down the street.

It's odd to be taking a trash can far from its home, but not as odd as dragging an unconscious person out in the open. No one calls the cops, and we stop on Forty-Third Street without exerting ourselves.

Not a bad plan.

BRISKO IS like a family dog—he's there when you need him, and he doesn't understand a word you're saying when you spill your soul and reveal your deepest woes.

He's also a decent driver. It's his one redeeming skill.

"Take us to Merrymore and Poppy Cotton," I say. "That's where my car is. I need something from the inside."

Jayden and Miles are in the far backseat of the van. Jayden falls in and out of consciousness—not because of choking him out, but because he's coming down from more than one substance at a time. He slurs his words and mumbles things in his sleep, but it's too hard to distinguish. Miles keeps him close and offers reassurance. He's too damn nice for his own good. Jayden doesn't deserve the attention or affection.

Brisko keeps his eyes on the road, his head-sized hands choking the steering wheel.

The sun sets in the distance, disappearing behind a looming black storm cloud. Rays of red and purple signal the dying of the light, but it's quick and depressing to watch. It reflects my mood well, considering everything I've been through. There are some days I wish I could wholesale forget. Today would be one of them.

I close my eyes, and by the time I open them, we're halfway into town and near our destination. Where does the time go? Or maybe I'm more exhausted than I thought I was.

Brisko turns the van wide and parks it alongside my dark red Landau. I reach for my keys and realize Santiago, or some other thug in the Cobras, must have them. I let out a long and painful sigh. I'm gonna have to break a window.

I step out of the van and gather a rock from the edge of a nearby property. I glance about, certain that Cobras must be in the area, and listen to the sounds of a sleepy city. Nothing. Once certain I won't be attacked, I return to my task and pick the rear right window.

The glass breaks after the third strike, shattering into a million pieces and raining onto the sidewalk and backseat. My hand gets cut a couple times, but I don't care. I'm more disappointed it took me three swings to break glass. My arm isn't in the shape it should be.

With an exhale I snatch up my cell phone. I scroll through the messages—through the death threats left by Anita—and go straight to the more recent calls. I take note of a number I've never seen before. I dial it back and wait.

"Hello?" a man answers.

Rodger.

"Where are you?" I bark. I realize I should keep my voice down, and I clear my throat. "You're not safe."

"I walked to the hotel next to the country club, and I've been relaxing ever since."

"Have you told anyone where you are?"

"No."

What a crazy, lucky son of a bitch.

I guess the Cobras don't know my vehicle. It might have something to do with the fact I switch between a handful on a regular basis, but still. *If* they had come for my car and found my phone, they could have found Rodger in a heartbeat. Why wouldn't he seek safety?

I rub my good eye and shake my head. "What is your problem? You couldn't think of a better place to go? Why not *go home*? Your father is looking for you as we speak. Your mother is calling me nonstop."

"Oh, I'm not ready to see my parents yet," he replies, his blasé demeanor shining through.

"Why not?"

"I need to find my fiancée before I return."

It takes a life of luxury and leisure for someone to be so detached from reality. After a day of running from gunmen and hiding from gangbangers, he's decided he needs to find his woman before seeking a place of safety—and by "find" I mean "wait until someone else finds her for him." Rodger's bank account might be impressive, but his mental debit card has insufficient funds.

"Which room are you in?" I ask. "I'm coming to get you."

"I'm in room 1-A. It's a lovely little thing with a bay window and a—"

I end the call.

Tucking my cell phone into my pocket, I walk back to the van and slide into the front passenger seat. Brisko turns to me, and I point to the road leading to the hotel. He takes off.

"You okay, Miles?" I call to the back.

"Yeah," he replies. "Don't worry about me. I'm just looking after Jayden."

"All right. Let me know if you need anything."

I DON'T want to go home. The Cobras have never hit my flat, but I'm nervous by default. I've slept in the same bed for months now; it's not unreasonable to think someone could be staking the place out, waiting for their moment to pounce.

And, since I have Rodger in tow, I need a bigger place.

"Where're we going?" Rodger asks.

I suck in a long yawn and motion to the road ahead of us. "I know a place. It's a beachside house—those places that rich kids rent when they want to go camping but they can't stand the thought of getting dirty."

"A house on the beachfront of Lake Michigan? Beautiful. The lake is a mirror of the sky at sunset and daybreak."

I grab Brisko by the arm and point to the nearest street corner. "Stop there."

The beast of a man grunts and pulls the car up to the place I indicated. There's a phone booth sitting idle. I grab a few coins and step out of the van, greeted by a chill gust of wind. I miss my jacket, but I carry on regardless. For some unknown reason, Rodger jumps out of the vehicle as well.

The pay phone booth doesn't have a door. I step in, grab the receiver, plunk in a couple coins, and hesitate. Again, who am I gonna call? If I call Nick, he's going to demand I return Rodger—and I know Rodger will fight the decision the entire way. Plus I don't want to deal with his wife, and Rodger is safe with me for the time being.

I dial Jeremy. At least me and him have a side project going on, and I need to confirm everything is going down according to schedule.

The phone rings twice before Jeremy answers.

"Yes?" he says.

"Jeremy," I reply, breathing a sigh of relief. "I need to talk to you."

"Pierce? You're… calling me? What a pleasant surprise."

"Yeah. Listen. I found your brother. I'm going to hide out with him for the time being. Just until I can find his fiancée or I go to see Nick, whichever is sooner."

For a moment all I hear is chortling. I'm not sure what's so funny or why he would get a kick out of my irritated tone and terse speech, but whatever floats his boat, I guess.

"You're always so impressive, Pierce. I guess it shouldn't shock me anymore." He pauses for a moment before adding, "Did you say fiancée? As in, my brother is *getting* married or *has gotten* married?"

"Do we really need to do this? You know the definition of words."

I shouldn't be so curt with him, but I'm in no mood for anything. Fuck everything and everyone that's stopping me from recovering. It's not worth it. In a week and a half, I'll be skipping town anyway. What does it all matter? Jeremy can be pissed all he wants.

"Sometimes my brother is flighty," Jeremy replies. "I just wanted to make sure he hasn't married anyone without a prenup. Or, at the very least, without Mother's approval."

"Everything still a go for Harlan's fight scene?"

"As far as I know, yes."

"Good. I'll be taking care of it like we planned."

"Pierce, can I speak with my brother for a moment?"

I turn on my heel and motion Rodger close. He ambles over, not a care on his mind, and I hand him the phone. "It's Jeremy," I say. "He wants to talk."

I leave the brothers to their discussion and return to the van. Brisko is tapping his fingers to the music on the radio and singing a woman's song with the voice of an orangutan. Its happy pop beat intensifies my already debilitating headache. Brisko doesn't notice—perhaps he doesn't care—and continues on as though he were the next sensational idol.

I hate being around so many people. This is why I live alone in a flat. Everyone's got a tick, and they all rub me the wrong way.

It takes Rodger an eternity to finish his call. When he gets back to the van, Brisko stops his singing, and I glare at Rodger. "What took you?"

"I tried calling Luna at all her usual haunts, but she's not there." Rodger slumps back into his seat and stares out the window with a vacant expression.

Who names their kid *Luna*? They might as well have gone all the way and named her *Moonbeam*.

"Was she part of your cult?" I ask.

"She's the Elder's daughter. And it isn't *a cult*. It's a beautiful community that helps you understand the fabric of life."

Yeah. Moonbeam would've been an appropriate name.

I signal Brisko to continue. He drives the van up the long road out of the city and heads straight for the "camping cabins." I've rented one or two in the past, whenever I've felt insecure about the safety of my living quarters, and I appreciate the place, not because of the fancy view, but because few people are in the area.

When I leave Noimore, I'm going to find the smallest, most Podunk town on the map and live there for the rest of my days. Anyplace with a population of forty or less. Anything to get away from people.

I suppose I'll have to go into a major city from time to time to get my rocks off, but that's a trade-off I'm willing to make. It's more acceptable to be out and open these days—I'll find a gay bar and buy a couple drinks….

I laugh to myself when I imagine the scenario. I've never been a guy to go to a bar for a purpose other than getting shit-faced. That'll be different.

Brisko pulls the van into the cabin's driveway, and I slide out, my legs weak. The camping houses are locked with codes instead of keys, and when I set up the reservation, they gave me this week's numbers. I like this place. They have my info on file, and I don't have to deal with anyone in person.

I get up to the front door, type in the code—twice, as my vision is blurred—and stumble inside. Brisko comes in after, and I take the man by the arm and pull him aside.

"Watch the Asian kid," I say, my tone and posture weak. "Don't let him leave no matter what."

"Miles?" he asks.

"Not *Miles*. His brother. Watch his brother. I don't care if you need to tie him down, just make sure he goes nowhere. Understand?"

"Yeah. I got ya. I'll make sure he stays."

With my last bit of strength, I walk to the back master bedroom and shamble to the bed. I toss off my stolen hat and shirt, disgusted with the aromas that linger on my body, but I can't muster the *giving a damn* to do anything about it. I throw myself on the bed and roll into the covers, enjoying the soft caress of down-filled blankets.

Nothing beats the quiet of a house far from civilization.

Sometimes the natural music of the city can be pleasant, but lately it reminds me of gunshots and violence. All I want is to relax—to feel like myself again. Why am I never content? Something is off and I can't quite fix it.

The coolness of the room envelops me. I think the bed has pillows, but I don't need them. Everything is as it should be.

Except for the sun.

I cringe and roll over, shielding my face from the heat. The coolness is gone....

So soon?

I open my eyes and meet the afternoon light streaming in through the windows. I push myself up onto my arms and gawk, stunned that I somehow slipped into sleep and then back into consciousness without even realizing it.

How long have I been out?

I rub my eyes and feel the crustiness of a deep slumber. I'm starving. My body aches and trembles, urging me to return to the bed and sleep once more. The door opens and I flinch away. Miles steps into the room with a plate in hand.

My heart rate accelerates, and I glance around in mild confusion. It's nothing fancy—the wood of the floor and walls is kept bare to highlight its natural beauty. The curtains, blankets, and rugs are all white. I assume it's so the place feels clean and modern, but I don't know for sure. I didn't take note of the details when I entered earlier, and I give myself a moment to ponder them.

Miles walks over and takes a seat on the bed next to me.

"Here," he says, holding the plate out. "You hungry?"

I spy a peanut butter and jelly sandwich. I eat half and feel the weight of exhaustion settle itself back onto my being. I lie down and stare at the ceiling.

"You gonna be okay?" Miles asks.

I nod. It's all I can do.

"I'll shut the curtains."

I want to tell him thank you, but by the time I gather the energy to do so, the curtains are drawn and the room sits dark.

I slip into sleep once more.

CHAPTER EIGHTEEN

I WAKE on my stomach, my internal clock ringing at the crack of dusk.

It's night. I know it to be true. It's time for me to get up.

A pair of hands runs the length of my back. I stiffen and arch up, but whoever it is pushes me back down with gentle motions.

"It's just me," Miles murmurs.

He straddles the back of my legs and runs his hands over me a second time, raking his fingertips across the skin. I shudder beneath him, confused but enjoying his touch. He grazes one of my injuries—a bruise on my ribs—and I gasp. Miles pulls away and avoids the spot, keeping his kneading close to my spine. Once the dull pain subsides, I relax into the caressing. I'd purr if I could.

"You've been sleeping for a long time," he says in a low and soothing voice.

"I needed it."

In comparison my voice is gruff and rusty. It doesn't help that I speak into the blankets, half lying in a pool of my own sweat.

I attempt to stir and get up, but Miles urges me down with his hands. "I should shower," I say.

"I don't mind."

I rest back on the bed. "How's your brother?"

"He's upset that we don't have any hits for him. And that he can't leave. And that we kidnapped him. He's in a constant state of… anger. To put it mildly."

"I can imagine," I drawl.

"I'm gonna try talking to him once he's detoxed a little."

"Heh. Good luck."

Miles massages my shoulders and the nape of my neck. I moan into the bed. He's good at pleasing me, that's for sure. I sigh and stretch my arms above my head. I get hard thinking about his affections, and I realize I'm still wearing my pants. Damn. I hate sleeping in clothes. I must've been desperate.

"Did you rest at all?" I ask, wondering about the day that took place without me.

"Yeah. This is a nice cabin."

"I enjoy it."

"I thought you liked the city more."

"Depends on my mood. I'm not feeling the city life much lately."

"You're planning on leaving, aren't you?" Miles's tone is more accusatory than anything. He doesn't stop with his hands, but I feel the shift in his mood. I tense under him. I don't want to have this conversation.

"Nothing's set in stone," I say. "Whatever happens, I'll make sure you're taken care of."

Miles stops his hands. For a moment the room is mute. I hear him sigh, and he leans down to kiss my back. "Think about it long and hard, okay?" he whispers. "I'd rather have you with me than be *taken care of.*"

I don't reply. He deserves something better than me—he just doesn't realize it. Once he has a fat stack of cash, a lot of his problems will disappear. He can have the life he always wanted, and I can go die off in the wilderness somewhere, most likely from lung cancer. It's the ideal scenario.

I sit up on my elbows. "I gotta piss."

Miles gets off me and I roll to the side. My bladder can't take much more. I feel like a racehorse that's been holding it for over twenty-four hours. I hustle to the bathroom and unzip my pants. I wait a long moment—being hard makes it difficult to unload—but eventually I groan in sweet release.

I finish and go to the sink to wash up. My skin has a fine layer of sweat and grime. I need a shower.

I shed the last of my clothing and step into the spacious stall. I flip on the water—it's freezing and I jump away—but the heat comes within seconds. I splash and scrub my body clear of the drunken hobo scent and replace it with whatever lavender bullshit the cabin rental place stocks.

Despite feeling clean, my body still aches. My injuries won't disappear as easily as they did on Miles. I grab a towel and dab the water away, careful not to touch anything sensitive. I toss the towel when finished and walk back into the bedroom.

Miles waits for me on the bed, leaning back with his legs spread. He's dressed in casual attire—he must've gone out for clothes at some point because everything he has is brand-new—and I enjoy the way his jeans hug his thighs and his T-shirt clings to his lithe body. His short hair is slicked back, and he has a sleek handsome look about him that's hard to describe. It's suave. I like it.

Miles catches me staring. He widens his legs farther and motions to the bed with a tilt of his head. I walk over, crawl onto the mattress, and take a seat with my back against the headboard. Miles jumps onto my legs, his knees on either side of my hips, and pins me back, forcing his tongue into my mouth.

His rough urgency excites me. If I had known he was so pent-up, I would've rushed through my shower.

He tastes good—minty—and I suck on his tongue. Miles presses hard against me, trapping my head in place and scraping his teeth against mine. I tilt to the side to get deeper and enjoy the way he offers soft moans with each new position. I turn away and breathe before licking his lips. The look in his eye is exhilarating.

Miles pulls off his shirt and tosses it to the floor. I run my hands down his sides and circle my thumbs on his firm flesh.

"Wanna ride me hard?" he asks. "I've been thinking about it for the past few days."

I chuckle, my breaths husky. "I always wanna ride you hard. But I don't think I can do it tonight." Then again, maybe he should ask me halfway through, when I'm not thinkin' straight and all I can feel is my throbbing cock.

"What do you wanna do, then?" he asks, unbuttoning his pants and exposing the fact he isn't wearing anything underneath.

My mouth goes dry as I run my tongue along my teeth. I love his eagerness. He's erect and leaking onto the front of his jeans. I don't have much time left with Miles, and the fact hits me hard. My mind goes to some odd places when I'm aroused, and I decide that tonight we'll do something different.

"Lie down on your back," I command.

Miles jumps off me and removes his jeans. He gets back on the bed and complies, propping one leg up and flattening the other. I crawl on top of him, trailing my tongue and teeth across his stomach, chest, and neck, before flipping around and positioning myself over his mouth, his own erection in front of me, twitching and wanting.

Sixty-nining with a guy has never been on the top of my to-do list, but I want the experience of tasting Miles—I like that's he's tender and beneath me, his flesh inviting.

I lower my hips and he reaches up with his mouth to take my cock, licking the top and underside as I get situated. Once down he swallows me to his gagging point and holds my hips with his trembling hands. The warm chasm of his mouth is slick and welcoming. I thrust slow and deep, and he angles himself to better allow me access to his throat. He's a good boy—I love it when he does what I want without me telling him.

I reward him by dragging my lips along his shaft. My heavy breathing gets him shuddering, and I take my time. I don't know if he's ever had another man's mouth, but I intend to make sure he remembers this.

With gentle motions I cup his balls and massage them between my fingers. I've done stuff like this in the past, but it's been a long while and the newness of it gets me worked up more than before.

I lick the tip of his dick and take the precome in one go. Miles whimpers—he's desperate. How long has it been since he came? I don't focus on it much with his tongue circling me, though. I thrust faster and deeper, pushing the limits on what he can take without gagging to the point of pain.

Miles spreads his legs and trembles. If he could, I'm sure he'd be begging. I close my mouth around him and suck down to the base of his full erection, thankful he trims his hair. The salty flesh and heat of it all tastes erotic. Precome and saliva slick my mouth. I caress his cock with my tongue and I toy with the rim of the edge, knowing full well I get a whole new range of feeling whenever it's played with on me.

His moaning around my cock is heaven. He imitates my strokes and brushes the head of my dick with his tongue. It's my turn to moan into him, and I bite back the urge to fuck his face hard. I do ease myself all the way to the base, slow enough to avoid him kicking back the intrusion to his throat. The grip around my cock is tight the deeper I go. His throat is untested, and I enjoy the feeling of it stretching to accommodate me.

I pick up the pace with my mouth, careful to avoid cutting him with my teeth but getting it close enough to "threaten" injury. He quivers each time my canines run the length. I'd never hurt him, but even when I'm sucking his cock I like to think I have him controlled under me.

I move my hands from his balls down the cleft of his ass. Saliva from my efforts runs in rivulets down to the bed, coating his ass and getting things wet enough for play. I take my time inserting a finger—slow enough for the experience to be pleasurable the whole way through—and he groans in satisfaction.

Lust gets the better of me and I thrust hard and quick. Miles doesn't protest. He goes as limp as possible and takes me all the way, digging his fingernails into my skin as he suppresses his urge to gag. While fully planted in his throat, I feel a tightening in my lower gut and clench my whole body with the wave of release. My mouth closes around Miles in a tight embrace as I empty my seed deep inside him.

I pull out as he coughs for air. He doesn't make a move to get up, and I continue my work on his erection. Without my cock in the way, he moans aloud with each full descent along his shaft.

"Pierce," he whispers. "You're really good at that…."

I slowly insert a second finger and pick up the pace. I'm tired—awash in afterglow delight—but having his cock in my mouth keeps a bit of the heat alive in my gut. I'm half tempted to put my flaccid dick back into his mouth and have him suck me hard for a second round. I doubt it would work, considering my busted-up condition, but the thought excites me.

I don't dwell on it long, however. I can feel Miles swell for release. He arches his back, and his balls tighten as I take him deep. He comes into my mouth, and I allow the tangy flavor to flood my senses. I don't get excited over semen, but Miles is a different story. I like knowing what he tastes like.

I swallow and lift off him as I roll to my side.

Miles scoots close and locks his mouth with mine, the flavors of sex mingling in our kiss. It's erotic in a way I haven't experienced before. I pull away and run a hand over my mouth, rubbing the edges to relax them after a prolonged period of use.

"What got you into that?" Miles asks, tucking his hands behind his head.

"I wanted to try something different," I say between long breaths. "You like it?"

"Y-yeah. I mean, I didn't think you'd do something like that, but… I enjoyed it. I wouldn't mind if we did it more often."

"Hm."

I crawl my way up the bed and rest my head back on a pillow. Miles chases after me and tucks his head between my arm and chest.

"Why do you think the Cobras are after Big Man Vice's kids?" he asks.

I snort. "I have no idea. To fuck with him, most likely. Anita would have a conniption fit if her children were harmed."

"Maybe. Why didn't they want to kill you?"

"I suspect they were going to once Diver spoke to me. This is the Cobras we're talking about. He probably doesn't trust his underlings to do anything meaningful."

Miles nods. I keep him close.

I POCKET the key to my safe deposit box and exit the bank.

That's it. Everything is done. All that's left is the grand finale.

I glance around Noimore as I get into Brisko's van. The muted rays of sunlight filtering through the overcast sky reflect off the chrome of a thousand cars going to and fro. Once I set off Jeremy's trap, I'm skippin' town and never coming back. Nick won't be looking for me much as the turf-war bullshit settles down. By the time he realizes I'm missing, it'll be too late.

I finger the key in my pocket as I drive through town. I hate rush-hour traffic, but my mind is preoccupied. People could be flipping me the bird and I doubt I would notice.

My only regret with this ordeal is leaving Miles. I think about him all the time—for the past five days it's the one thing I fluctuate on. A piece of me wants to tell him everything. A piece of me also wants him to forget I even existed. What would a younger version of me want? I don't know. It's bullshit thinking like that, which is messing me up.

I pass by the Nightquarter Café and see the establishment is closed. It doesn't surprise me. The fights happening in the basement are illegal. Setting it up with customers in the main room would be a hassle.

The laundromat is set and ready to go. I finished the wires days ago, and now all I'll have to do is walk in and trigger the explosion at the appropriate time. It feels good to get things done early.

A damn storm is lingering over the lake. Winds bluster in at odd times and the rain comes and goes without any definite beginning or end. It's typical weather, but I'm in a better mood than most days and wish the surroundings would reflect that. It's easy to get worked up on life after avoiding death twice in a row, after all.

I pull up to the safe house and step out of the vehicle. I open the front door and a wave of smoke hits me, dispelling any jovial feelings I had seconds before.

"What's going on?" I yell.

"Everything is under control," Rodger shouts back from the cabin's kitchen.

I doubt that. Common sense is in short supply these days.

Rolling my eyes I storm into the kitchen and find the oldest Vice boy attempting to cook. It doesn't look like anything difficult—a few pancakes and eggs—but somehow he's burnt half of them and undercooked the others. I rip the spatula from his hands and shove him away from the utensils. The problem is apparent the moment I glance down. The heat on the stove is set to the max.

"Have you ever done this before?" I ask in a condescending tone.

Rodger shakes his head. "No. It doesn't look that hard, though. I'm sure I'm just missing an easy trick."

With one part sarcasm and one part melodrama, I slide the heat to a lower setting. Rodger frowns.

"Perhaps we should order out," Rodger says.

I snort back a laugh. "Best idea you've had so far."

"Three pizzas, then? One for us and two for Brisko?"

"I don't care. Anything but you cooking."

The place is a mess, and I straighten things out, if only to avoid a fire starting. Rodger watches me with an intent focus, and I glance back at him with a glower. He doesn't pick up on my cue of irritation and instead gets in closer.

"I managed to get ahold of Luna," he says. "It turns out she'll be leaving the state soon."

"And you didn't know?"

"No."

"Sounds like you have a wonderful relationship with your *fiancée*."

"Apparently she doesn't want to go back to her father," Rodger drawls, staring at the oven but likely not seeing a thing. I hate to inquire, considering Rodger's tendency to pontificate on matters I don't care about, but it's obvious he wants some sort of attention.

"How did you meet this broad?" I ask.

"Out and about in town. She was shopping, and I bought her some new clothes." He laughs. "I didn't know at the time owning personal effects was against her tenets in life."

So she was shopping but her religion doesn't allow her to own personal property? I already know the punchline to this entire story, and it churns my insides—Rodger has no idea what's going on.

This dame goes out shopping. I suspect she hates her father's way of life—it would explain the negativity in the paintings she made—but couldn't find a way out of her situation. Then she meets some rich kid who purchases her clothing—something she's probably never had much of—and falls for him, despite his lackluster qualities. They fool around, he goes to their cult house, *he falls for their cultist ways of life*, she doesn't like that and ends up running away again after he submits to their "you don't need money, give it to us" bullshit. And now she'll keep running until she finds someone else.

I pity Rodger. He should've eloped with the girl and been happy.

The thought stops me dead in my tracks.

Am *I* making the right decision? My situation is different than Rodger's, but my advice applies regardless.

No. It's different. It is.

God, I hate when I get pensive.

"Are you okay, Pierce?"

I turn to him with a lifted eyebrow. He motions to the countertop. I glance back and realize I've spilled pancake batter across the tiles. When did that happen?

"Get me a towel," I say.

Rodger shrugs. "I used them all already."

"Then give me your damn shirt."

He removes it on command, and I find myself unable to think for a second time during this conversation. Rodger's got a cut body—must have time to work out—and when he's quiet, he's delicious eye candy. I take the shirt from him and give the counter a hasty swipe, my eyes on him rather than my task.

"Something wrong?" he asks.

"No."

Miles procured all sorts of clothing, but nothing in the usual suit format. I feel lowbrow wearing jeans and a T-shirt, but they look nice on both Miles and Rodger. Especially Rodger when he's wearing nothing but jeans.

Then again, the thought of Miles stripping down also gets my blood hot.

I'm neck-deep in pancake batter with smoke swirling overhead, but my mind careens into the gutter regardless. It doesn't take much sometimes.

"Pierce?"

I jerk my attention to the other end of the kitchen and spot Miles staring. He's got his arms crossed over his chest, and he eyes Rodger with an odd expression. I nod to him and he motions me over. I throw down Rodger's shirt and walk to his side.

"How much longer are we going to be here?" Miles asks in a quiet tone.

"A few days," I reply. "Then we're all going to Big Man Vice's house."

Miles grips his arm tight and stares at me with a hard expression. I stare back, bemused.

"Do you wanna fuck him?" he asks.

I chortle and offer Miles a smirk. "Yeah. I do."

His honeyed skin gets flushed, and he turns his gaze to the floor.

"I'm not going to," I say, rubbing at the soreness that lingers on my neck. "Nick's made it clear no one is to touch his children. Besides, Rodger likes *the ladies* and not so much *the cock*."

"And if he was available? And wanted you?"

"I'd fuck him, then, sure."

Miles drills a hole in the floor with his eyes. "What if I said I didn't feel like sharing?"

Tsk. This is the exact reason I stopped fucking all my past flings. They start thinking they can tell me what to do—limiting who I'm gonna fuck or where I'm gonna go—or demanding I give them my time. It's a deal breaker for me. I don't let anyone tell me what to do outside of the hatchet work I do for the Vice family.

I open my mouth to explain but stop before I utter a single word. His grip on his arm grows tighter with each passing moment. I don't like the thought of relinquishing control to other people, but… I'm not gonna be with Miles much longer anyway. Why not give him what he wants? He looks like he needs it.

"If you don't want to share, I'll keep it in my pants," I drawl.

He snaps his gaze to mine, taken aback. "Really?"

"Don't look too surprised. It's what you wanted, right?"

"Y-yeah," he says. "I just… I mean, you're not angry or…."

This would be a different conversation at any other point in my life, but for now I revel in his excitement. "No, I'm not angry." I brush his chin with my knuckles. "But I do expect more from you if I can't get it elsewhere."

"Of course."

I already bed him to my heart's content, but I love hearing him admit he'll submit even further to keep me satisfied.

"You busy right now?" I ask.

"No."

"Good."

CHAPTER NINETEEN

It's hard to sleep during the hours leading up to a major assignment.

I watch the sun set from the balcony of the master bedroom. We have a couple hours before game time, and I inhale my cigarette as I mull over the details in my mind. Today is a turning point—not just for the Vice family, but for me.

Nothing will be the same tomorrow. It gets me anxious.

I exhale a long line of smoke and stomp out the rest of the cigarette before heading back inside. Everyone else must know I'm on edge, because they keep their troubles to themselves and their volume low. The cabin isn't as much of a cringe factory today.

I spot Brisko leaning against the wall in the hallway. He's guarding Jayden's room, and I'm glad I kept him for the week and a half. He does well given simple instructions.

"Brisko," I say as I approach him. "What's going on?" I motion to Jayden's door with my eyes.

"Miles is talkin' to him."

"Oh?"

"Yeah. Been talkin' for hours."

I stand by the door and stare. I've been avoiding Jayden the entire time we've been here. I don't care for the kid, and he thinks I'm gonna rape him if we're left alone together for longer than thirty seconds. It doesn't make for a great relationship.

I wonder what Miles is discussing with him.

"Hey, uh, boss?" Brisko asks, his voice slow and his mannerisms even slower. "What's goin' on tonight? Somethin's brewin'?"

He's a little more astute than I gave him credit for. "We're gonna go see Big Man Vice tonight once I finish my assignment."

"What assignment?"

I flash him a glare. "*My* assignment. You don't need to worry about it."

"Right. I forgot."

"Brisko—why don't you take a break and watch TV? I'll stay here for the time being."

Brisko stares down at me for a long moment. I don't know if he's processing my request or zoning out, but once he's done he nods. "If that's what you want."

He lumbers away but I grab him by the arm. "Hey. I need you to drive for me tonight. You good with that?"

"Yeah, boss."

"Stop calling me boss. I'm not the boss."

"You're the boss right now."

I release his arm and motion him to the living room. "Well, then, I'm ordering you to rest up."

"Right, boss. I'll get on that."

Heh. I think I might actually miss seein' Brisko from time to time. He's grown on me.

I shake the thought from my head and return my attention to Jayden's room. Once Brisko leaves, I lean up close and listen. I'm curious—I want to know what Miles plans on doing with the little gangbanger. What could he be saying to sway this kid's mind? What if Jayden is harassing him and Miles isn't saying anything?

Their voices muddle together, but I can identify them through context.

"—and they live out of town now," Miles says.

Jayden scoffs. "She always hated Noimore."

"They have a nice house too."

"Good for them. I don't care. She doesn't give a shit about me."

"I talked to her recently. She said she would take you back."

"She did?" Jayden asks, his voice betraying his hopeful disbelief. "When did she say that?"

"A month or so back."

The conversation lulls but I doubt it's because of anything bad. Miles breaks the silence by asking, "Would you at least give it a try? She seemed like she wanted you back in Lacy's life."

"How old is Lacy now?"

"I dunno."

"I remember when she was a baby. She was so adorable."

"Yeah," Miles replies with a hint of melancholy sadness. "I remember when you were a baby too."

Again, Jayden scoffs. "You do not."

"Yeah, I do. I was four, going on five. You were adorable then, just like Lacy."

I move away from the door. I don't know how Miles does it. I just don't have the patience… but he seems like he gets to everyone eventually. Charisma, I guess. Maybe it's his honesty. I'm not sure—all I know is that I don't have it like he does. I would've left Jayden, and we would've killed each other in a gang turf war, even if we were blood brothers.

Miles is different. He has a lot of traits to admire. A lot of good traits.

"Pierce, are you spying?"

I turn on my heel and face Rodger with a glower. "What is it?" I snap.

"Aren't we going to go kill Harlan soon?"

I glance around before lunging forward and taking him by the collar of his T-shirt. "Who told you we were doing that?" I ask.

Rodger holds up his hands in mild surrender. "Jeremy. He told me that I should help you out when the time comes."

"Why would he say that?"

"So that our father wouldn't be so furious at me for running off."

I take a deep breath and release Rodger. I guess that makes sense. He can walk in and claim he killed the King Cobra himself to get in good with Nick. That suits me perfectly. I don't need any fame or fortune where I'm going. Rodger can take it all.

"Get your things together, then," I say. "We're gonna be leaving soon."

I knock on the door to Jayden's room to signal our imminent departure. My blood pressure is high, and I know I'll be on edge until the mission is done. I walk back into the master bedroom and collect the few items I got from my house. A gun holster, a spare .45, some cash…. I glance at the key to the safe deposit box and debate about whether to give it to Miles now.

The box contains half a million dollars in various forms—Miles and I are the only names with access, and it's my parting gift to him. I could give it to him now, but then he'll know what's up. Instead I pocket the key and decide to tell him afterward. Right before I take off. I want the parting to be quick, and I don't wanna give Miles time to work his charisma on me, or whatever it is he has.

I throw on a jacket and head for the front door. The sun has set. Game time.

Brisko, Rodger, Miles, and Jayden are all waiting by the van. I give Jayden a sideways glance but dispel my thoughts afterward. We can't leave him here alone, so we might as well take him. I can leave him in the van with Brisko.

There aren't many words spoken as we gather up. Brisko takes the pilot's seat, I take copilot, and everyone else takes a seat in the back. We leave the rental cabin, and I'm sad to see it go. I guess I hate people, but this week and half wasn't as terrible as I had suspected it would be.

The pulse of life in Noimore is different tonight. Maybe everyone is on edge. Maybe everyone can sense it. Something big is gonna happen. It's Saturday but the traffic is that of a Wednesday or Thursday. There aren't any lights or parties on the streets. Nothing is right.

We zoom through town, avoiding known police beats, and circle our destination wide, avoiding anyone who might be watching for patterns. I light a cigarette to try and calm my nerves, but my unsteady hands betray my true feelings. I suck down the nicotine in record time and light myself a second. I should've taken a bottle of vodka.

Brisko parks the vehicle and nods to me. "We're here."

"All right," I say. "Miles, Rodger—you're with me. Brisko, watch Jayden, understand?"

"Right, boss."

I jump out of the car. My body hasn't fully recovered, but the tension in the air stifles all other feelings. I unlock the laundromat and allow Miles and Rodger inside.

The place has all the welcoming warmth of a horror movie. The cold, unused washing machines cast long, dark shadows, and the place smells of mold. We walk through, our footsteps echoing. I pull my gun and Miles follows suit. It seems we're alone, but who can tell for sure?

The back room has our false door and tunnel. I pick up the trigger left sitting on an old basket and fiddle with the simple controls. I glance at my phone. Jeremy said he would send me a text once everything fell into place. All I need to do is wait for the signal.

The text comes sooner rather than later.

The buzz of my phone causes everyone to flinch, and I rip the device from my pocket with a sweaty palm.

The message reads: *now*

No punctuation, no other words. It's a simple command.

I glance between the trigger and Rodger. "You wanna do the honors?" I mutter, keeping my voice low out of paranoia rather than necessity.

"What's going to happen when I activate it?" he asks.

"You're gonna kill a handful of drug-running gangbangers."

Rodger holds out his hand, his expression less than enthusiastic about the matter. Miles turns to me and indicates he would be willing to flip the switch, but I give him a curt shake of my head. If anyone is going to taint their soul with the death of scumbags like Harlan, it's gonna be me or Rodger. Miles doesn't need this kind of weight on his conscience.

I hand Rodger the trigger. He flips it without a second thought. Moments later the ground beneath us shudders and the dust of a well-settled building rains down upon us. I wait and hear the tunnel beyond the false door rumble. The wall cracks and wood splinters outward. A rush of air and thick particles fill the cramped space. I cough and wave my hand around to clear my vision.

"That was mighty anticlimactic for the gravity of the situation," Rodger says between heavy rasps.

I force a chuckle. "Yeah. Let's get outta here."

We walk as a tight group into the front room and out to the road. No signs of trouble. No Cobras. Nothing. I'd say we're lucky, but my sense of dread has yet to leave me.

I pull myself into the van and dial Nick. There's no longer a reason to hide anything from him.

The phone rings once and he answers.

"Pierce," he says.

"Nick," I reply. "I'm on my way over. Your son Rodger triggered the explosives. If all went well, Harlan is dead, along with all his major lieutenants."

"Good work."

He's more terse than usual, and I can't get a read on his mood. Perhaps he's irritated I haven't contacted him in a few weeks. I wait for anything else he may have to say. Nothing.

"Rodger is coming back with me," I say.

Nick doesn't answer.

"We'll be there within the hour."

Again, he says nothing.

"Is there anything else you want me to do?"

"Just get here." He ends the call with a sharp click.

I hadn't anticipated Nick being upset with me. It might delay my flight from the city—but not for long. I'm sure he'll be pleased by the outcome of the turf war, if nothing else.

Brisko starts up the van, and we head straight for the Vice family compound. I spot Jayden in the rearview mirror as he fidgets around like only tweakers do when they haven't had their fix. Miles calms him with a few words under his breath, but I know the younger brother will be trouble. I hope Miles follows through with the rehab program.

"Was my father upset?" Rodger asks, cutting the silence with his voice.

"Seems like," I reply.

"I thought he would be proud. I've never done anything to help his organization before."

"He's been under a lot of stress lately."

Stress….

I can't seem to relax.

The van pulls up to the Vice family gates, and they open to let us up the long driveway to the house. A whole handful of cars are parked outside—more company than I've seen in years—and all varying makes and models, not just the vehicles of the aristocratic elite. I stare at them as Brisko finds a place to park. Enforcers stand at the doors and behind us near the gate.

"What's going on?" Brisko asks.

"A celebration," Rodger answers before I do. "Perhaps thanks to our victory over the King Cobra himself."

Yeah, maybe. Seems a little premature. What if Harlan survived? Doubtful, but still a possibility. Or perhaps some other gangbanger will take his place in the void and the power struggle that is soon to take hold of the streets. In an ideal situation, the Vice family would reacquire their holdings, but there are a myriad of possibilities.

I shake my head to dispel my dark thoughts. I'll speak to Nick himself. He's always straight with me. I'll get to the bottom of this.

With a heavy sigh, I step out of the van. I motion for Rodger to follow, but I shake my head at the others. "Wait here," I command.

They all mutter acceptance, and I slam the door behind me.

The two men at the front door are the same enforcers I saw at Jeremy's strip club. What did Miles say their names were?

The men flinch back as I draw near, their hands on their guns and their expressions so suspicious it's like they expect a chest-bursting alien to fly from me at any moment. Perhaps they don't know who I am—perhaps it's too dark. I glare at them and piece together their names from fragmented memories.

"Dorian, Lucky," I say with a nod. I'm not sure who is who, but that's their names.

The moment I speak casually, they relax. Both return my nonverbal greeting and force one-sided smiles, opening the front door for me as I walk by. Rodger shadows my steps and gives the men an openhanded wave.

I gawk at the interior of the home. It's lit up bright, and the housekeepers hustle about in a panic. There are more enforcers inside than out—they stand at major entrances and hallways and they're bullshitting with each other until they catch sight of me. Then they clam up and get tense.

What's going on? I glance at Rodger and his expression mirrors my internal thoughts. This is bizarre behavior.

"Where's Nick?" I ask the first guy I roll across.

He motions to the ballroom. I walk by and head straight there. I throw open the ballroom doors and freeze, my breath caught in my throat.

CHAPTER TWENTY

"P‌IERCE! Y‌OU made it!"

The room is a giant open floor with a hundred individuals gathered around the sides. They leave a wide-open space in the middle—a space already coated in fresh blood, brain matter, bullet holes, and hunks of raw flesh—while enjoying booze and hard liquor displayed on long tables. Jeremy steps from the crowd, his arms wide.

"Come over here!" he calls out. "I've been waiting for you!"

My eyes linger on the guests. I recognize half—friends of the Vice family—but the other half of the crowd…. They're not people I would associate with Vice holdings. They're street thugs; there's no other way of calling it. Some are a little more well-to-do than others, but they all stick out like sore thumbs. Most are already drunk.

I see other familiar faces as well. Donny, Santiago—other men from the streets. A man I don't know pushes me farther into the room and swipes my handgun from the holster before I can offer any protest. I don't fight for the weapon… not when I can feel the bloodlust of a hundred armed individuals pulsing through the crowd.

"Jeremy!" an enforcer by the door shouts. "These three were left in his van!"

I wheel around. A squad of muscle-bound goons shoves Miles, Brisko, and Jayden into the ballroom. They're stripped of their handguns and have rifles in their back.

I return my attention to Jeremy. I'm at a loss for words.

Rodger steps forward. "What's going on?" he asks, his voice a little too innocent for the occasion. I grab him and pull him back. This isn't going to end well.

"I'm glad you asked, brother," Jeremy replies. He straightens his designer suit and smooths his tie. "I've decided that our little turf war has gone on long enough. And, since our father was going about it all the wrong way, I handled it myself."

The guests whoop and cheer.

"What do you mean?" Rodger asks. "Where's our father?"

Jeremy snaps his fingers, and Nick is dragged from the back corner of the room, his hands bound behind his back and a strip of duct tape tight around his head and firmly into his mouth. He looks like he's been struggling—his hair is clumped together with blood—but he's still alive.

"Dad?" Rodger asks. He goes to step forward again, but I keep my hold on his arm.

Jeremy smiles a dark smile. "With Harlan gone, it's just the Vice family in charge. But I think it's time for a change in management."

He pulls his heavy .45 and blows a hole in Nick's head before anyone can voice their opinion. The room explodes into laughter and clapping, but I hold my breath. Nick's limp body slumps into the pool of body parts that fills the center of the room. The bang of the gun rings in my ears.

"*Jeremy*!" Rodger barks, his voice cracking with newfound rage. "*How could you*?" He struggles to get out of my grip, but I hold him back. Doesn't he see what's happening?

"Bring him over here," Jeremy says with a laugh. The incessant cheering makes it difficult to hear, but Jeremy's voice is distinct.

Enforcers circle me and Rodger. They take Nick's oldest son, and I remain standing where they left me. They manhandle Rodger and throw him into the middle of the room. Before Rodger can plead, argue, or debate, Jeremy cocks his gun and does it all over again—another harsh bang fills the ballroom, and Rodger jerks back and twitches to the ground, half his face missing from the blast.

"There's only one person who's going to inherit my father's estate," Jeremy says, eliciting another round of cheers as he holsters his gun. "And it ain't going to be my deadbeat of a brother or worthless sister!"

The "joke" is well received by the drunkards and scum that surround us.

Jeremy turns and motions to a man in the crowd. "Diver? You have anyone else you need to make an example of before we solidify our arrangement?"

The one-armed man—Diver—shakes his head and gestures for Jeremy to continue. "I had my fun earlier," he calls out. "Besides. Your main enforcer took care of the King Cobra himself. Everyone knows *I'm* in charge now."

I've never spoken to Diver, and I don't know much about the man, but I can put one and two together. He and Jeremy are two peas in a pod. They're both disgusting, ugly men, inside and out, who got shafted with second place, so to speak, and now they're working together to claim what's "rightfully theirs." They made an alliance. Jeremy would kill dissenters to Diver's rule, and Diver would kill dissenters to Jeremy's rule, all in the name of a turf war. Now, with no one left above them, they've come together to claim the city like a pair of fucked-up lovebirds.

This isn't a party. It's an execution of everyone who still harbors loyalty to the old rulers.

They're gonna shoot us all one at time.

"Brisko!" Jeremy says, mimicking a game show announcer. "Come over here. I need you to stand in the middle of the room, buddy."

Brisko hesitates. He glances around, his drifting eyes scanning the faces of the crowd as if looking for the solution to his problem. The correct course of action is to do whatever the fuck Jeremy tells him. It's not like he's going to ham-hand his way out this situation.

Brisko comes to the conclusion by himself and walks into the center of the room with heavy steps.

"How long did you work for my father?" Jeremy asks.

"Four years," Brisko replies through a thick mouth-breathing huff.

"Why did you start working for him?"

"Money."

"You still want money? You gonna work for me?"

"Yeah."

The infantile way Jeremy speaks to Brisko is so patronizing it's laughable. The audience gets it too. They snicker and point, and someone mutters something about "shooting the giant retard." I grit my teeth.

Jeremy answers with a slow nod. "That's what I wanted to hear, big guy. Get in line and enjoy the benefits of better business. We're a bigger organization now. The cash flow will be unstoppable."

More cheering. More whooping. More drunken toasts.

I understand what Santiago was talking about now. He knew this would happen. He knew.

"Pierce," Jeremy says, drawing me back to reality in a painful way. "I really am impressed. You killed Malloy *and* escaped the Cobras. I knew you couldn't be stopped. I told them not to kill you, but I never imagined you'd be such a thorn in their side. My father was right to keep you around all these years."

The audience gets quiet, and I can hear my own heartbeat. I wasn't afraid of dying in the Cobras' den, so why am I now? I mentally chuckle to myself. I know why. I was so close to getting out of this business that I started to believe I would leave Noimore behind for good. I should've known better. I should've known I'd never get out.

I stop myself from glancing back at Miles. I should've sent him away before this. It's my fault he's here.

"You sure this enforcer of yours is going to stay loyal to you?" Diver drawls, his gaze locked on me and his only hand gripped tight on a bottle of wine. "He hasn't said a damn thing since he's arrived. He's shell-shocked."

Jeremy chortles. "Oh, don't worry. Pierce—tell them. Where do your loyalties lie?"

All eyes are on me.

I swallow and take a deep breath. "The Vice family," I reply, my voice unsteady.

"That's right. *The Vice family*. And who's in charge of the Vice family?"

I don't see Anita, but I don't doubt she's dead. "You."

"That's right. Me. Remember how we talked about your loyalty once my father died?"

"I remember," I force myself to say.

I get it. He's trying to save face while saving me—if only because he wants me for his own personal reasons—so why am I still shaken?

Miles. It's because of Miles. What reason is there to save him? Why *wouldn't* Jeremy kill him? What am I going to do about it?

Diver gestures with his head. "He's dangerous. How're you sure he's not gonna turn on you? He was Big Man Vice's *right-hand man* for two decades. That's a long fuckin' time."

The audience absorbs the drama like a sponge. They watch intently, and I can feel the hate from half the crowd. Some men here want me dead. Others just want to see me beg. I don't have many friends—not with Nick dead.

"Jeremy," I say with a chuckle, the sound more nervous than jovial. "I didn't know you had it in you to orchestrate all this."

He narrows his eyes and waits.

I take a step forward and spot a handful of thugs reaching for their guns. I continue on regardless, sauntering over with my hands in plain sight.

"To be honest, I thought you were more like Rodger." I gesture to the corpse without looking at it. "But I can see now you're more shrewd and cunning than even your father."

His eyes light up as he attempts to restrain a smirk. He loves eating up compliments.

I walk through a small pool of blood, careful not to slip on the warm, slick substance. I stop once I'm in front of Jeremy—only a foot away—staring down at him with an easy smile.

"You know how I have a weakness for strong men—men like you."

Jeremy runs a hand along his flushed and hideous face. "Yes," he murmurs with a husky breath. "I do. I knew you would come around once my father was out of the way. You're attracted to power."

"Exactly."

"So now I want you to prove it to Diver."

I lift my eyebrows. "What?"

"Get on your knees, Pierce."

The crowd murmurs in anticipation. I suspect most don't care for "man on man" action, but they *do* want to see me grovel or—in some cases—they get their rocks off on humiliation of the worst degree.

I hate Jeremy with an ever-growing passion but… this isn't about me.

I fall to one knee and then the other, my breathing shallow. Eyes focus in like a harsh spotlight. With shaky hands I reach for Jeremy's belt.

He stops me and utters a *tsk tsk tsk*. He grabs my chin and forces me to stare up at him. He's excited—the bulge in his pants isn't going away anytime soon—and his eyes have a lustful glint I've never seen before. Before I can ask what he wants of me, Jeremy pulls his handgun from his shoulder holster and runs it along my lips.

I drag my tongue along the underside of the barrel. Jeremy *really* likes that. He forces the weapon into my mouth, and the cold, jagged metal cuts my cheek. I suck on it regardless, ignoring the roar of exuberant cheering and laughter as the gangsters get a kick out of my submission.

I block out the reality—if Jeremy wants me to blow his gun, I'm gonna blow his gun.

"Heh," Diver says once the crowd dies down enough for conversation. "I knew he was a sick fuck, but I didn't know he was *this* flavor of whore. No wonder Big Man Vice kept him around."

Another roar of laughter. Jeremy withdraws the gun barrel from my mouth and wipes it off on my shirt. "Get up, Pierce," he says, his voice quiet enough for me alone. "We'll have fun later, I promise."

I stand—a cold calm permeating my being.

"Who are these two?" some asshole from the crowd says, motioning to Jayden and Miles.

The crowd turns to them. Miles attempts to hold back his brother, but Jayden seems to have something to say.

"I'm with the Cobras!" Jayden shouts. "I am! I should be celebrating with you guys." He glances around until he meets the gaze of someone he knows. "Tell 'em, Tony."

The man he called out to doesn't say anything. Jayden turns his attention to another. "I'm one of you!"

The kid's never been in a gang before. Gangsters will help each other out when it's good for them to do so, but they don't help you when it's gonna jeopardize everything. Anyone who vouches for Jayden is running the risk of getting thrown into the center of the room for another bang-n-splat performance.

Jayden learns his lesson under the gaze of a few hundred eyes—the sting of embarrassment a terrible punctuation. Miles doesn't care. He pulls his brother back and shields him, his own expression unreadable. He knows he's in danger, and he turns his attention to me.

Diver shrugs. "Isn't one of these kids Pierce's boy toy? What're you gonna do about that, Jeremy? Let him keep a side thing?"

He's a comedian as far as the crowd is concerned. They laugh at every little taunt he has to say.

"I don't care about fuck-things," Jeremy says with a shrug.

I take a deep breath, but my relief doesn't last long.

"He's no fuck-boy," Donny chimes in from the other side of the room. "I've seen them together. They've been kissin' and starin' into each other's eyes like they're lovers! It's true! I saw the whole thing!"

I think most people in the audience are drunk, or else they're just cruel, as even that line of reasoning gets another round of laughter. I knew they wouldn't appreciate an actual relationship between men—I told Miles we couldn't be like that in front of others—I just didn't think *Donny* of all people would be the one to throw me under a bus.

While the crowd has its outburst, I turn and lean in close to Jeremy—close enough to have my breath on his neck. "Let him go and I'll make it worth your while."

Jeremy smirks up at me. "I'm the jealous type, Pierce. I don't want you straying."

"You wanna see me beg, right?"

"I'd like that."

I get in close and lick the ridge of his ear. "I'll do it every night if you do me this one favor."

I'd threaten, but I know Jeremy. He's got an ego that can't be satisfied. He'd never go for a deal that involved him looking weak.

Jeremy pushes me back and motions to the corner of the room with his personal thugs. "Wait over there, Pierce. I have a business to run."

The energy in the room gets explosive once again. Miles and Jayden are sacrificial goats. Diver gestures for Jeremy to continue, and the youngest Vice boy pulls his handgun up and aims.

For a split second my heart stops. He pulls the trigger. I'm on the verge of leaping at him to sink my teeth into his throat for a savage animal kill when I realize what he's done.

Jayden hits the floor on his back, his legs sprawled. Miles ducks down and grabs him—the bullet had hit Jayden's chest. With a few quick breaths, Miles suppresses a mild case of hyperventilation. The surrounding men laugh.

"I never liked that kid anyway," Tony says, pointing.

"There we go," Jeremy says. "We split the difference. One whore can remain and the other is gutter trash."

"Did you get Pierce's boy toy?" Diver asks, earnestly confused.

"Eh. Who can tell Asians apart. Am I right?"

Drunken laughter rings in my ears. I know it to be a lie—Jeremy took my offer. Jayden and Miles might look damn near identical, but Jeremy knew Miles before. Jeremy says what he has to in order to save face.

The muscle of the party goes in to move the corpses off the floor. I grab Brisko and point him toward Miles and Jayden. "Take them out of here," I command. "And give Miles this." I shove the safe deposit box key into Brisko's mighty hand and urge him to hurry with a forceful shove. The man nods and hustles over to help with the lifting.

Jeremy walks to my side and gives me a knowing smirk. "If I see you two together, it'll be a different story," he mutters.

"I know."

"Don't think I won't have men follow him either. I'll always know, Pierce. This is my city now."

CHAPTER TWENTY-ONE

The Crystal Floor Nightclub isn't what it used to be.

Music plays, sure, and drinks are served to the guests, but the place has a seedy feel akin to a porno theater or "massage parlor." The waiters and waitresses are treated as objects for amusement, the floors are sticky, and the smoke overhead is a mix of chemicals. It's like the establishment is reveling in its debauchery rather than trying to maintain an air of class and sophistication.

But I don't fuckin' care.

I stare out across the dance floor without seeing the people around me. After one cigarette I pound down a few shots and chase it all with yet another cigarette. If I'm not burning my taste buds, I'm drowning them—either way it doesn't help get the foul taste out of my mouth.

Jeremy runs his hand up my inner thigh. I let him touch me as he pleases, numb to the sensations.

"You've had enough for one night," he says, motioning the waiter away when he comes to refill my drink. "I want you sober for later."

I take a long drag of my cigarette and exhale through my nose.

"We had problems down at the docks last night," Diver says. "Some cops are getting in the way of operations."

Jeremy rests back onto the leather seat of the booth. "We'll have to find a way to deal with them, then."

"How did Big Man Vice deal with cops that got uppity?"

"What does it matter how my father handled it?" Jeremy growls. "*I'm* in charge. *I'll* deal with it."

His anger is amusing in a pathetic way. He doesn't know how his father dealt with things—if he did, this situation wouldn't have become a problem.

Oh well.

The dim atmosphere messes with my sight, but I know the Cobras from the old Vice family enforcers by the way they hold themselves. A

Cobras stooge rolls up to the booth and attempts to take a seat next to me. I rear one leg up and kick him hard, sending him to the floor in one violent shove. He gets to his feet, gun in hand, but I already have mine out and ready.

"Pierce, behave," Jeremy says.

I return my gun to its holster and continue with my smoke. It's hard to feel much these days, but anger still gets my heart rate going. I like getting angry, which is an odd thought, and Cobras punks just give me an excuse.

Jeremy addresses the newcomer with a one-sided smile. "Never mind my dog. What did you come here for?"

The man doesn't attempt to sit. Smart move.

"Guinevere called," the guy says. "She's on her way from the airport. She'll be here shortly."

I perk up at the mention of her name.

Jeremy waves the guy away. "Good. Bring her to my table when she arrives."

Guinevere… I had hoped she would stay away. Jeremy hadn't been able to find her, and I thought she'd stay hidden forever, but news of her parents' death must have reached her, because she called out of the blue to see if the rumors were true.

She and Jeremy had a long talk. At first he wanted to kill her—to take the Vice family estate for himself—but after their little discussion, he changed his tone. He wants her help.

I laugh and take another long drag. It's probably because he's floundering. Running a mob isn't like running a McDonald's, that's for sure. Jeremy doesn't have the experience, even if he likes to think he does.

I glance around the nightclub and take stock of the individuals. A lot of "leaders" came to meet Guinevere tonight.

That's another problem with the streets these days… too many people think they're in charge. With Nick you *knew* who had the authority. With Diver and Jeremy, it's hit-or-miss. They don't have a handle on it like they should.

Diver holds a girl close to his side—a different girl from last night—this one the youngest yet. I don't know how old she is, and I'm not gonna ask, but whenever she turns to me I feel obligated to help her. She's quiet and motions to a glass without uttering a word. She's thirsty. I flag one of the many waiters.

"Water," I bark.

The man scurries away and returns moments later with a cool cup in hand. I take it and slide it across the table. She thanks me with a reserved smile.

Diver doesn't appreciate my actions. He eyes me like the jealous and insecure man he is. I don't even fuck women, yet he's gripping her side tighter than before.

He nudges Jeremy and motions to me. "Didn't you have your little toy tattooed?" He forces a laugh and turns to his girl. "You're gonna like this. Jeremy's bitch got marked."

Diver likes calling me that. *Jeremy's bitch.* I don't feel anything anymore when he says it, but for a short while it got under my skin.

Jeremy points to my jacket sleeve. "Show them," he commands. "As a matter of fact, why don't you keep your sleeve rolled up? It's better that way."

I roll up my sleeve and flash the tattoo. It's nothing fancy—six inches of stark black text straight to the skin—but I guess the font has a nice old-world feel to it. It reads: VICE HOUND. I keep my sleeve up and return to my cigarette without commentary or reaction, much to Diver's displeasure. I think he wants a rise out of me, but I don't have enough fucks to give in order for that to happen.

"I let him pick the spot," Jeremy says. "He wanted it on his left forearm. Isn't that right, Pierce?"

I exhale and nod. I got the tattoo right over that scar I hate so much—the baked beans can scar. I laugh to myself remembering the event and conversation with Miles. This isn't the tattoo I would have picked first to cover it, but it's not bad, I guess. My life has been defined by my service to the Vice family. This is just the visual representation of that.

But Miles....

Miles.

I slide out from the booth, and Jeremy glares. I motion to the restroom. He waves me away, his permission granted for a leave of absence. With my half-smoked cigarette, I shuffle into the men's restroom and close the door behind me.

Miles....

I wonder about him every day. My fear for his safety has gripped every part of my body like I've never experienced before. I worry that if I try and find him, Jeremy will hurt him. I worry that if I kill Jeremy,

Diver or the others will come after me or Miles. I worry that if I just run, Jeremy will find Miles and use him to lure me back out.

Miles. Miles. Miles.

All my fuckin' thoughts and concerns and fears revolve around *Miles*.

Sometimes I think I should wait until Jeremy gets tired of me and then slip out in the dead of night but…. Does Miles even think of me? Would I be doing him a favor by running to him? I'm some criminal through and through. He needs my presence like he needs the plague.

I pull my Colt .45 handgun and turn it over in my hand.

I've also thought about just shooting Jeremy and then shooting myself. Of course, that doesn't ensure that someone won't go fuck with Miles anyway. I mean, why would they—I'd be dead—but maybe they would, and the irrational fear halts my actions.

What is this? He's all I can think about.

I sigh and toss my cigarette into the dirty sink. Maybe I can talk to Guinevere… maybe she can help me with this somehow. Or, maybe—

Movement outside the bathroom window catches my eye. I turn and stare. The frosted glaze over the tiny rectangle window makes it impossible to see outside, but the shadowy blur of movement is distinct enough. Once upon a time this would get me paranoid, but now I regard it with a mild amount of curiosity.

Odd.

The door to the restroom opens, and Brisko ambles in, his massive body almost too much for the tiny doorframe. I didn't know he would be here tonight. I nod to him. He nods back.

"We should go," he says.

"Go where?" I drawl. What a lovable doof. Doesn't he know Jeremy is here? He's not about to let me leave.

The restroom window shatters inward and a tear gas grenade hits the floor, exploding into a cloud all around us. I stumble back, caught off guard by the event, and soon my vision fails me.

"This is the police!" I hear past all the commotion. "We have the building surrounded!"

Holy shit. Since when do the police do raids on Vice family territory? I cough and hack as I stagger to a stall. My eyes are on fire and my lungs constrict as though they're incapable of taking in air.

Brisko grabs my shoulder and forces me out the bathroom door. The patrons of the Crystal Floor Nightclub are on their feet, guns in hand, ready to fight the cops—at least that's what I think I see, but my vision is a blur of water and pain. There are so many higher-ups here I'm surprised more precautions weren't taken.

If the place really is surrounded….

Heh. I always thought I would die long before going to prison.

Brisko continues to manhandle me. He guides me through the nightclub, and I allow it, but I can't see shit. Where are we going? At one point someone tries to stop us, and all I can do is cough.

"Pierce?" Jeremy asks.

I could detect Jeremy's voice from a mile away at this point. God, I hate his grating tone.

"Pierce, what's going on? Get me out of here!"

The ensuing scuffle is between Brisko and Jeremy—which ends in a powerful huff from Brisko and a sick crunch of bone from Jeremy. I pull my handgun and hold it out. Brisko takes it.

"Shoot him for good measure," I say.

"This way," he replies, ignoring my command. He pulls me to the back and, just when I think the excitement couldn't get any more thrilling, he lights a match and catches something on fire—something *extremely* flammable. The whoosh of flame echoes in the room, and everything gets hot.

"What is that?" I ask.

"Chemistry," Brisko says.

"What?"

"You need to leave your blood here."

"*What?*"

He punches me across the face. I hit the concrete flooring.

Everything is black.

I WAKE several times, each instance clearer than the last, but still confusing.

I'm on a bed. Under covers. My head throbbing.

What's going on?

I open my good eye and tense when I realize I'm not in a familiar setting. I close the eye and try to imagine what happened. What *did* happen? Brisko… fires… chemistry… the police….

"You awake?"

"Miles?" I croak.

"Yeah."

I get up on my elbows despite my spinning head and glance around. Sure enough, like a lucid dream, I spot Miles sitting on a chair next to my tiny bed. It's a hotel—the place is plain and the smell of overused cleaning chemicals is high.

He gets off the chair and takes a seat on my bed. The squeak of the mattress hurts my ears, but I don't give a damn.

"How did you get here?" I ask in a rusty voice.

"In a car," he replies with a smile.

What a smartass. Is now really the time?

He chuckles. "Don't worry. You're safe here. We both are."

Before I can ask more questions, Guinevere comes into my vision from the far end of the room. She smiles down at me, her long black hair pinned back, revealing the entirety of her face and emotions. I'd say she's close to tears, but her smile cuts through it all.

"I'm so sorry about Brisko," she says. "We gave him a set of instructions, and I guess he went with punching things instead."

"He had chloroform too," Miles chimes in. "He didn't have to punch you."

I glance between them, my thoughts a wreck. "What happened?"

Guinevere rests her cheek in the palm of her hand. "Miles called me and told me what happened."

"He *called you*? How? He didn't know where you were."

"You gave me her number, remember?" he asks. "You had it on an index card. I kept it… just in case."

Guinevere continues, "And I set up a meeting with my poor, stupid younger brother and convinced him I knew the ins and outs of the business he didn't. I told him I wanted to meet the men in charge, and he complied."

"I called Detective Ambers," Miles says as he turns away from me. "I told her I knew about you, and she had a team of people stake out the Crystal Floor Nightclub. When you got there, and the other Cobras guys got there, she had enough to get some SWAT members together and… raid the place, basically."

Guinevere claps a single time. "And Miles here called in a favor with Juliet. You remember Juliet, don't you? The nice old mortician?"

"Yeah," I mutter. "What kind of favor?"

"We needed you to look dead from a distance and, well, she helped us get a corpse to look like you. Long story short, the Noimore police think you're dead. It turns out you don't have dental records on file, and with enough DNA evidence and some fire damage, it's a case no one wants to bother investigating further."

"She does that?"

"That's all she did for my father back in the day. Well, that and be an honest mortician."

I smack my chapped lips and turn to Miles. "You set up the fire?"

"Yeah," he replies. "There are plenty of gases and chemicals that spread fires. I tried to explain it to Brisko, but he just kept repeating it back as *chemistry*." Miles laughs and then quiets himself with a melancholy expression. "I'm sorry it took me so long to get you out of there. I should've gotten a plan together faster, but Jayden… he was in critical condition for a while. I… I'm sorry."

I shake my head.

He thinks he has a duty to save me? I never thought he would—I never even imagined it. I just assumed he would take off and… live a better life.

"Why did you come back for me?" I ask.

Miles turns to me, confused. "You were there for me when I needed it. I told you. I owe you a debt I don't think I can ever repay, Pierce. I've got your back. From here on out."

Guinevere turns away and walks from the room, no doubt thinking her presence had somehow diminished the moment. I wait until the door shuts before I speak.

"I didn't do anything significant for you, Miles. You don't owe me anything."

"Pierce… I can't count the number of times you went out of your way for me. The amount of times you took the beating for me… the times you got the money for me… the times you gave me the confidence… or helped my brother…."

He turns away and glares at the floor. I remain silent.

"You really are the only one," he whispers. "No one else even compares. It's not *nothing*. It's *my life*." His last few words come out with a crack. "And… even if I *don't* owe you anything… I want you in it."

The statement almost breaks my composure.

"Miles…," I say in a weak tone that betrays my floundering. "I…."

He moves his hand over to grip my knuckles. It's like we never parted—like a piece of me returns and I feel things again.

I take in a deep breath. "I got your back."

He smiles. "And I yours."

S.A. STOVALL grew up in California's central valley with a single mother and little brother. Despite no one in her family having a degree higher than a GED, she put herself through college (earning a BA in History), and then continued on to law school where she obtained her Juris Doctorate.

As a child, Stovall's favorite novel was Island of the Blue Dolphins by Scott O'Dell. The adventure on a deserted island opened her mind to ideas and realities she had never given thought before—and it was the moment Stovall realized that storytelling (specifically fiction) became her passion. Anything that told a story, be it a movie, book, video game, or comic, she had to experience. Now as a professor and author, Stovall wants to add her voice to the myriad of stories in the world, and she hopes you enjoy.

You can contact her at the following addresses:

Twitter: @GameOverStation
E-mail: s.adelle.s@gmail.com

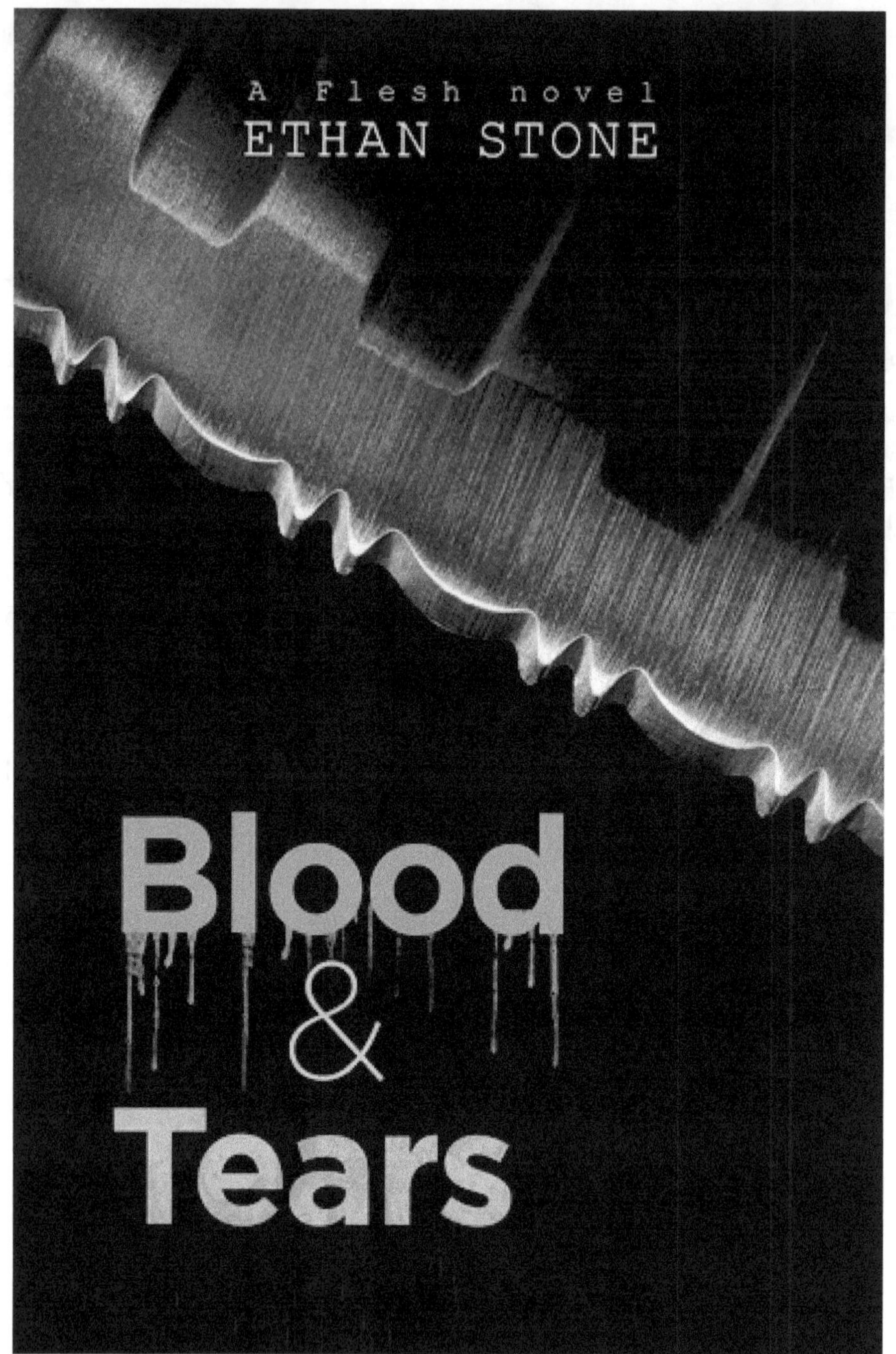
A Flesh novel
ETHAN STONE
Blood
&
Tears

A Flesh novel

The last thing Gabe Vargas wants to do after nearly dying is to leave his young son. But that's exactly what FBI Agent Drew Bradley is asking him to do. According to Drew, the only way to protect Gabe and find his wife's killer is to fake Gabe's death.

With an already established adversarial relationship, protecting a hothead like Gabe isn't exactly a picnic for Drew either. But Drew lets his guard down and a desire for Gabe leaves him confused. Before the crime can be solved, Drew will have to risk more than his life. He'll also have to risk his heart.

www.dsppublications.com

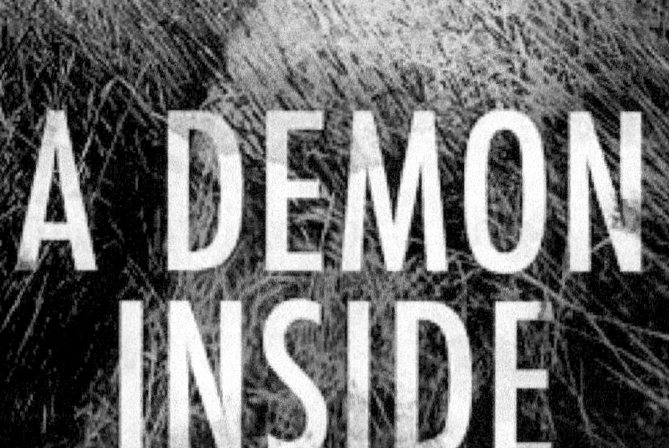

A DEMON INSIDE
AN INTENSE, MACABRE, EDGE-OF-YOUR-SEAT,
DON'T-READ-IT-IN-THE-DARK THRILL RIDE...
—THE NOVEL APPROACH
RICK R. REED

Hunter Beaumont doesn't understand his grandmother's deathbed wish: "Destroy Beaumont House." He's never even heard of the place. But after his grandmother passes and his first love betrays him, the family house in the Wisconsin woods looks like a tempting refuge. Going against his grandmother's wishes, Hunter flees to Beaumont House.

But will the house be the sanctuary he had hoped for? Soon after moving in, Hunter realizes he may not be alone. And with whom—or what—he shares the house may plunge him into a nightmare from which he may never escape. Sparks fly when he meets his handsome neighbor, Michael Burt, a caretaker for the estate next door. The man might be his salvation… or he could be the source of Hunter's terror.

www.dsppublications.com

MAD
LIZARD
MAMBO
RHYS FORD
BOOK 2 OF THE KAI GRACEN SERIES